Readers love the Snow & Winter series by C.S. POE

The Mystery of Nevermore

"The romance was sweet and hot, the mystery was well thought out and researched, and the ending was quite satisfying."

—Joyfully Jay

"This book has an embarrassment of riches—an engaging plot that will hold your interest to the final page, two intriguing main characters with a sizzling sexual chemistry, a top-notch mystery with plenty of red herrings…"

—Gay Book Reviews

The Mystery of the Curiosities

"For mystery lovers, this is a must read full of action, suspense, danger, and a not-so-easy solving of the crimes."

—The Novel Approach

"The attraction between Sebastian and Calvin sizzle off the pages. The author writes an interesting mystery and a wonderful love story… Pushes all my buttons…"

—Paranormal Romance Guild

By C.S. POE

Southernmost Murder

SNOW & WINTER
The Mystery of Nevermore
The Mystery of the Curiosities

Published by DSP PUBLICATIONS
www.dsppublications.com

SOUTHERNMOST
MURDER
C.S. POE

DSP PUBLICATIONS

Published by
DSP Publications

5032 Capital Circle SW, Suite 2, PMB# 279, Tallahassee, FL 32305-7886 USA
www.dsppublications.com

Southernmost Murder
© 2018 C.S. Poe.

Cover Art
© 2018 Reese Dante.
http://www.reesedante.com
Cover content is for illustrative purposes only and any person depicted on the cover is a model.

ISBN: 978-1-64080-076-2
Digital ISBN: 978-1-64080-077-9
Library of Congress Control Number: 2017911501
Published January 2018
v. 1.0

Printed in the United States of America
∞
This paper meets the requirements of
ANSI/NISO Z39.48-1992 (Permanence of Paper).

For Lynn and Trish.
Thank you for everything you do.

AUTHOR'S NOTE

FOR CURIOUS readers, *Southernmost Murder* takes place between the events of book two and three in the Snow & Winter series but can be read entirely as a standalone.

SOUTHERNMOST
MURDER
C.S. POE

CHAPTER ONE

PEOPLE USUALLY said to me, "Mr. Aubrey Grant, what a strange life you live."

Which was a fairly accurate assessment.

I had once been held at gunpoint by an angry ex-wife (not mine, mind you) wielding a loaded elephant gun—long story. I'd punched a clown in the face—longer story. And I'd very briefly been part of a knife-throwing act in a traveling circus—this is unrelated to the clown. I'd seen and done enough in my thirty-eight years to not be all that shocked by what was often waiting around the corner.

Except for dead bodies.

I could positively say that I'd never expected, nor prepared myself to deal with, very dead people.

And not funeral dead.

I mean, skeleton-in-the-closet dead.

Like, a *real skeleton*.

I raised myself up on my elbows from where I'd fallen to the floor after screaming and tripping. I stared through the open doorway.

He... she? Our dearly departed was slumped forward, dangling out of a false wall I'd just now discovered, despite managing the historical property for two years. And it was only because the wallpaper was inaccurate for the time period and I was finally removing it.

I swallowed a few times and tried to get my breathing under control before I started hyperventilating. My entire body felt weak, and I dropped back to lie on the floor and stare at the ceiling. Freaking cataplexy. The involuntary loss of muscle control was a unique symptom of narcolepsy. It usually happened when I laughed a lot, but sometimes... yeah, nearly having the bejesus scared out of me could make it kick in.

The house was eerily silent after my scream. There must not have been any visitors inside, odd for March—the height of tourist season—although it *was* only a little after eight in the morning. The tour guide downstairs didn't respond either, and I knew I screamed loud enough to rattle a window or two. Goddamn Herbert. He was probably asleep in one of the rocking chairs on the front porch.

I looked at the closet again.

Skelly had nothing to say about the situation.

Okay, everything's cool. It's just a dead dude. Or dudette. Or—fuck, it doesn't matter.

I climbed to my feet again, then took a moment to steady myself before stepping toward the closet. Dust—over a hundred years' worth—floated about in the morning light, finally disturbed when I'd found the hidden switch that threw the false wall open. I coughed and waved it away.

I couldn't believe it. There was a skeleton hidden inside the Smith Family Historical Home in Old Town, Key West. Down here we were known for our gay pride, key lime pie, and the local authorities looking the other way when open containers came out to play on Duval, not whatever *this* was! I mean—fuck! Who was this? How'd they die? When did they die? *Why* were they inside my goddamn walls?

I'd spent the last two months on an intensive restoration project, which included testing the walls, to create a custom paint that would match the original color from 1853, the year chosen to represent the home. The out-of-place wallpaper in the closet, antique and beautiful as it was, was historically a no-no. I had no records of who placed it there, so unfortunately it had to go. And it figured. I did a little home improvement to satisfy the historian in me, and got a dead guy for my effort.

Like I said, I took what life gave without much gripe and a healthy dose of humor. But dead things? *So* not my field of preference. I couldn't even handle the occasional roadkill without getting weird. This was the sort of bullshit an antiquing buddy of mine in New York got mixed up in, not me. I kept my nose clean and didn't snoop into dead people *anything*, so I really didn't appreciate this guy dropping into my life.

"Okay," I said. "I need… to call someone. Like… police, probably. Good start."

Right.

I spun on a heel and took off down the stairs like a bat out of hell.

I made a brief circuit through the second and ground floors to ensure it was completely empty before racing out the front. I yanked shut the heavy, solid wooden door and then closed the hurricane door behind it. I crouched down to lock it into place.

"Aubs?" Herb asked from his chair.

I looked sideways, catching him blinking sleep from his eyes. He was semiretired and worked as a part-time tour guide because, and I quote, "I'm bored and got nothing else to do but sit around and wait to die." I stood and pocketed the ring of house keys. "There's a skeleton in the third-floor closet."

Herb pursed his lips, rubbed his thick, straight mustache, then said, "Okeydokey."

I cocked my head to the side. "What?"

He waved his hand idly. "I know you have to leave early today, but if you were going to lock up thirty minutes after opening, why'd I bother dragging my ass here?"

I stared in disbelief for a minute. "Herb! There's a *dead guy* in my storage closet!"

He settled back comfortably in his chair. "Are you drunk, Aubs?"

"*No!*" I shouted, maybe a bit louder than necessary.

"You're more wound up than an old watch. Good thing that man of yours is flying in today. I swear, we've been saying it all month—you need a vacation."

I felt like I was going to burst a blood vessel. I raised my hands, because even though I liked Herb, I was going to strangle him. "The house is closed off right now. I have to go make a phone call."

"Uh-huh." He shut his eyes and rocked the chair.

I jumped off the porch steps and raced through the gardens. That Wednesday was tropical-paradise perfect. Between the beach-going sunshine, balmy breeze, and vivid beauty of all the flowers in bloom, it was almost possible to forget about Skelly lounging around in the closet, making friends with the store-brand cleaning supplies.

Almost.

A shiver of *ick, yuck, ew, oh my God* went up my spine, and I ran a little faster to a building that served as our ticket booth and gift shop. I entered through the back door and walked along the messy corridors created solely out of inventory because Adam Love, who manned the inside, was seemingly unable or unwilling to put anything away.

"No ticket sales today!" I said, rushing into the main room.

Adam startled and turned from the register to give me a look. He was a huge guy. Like, linebacker huge. A regular bull in a china shop, although to his credit, he'd yet to break a single tacky knickknack on the shelves.

He was the newest hire, about four months ago now. And young—I think twenty-five at most. The kid had moved to the Keys to start an adventure. I wasn't sure if Adam considered selling fifteen-dollar tickets to an old house particularly exciting, but hey, beggars couldn't be choosers.

"Why not?" he asked.

"There's a—long story. But no visits to the house, okay? Garden tours only."

"Sure," he slowly said.

I walked into the mess of the backroom and toward the nook that served as my office. The walls around my desk were merely boxes of holiday decorations, old stock we couldn't move, and various antiques coming and going to the home. I sat in my chair, took some more deep breaths, then picked up the landline. This didn't seem 911-worthy. Frankly, Skelly looked to have been there for a while. If he hadn't been, we'd have all smelled a decaying body.

Once, I had a dead opossum in the walls of my apartment back in New York City. What the fuck an opossum was doing in Brooklyn, let alone in the walls of my apartment, I had no clue. But it reeked, and the super had to tear through the drywall to fish it out. So yeah, Skelly was old news. Still bad news that needed to be handled immediately, but not like he-might-still-be-breathing kind of priority.

I called the main number to the local police department instead. "Yes, hello. My name's Aubrey Grant. I'm the property manager of the Smith Home on Whitehead Street. I have a rather unusual situation. ... No, no. No drunks on our porch, but thank you for sending an officer last week."

Tourists had a tendency to get trashed on Duval Street, get lost looking for their rental cottage or B&B in the middle of the night, and then end up passed out on my front steps. Such was life.

"There's a very dead person inside my supply closet."

"There's a *what*?" Adam shouted.

I jumped and turned to see him hovering in the doorway, watching me with bug eyes. I shooed him, but he didn't budge. "What's that? ... Yeah. A dead—yes. It's a skeleton. I found it inside a false wall."

"What the shit?" Adam asked.

I made a face at him. "Sorry?" I asked the person on the call. "I'm being interrupted by an employee, say that again?" I sighed and shook my head. "No ma'am, I am completely sober. Thank you for checking."

"Aubs!"

"I don't want to talk about it until the cops arrive," I answered.

Adam had locked the gift shop and followed me out the back door after I'd finished the phone call and had collected myself in the bathroom. He ran ahead of me, put a firm hand on my chest, and stopped me like I'd just walked into a brick wall.

I referred to myself as fun size. Like the candy at Halloween. Adam was movie-theater size. And my supercool, not-exactly-boyfriend, who was arriving around 10:00 a.m. to visit me, fell somewhere around share-size candy.

I was fixated on candy.

I quit smoking a month ago. It was fucking killing me.

Anyway. I was five feet three when I didn't slouch and probably weighed a hundred and twenty pounds soaking wet, so Adam had no trouble stopping me with a finger jab. Sometimes I wondered if me being his boss bothered him. He's younger, sure, but I *so* don't assume a managerial appearance. Adam dressed like—I don't know how to describe it. Like a good boy. Me? I'm pushing forty and still wear dirty Chucks, skinny jeans, and at times, tastefully offensive T-shirts. My hair was bleached white, I wore zero-gauge plugs and a nose ring—but *Key West*. The number of people who care, I could count on one hand.

"Is there really a dead man in the home?" Adam asked, his voice a loud whisper.

I put my hands on my hips. "No, I'm just drumming up new publicity!" I whispered back.

Adam crossed his huge, beefy arms.

"Sorry, sorry. It really freaked me out. I don't know whether to ask for a cigarette or a Valium."

"You *are* pretty worked up," he pointed out after a beat.

"Add a blowjob to my list of needs."

"I can offer one of the three, but you'll have to guess which."

I shook my head and waved him off. "I've gone a full month without a cigarette. I don't want to light up a few hours before Jun arrives."

"I wasn't offering a cigarette." Adam smirked.

I laughed. "Watch it, dude."

He stepped aside, no longer blocking my path. "A skeleton behind a false wall?"

I started walking toward the porch of the home. Herb was still passed out in his chair. "That's right."

"Was it old?"

"Hmm?"

Adam stopped walking. "I mean… did it have any… *flesh*?"

"No! That's gross. It was old. All discolored and dusty."

He glanced up, eyeing the third-floor windows. "Who the hell put him there?"

I shook my head. "No idea…."

"Think he was murdered?"

"Murdered?" I echoed, looking up at Adam. "Why would you assume that?"

"Someone went through the effort to hide the body," he answered. "Who does that if the person died of natural causes?"

"I guess you have a point." I caught Adam giving me a few nervous glances. "What?"

"I know it's just local superstition—"

"No," I interrupted. "Don't say it."

"But everyone says that the house is haunted!" Adam protested.

"No. Tess at Key Lime & Forever says that." I motioned across the street at our dessert shop neighbor.

"Everyone does, Aubs," Adam insisted. "All the locals say it's Captain Smith."

"Herb doesn't," I replied, pointing to the porch.

Adam rolled his eyes. "Herb also doesn't believe in antibacterial soap."

"Wait, what?"

"All I'm saying is—*if* ghosts were real, I'd have a reason to haunt this place, knowing my body was crammed into some wall for over a hundred years."

"Adam," I began, "I've been managing this home for two years. I spend more time here than I do in my own house. I can absolutely assure you that it's not haunted."

"You're a cynical New Yorker—what else would you say?"

"I'm not cynical."

"I've seen things," Adam insisted. "Not here, but at my grandmother's house. It was old. We're talking Revolutionary War old. And sometimes, at night… I'd hear someone walking up and down the stairs in heavy boots. It was just the two of us there, and my grandma's as big as you. No way she was clunking around like that. One time," he continued, "I decided to get up and follow the sound."

A breeze rustled the leaves of the sapodilla trees. A few fruits loosened and fell to the paved walkway with a splat. The morning chatter and the laughter of tourists were beginning to fill the streets just past our white picket fence, but it sounded… distant. Like a bubble had encased us.

"A man was standing in the living room," Adam said. His face had gone pale, and he licked his lips. "He was just *standing there*, Aubs. With a musket over one shoulder and an old hat on his head. He turned and looked right at me, and clear as day, he said, 'I've got to go fight.'"

I didn't believe in ghosts.

And I didn't believe Adam.

But we were fairly friendly at this point, and the guy was too sweet to lie, so his story left me… puzzled.

An unwelcome shiver crept up my spine.

"Mr. Grant?"

I jumped at the call of my name, and Adam grabbed my shoulder. The bubble around us burst, and the roar of a busy Key West morning invaded the garden. There was a plain-clothed officer standing outside the fence.

"Oh yes! That's me. Thank you for coming." I left Adam and hurried to unlock the gate and allow him into the garden.

"Detective Tillman. I was told there was a body on the property," he said. He was a tall (well, everyone was, by my standards), lean guy. Brown hair, a light tan, and no features that really stood out. He wasn't ugly or anything, just sort of someone who blended into a crowd. Except his eyes. They were sharp like broken glass. Definitely a cop, even in trousers and a button-down shirt.

"Believe me, if it had been closer to October, I'd have thought someone was pulling my leg. But this is very real."

"Been around a lot of bodies, Mr. Grant?"

I raised an eyebrow. "I have enough understanding of human anatomy to know the difference between a plastic skeleton from Kmart and the real deal."

Tillman's mouth tightened.

Yeah, I could be sassy too, buddy.

"Mind showing me?"

I nodded and led the way up the porch steps. I unlocked both doors, ignored Herb's snoring, and walked into the house. "It's on the third floor," I said, starting up the stairs.

"How exactly did you come upon it, Mr. Grant?" Tillman asked.

"Aubrey," I insisted over my shoulder. "And I was getting ready to remove old wallpaper in the closet. I guess during the process I uncovered some sort of latch, the false wall gave way, and Skelly—uh, he or she came tumbling out."

"Find many hiding places in this house?"

"Not exactly a regular habit, no."

I led Tillman across the hall of the second floor and up another set of stairs. When we reached the landing of the third floor, I walked over to the closet.

The skeleton was gone.

CHAPTER TWO

DETECTIVE TILLMAN raised an eyebrow.

"Wait! It was *right here*. How did…?" I stepped into the cramped closet and turned a full circle. "I don't understand. It was here. See, this little nook," I protested as I pointed to the empty space inside the wall.

"I see," Tillman said in a *so* very unimpressed tone.

"I'm not joking! As soon as I found it, I immediately ran outside. The house was locked—you saw yourself. No one went in or out until you got here."

"With Herb watching the front door?"

"Well, yeah, but—"

"He'd sleep through a hurricane," Tillman answered.

I stepped out of the closet and turned to stare into the dark space. "It *was* here."

Tillman let out a deep breath. "I've heard around that you have narcolepsy, isn't that right?"

"Excuse me?" I looked at him. "How is that at all relevant?"

"I've heard narcolepsy can cause hallucinations."

"Not hallucinations while I'm fully awake and going about my daily routine," I argued. I could feel my cheeks getting warm as my blood pressure rose. "It's called hypnagogic and hypnopompic hallucinations. They happen sometimes when I fall asleep or am just waking."

"Perhaps you were falling asleep, then?" Tillman suggested.

"I was perfectly awake," I spat. "And with all due respect, my sleep disorder is none of your business."

That was true enough. But at the end of the day, Key West was a small town and people knew all sorts of shit about one another. And since I was the property manager to one of the most important historical attractions on the island, basically everyone knew of the dick-loving narcoleptic who drove a pink Vespa. It was inevitable.

Tillman put his hands on his hips. "I'm not sure what you expected to gain by having me sent out here."

"There was a skeleton!" I shouted, waving my hands at the closet.

"I'd ask you to mind your tone."

Oh, this was not going to end well if Tillman kept talking to me like I was twelve. Some locals really hated us transplants. Maybe Tillman was one of those guys.

"It *was* here," I said again, because what else *could* I say?

"What would you like me to do?" Tillman asked in a tone I chose to ignore.

"I don't know."

"Do you have security footage that can be reviewed?"

I looked up. "We have cameras, but they're trained on specific artifacts in the house. Maybe I can run through them anyway. Perhaps whoever got inside moved into one of the camera's points of view while looking for the skeleton."

"Maybe," Tillman agreed without sounding like he *actually* agreed at all. "How long was the house locked up?"

"Fifteen minutes? And before that, I got in at six and we opened at a quarter to eight."

"Why'd you arrive so early?"

"I'm leaving at ten today and taking some time off. I wanted to get work done before that."

"Going somewhere?" Tillman asked.

"No. My… uh, friend is visiting."

Tillman gave me a curious expression.

"He's a friend," I insisted again, which was only half-true but also not Tillman's business either.

Tillman sighed and turned to go back down the stairs. "I'll check the locks on the doors, see if they've been tampered with, before doing a walk around the perimeter of the property."

"And if you find nothing?" I asked, following him down to the second floor.

"Without any evidence of this so-called skeleton in the wall, there isn't a hell of a lot I can do."

"Yeah, but—"

"Did you recognize the deceased?" Tillman asked, still walking.

I paused on the last step. "Skeletons don't typically have faces."

"Then believe me when I say that if it was really there, no one's been missing him."

"Isn't stealing a body illegal?" I continued, hurrying after Tillman. "And putting them in someone's wall?"

"Yes," Tillman said, halfway down to the first floor. "But there's been no reports of remains dug up from a cemetery, or anything ransacked from Native American grounds nearby." He waited for me at the bottom. "I have your word alone that it was even here at all."

"And how is that not good enough?" I asked.

"Mr. Grant," Tillman said firmly. "I'll take a look around, and I'll file a report, but if there was a skeleton here, it's gone now. So what did it do, climb out the window?"

I STOOD in the dining room that overlooked Whitehead Street.

Not that I actually believed Skelly had reenacted a scene from *The Mummy* and strolled out on his own, but Tillman's sarcastic comment gave me a thought. I'd locked the front door, and the back door had never been unlocked for tours by Herb—the lazy shit—so someone, *somehow*, got in and out while I was calling the police. And what other way than climbing through an unlocked window?

But it couldn't have been through the dining room, because it was off the front of the house, in full view of the street, now riddled with morning tourists, and Herb in his chair. Granted, he'd proven to not be much of a guard. So, the back of the house, right?

Right.

I walked through the dining room and exited into the hallway. Crossing to the parlor, I climbed over the rope that kept visitors from the disturbing displays. There were two windows that overlooked the back porch and lush garden. This section of property was heavily shaded from view. Between the countless sapodillas that surrounded the grounds and the heliconias, nearly as tall as me with their huge leaves, it was next to impossible to peer into the house or inner gardens from the cross street.

And considering someone was bold enough to sneak inside to steal a fucking *skeleton* in broad daylight, coming via this end would provide cover. The fact that my mystery intruder knew what I'd found, got to the house, and slipped out with the human remains in under twenty minutes was so disturbing, I didn't want to focus on those details quite yet.

So, the windows.

Besides my housekeeper needing to dust better, the one on the left looked undisturbed and was securely locked. We didn't open the windows of the Smith Home. There were no screens, Florida bugs were a bitch, but more importantly, the glass was antique. I'd be a very cranky boss if any were carelessly cracked or broken due to someone closing them too roughly.

I moved to the right window and found the sill had a stray bit of paint on it. I scratched at it in annoyance. "Fucking painters…." They'd finished renovating the downstairs walls two weeks ago. Clearly one of them wasn't liberal enough with the plastic sheets to protect the original wood finishing. I stood on my toes and checked the latch. Another spot of paint, and this time… a broken lock.

I turned and looked behind me. There was a camera in the room, but it was aimed toward the tête-à-tête seats and a table with several small artifacts placed on it. It would have been a tight maneuver, but someone could keep out of its frame if they wanted to.

How long had this window been unsecure? A day? A week? Since before the painters? Had one of them done this and not told me so they didn't have to pay for the damage? I couldn't imagine that it had been broken on purpose….

Maybe I *did* dream everything this morning. I mean, come on! A skeleton in the house, which someone broke inside to steal? Absurd. This *entire* morning was absolutely ridiculous.

Tillman tapped on the window from outside, making me yelp and jump. He motioned for me to join him with a finger wag.

I needed a cigarette so bad. Maybe I could smoke one and spray myself with Febreze before Jun got in….

I left the parlor and went out the back door.

"You're mighty jumpy this morning," Tillman stated.

"Did you find anything?"

Tillman crossed his arms, doing that cop-trying-to-intimidate thing. I knew the pose. Didn't matter what branch of law enforcement—they all did the same thing. "The locks on your doors don't show any signs of tampering."

"What about windows? The lock is broken on this one." I pointed.

Tillman ignored the question. "The grounds appear clean as well."

"That's it, then?"

"If something turns up, the police department will be in touch."

"I'm going to go through all of our security footage," I insisted.

"Please do."

Tillman left my side. He walked down the porch steps and disappeared into the garden as he made for the front gate.

Screw that guy. He was an ass. I swear it was like a prerequisite. *Are you a total dickwad? Here's your gun and badge.* But on the other hand, I had a constant hard-on for men in uniform, and it was my own fault. I grew up reading a lot of romance novels, and the cop stories were my favorite. Too bad I never seemed to find the sexy hero with a heart of gold and a naughty idea or two on how to use their handcuffs in real life.

Until Jun.

But I didn't want to jinx anything, so I knocked on the wooden windowsill behind me for good luck.

"Aubs?"

I looked to my left as Adam came up the porch steps. "Tillman leave?"

"Yeah."

"He's a jerk."

"I don't think he likes you," Adam agreed. "What did you do?"

"Nothing." My shoulders slumped. "The skeleton is gone."

"I didn't see Tillman with it."

"No, I mean it vanished."

"I… don't think that's possible."

"No shit." I stepped up to the window again and nudged the bottom of the pane.

"What are you doing?"

"Trying to break in."

"There's a door right beside you."

I rolled my eyes and looked back at him. "I'm testing a theory."

"Which is?"

"Not sure." I grunted and struggled to try to open the window without any of the leverage provided from opening it on the inside. "There's no way someone could get inside with the doors locked, yeah?"

"Yeah," Adam agreed.

"But this window? The latch is broken."

"You think someone climbed in and… stole the skeleton that no one knew existed thirty minutes ago?" Adam slowly asked. "Because that makes very little sense."

I paused to look at him again. "It makes *no* sense."

"Then why are you trying to get the window jimmied open?"

"Because—I know I didn't dream it," I insisted. "It was there. In all of its dead, bony glory. And now it isn't, and it's bothering me."

"I think you should be more concerned with what someone wants to *do* to a dead body that made it worth stealing."

"Gross, Adam." I heaved the window hard, and it groaned and squeaked loudly as it went up. I grinned triumphantly and pointed. "See? Look at that."

Adam got closer, setting a hand on the sill and peering into the parlor. "A big person would have trouble getting inside."

I nodded and was about to speak, but a wave of exhaustion hit me like a freight train. I reached out for the sill as a groggy fog started to take over. It's weird, when the sleep attacks come. It's like falling over in slow motion. There's usually enough warning to keep myself from getting hurt, but it's helpful when someone is nearby. I'd fallen asleep for only a moment, but woke to Adam holding me in a standing position, my weight of little concern to him.

"...hate it when you just topple over," he was saying.

"Huh?"

"You awake?"

"Yeah, sorry." Sometimes micronaps were a few minutes, sometimes only a few seconds. And I couldn't predict when they'd hit. I wiggled free from his hold after a beat, patting Adam's arm. "Thanks for that."

"It's why you pay me fourteen an hour."

I snorted and looked back at the open window. Now what was I… oh right! I leaned my head inside, looking around the floor. "No footprints or anything, and nothing was disturbed but a bit of dust." I moved back and swung a leg through the open window. I ducked my head in and did an uncoordinated ballet act to get the rest of me inside. "Ta-da!"

"Very impressive," Adam said as he gave me a polite golf clap.

I laughed.

"What now, detective?" Adam leaned down to look inside at me.

Good freaking question. I'd proven *what* exactly? That I had a broken window latch and could get it open from the outside. Not a single thing in the house appeared to be disturbed. Nothing was missing either. Nothing but the skeleton only I had seen.

"Adam?"

"Yup?"

"I'm not… crazy, right?"

He looked contemplative, which, oh my God, *rude*.

"A little," he said. "But it's like the cute, harmless crazy."

"What!"

Adam held his hands up in defense. "You dated an FBI agent once. I think that's fairly nuts."

"So?"

"So, aren't you dating his *partner* now?"

"We're not dating. We're still performing some weird mating ritual. And Jun doesn't work with Matt anymore."

Adam shrugged. "To each his own."

I'D FALLEN asleep three times scrolling through the home's security footage. It was boring as hell to say the least, but it was also a passive activity—my worst enemy. Watching television, reading, highway driving—they were all too relaxing to keep me engaged for any reasonable amount of time. I'd nearly flunked out of college because I wasn't able to stay awake during class and hadn't been correctly diagnosed as narcoleptic until I was twenty-three. So my professors had all thought I was lazy and unmotivated. What could I say in return to that?

That diagnosis was a blessing, because at least now I knew what was up.

I had to constantly be active and focused, otherwise the overwhelming desire to sleep took hold. Sometimes I could fight it, but usually not. It sucked when a micronap hit while I was in the middle of a conversation. Or eating. (In my defense, salads were boring.) Or repetitive chores—like washing dishes—which I kept doing even as I fell asleep. I'd broken so many dishes over the years due to automatic behavior, nothing matched anymore. But at this point, I'd learned to embrace my cupboards of eclectic, mismatching cups and plates.

It was difficult to explain what being narcoleptic felt like, other than my life was a constant state of extreme sleep deprivation. But I was coping. Considering I experienced all of the narcoleptic symptoms, from daytime sleepiness to sleep paralysis, I think I was doing a pretty decent job. It still sucked, but hey, could be worse. And at least I had a fancy medical bracelet that said NARCOLEPSY so those times I'd passed out alone in a public place, no one thought I'd had a heart attack or overdosed or… you know, something equally awful.

I groaned and scrubbed my face hard. A few more minutes of this and I'd be asleep on my keyboard again. It was taking forever because I'd decided to watch more than just this morning. What if someone had… hidden in the house overnight or something? I wanted to cover all my bases, even though so far no one but tourists had come into the view of cameras.

The *beep, boop, beep* of an incoming Skype call caught my attention, and I dragged my hands from my face. My webcam turned on and my trouble-prone antiquing friend, Sebastian Snow, popped on the screen. We'd known each other from back in the day, when I still worked in a New York pawnshop and he was only daydreaming about his own business. Now he ran a cool, albeit bizarre, shop in the East Village and was doing quite well for himself.

"Hey, cutie," I said. "You saved my life."

"I did?" Sebastian asked.

"Sure. I've been going through mind-numbingly boring security footage. You're looking great." That wasn't a lie. Sebastian had never been my type, but since he started seeing that new boyfriend of his, I'd noticed he looked healthier the last few times we'd talked business. And happier. He glowed, I guess. "Is that a blue shirt?"

Sebastian looked down briefly. "So I'm told. Why are you watching security footage?"

"What? No, *Aubrey, you're looking dashing as well?*"

"You look dashing," he replied. "What footage?"

"You've got a sick obsession."

Sebastian adjusted his glasses. "This sort of stuff sticks to me like shit on shoe treads."

"Now there's some imagery."

"Is everything okay down there?"

I frowned and leaned to the side to open a filing cabinet. "Not sure." I reached into the very back and retrieved a hidden pack of cigarettes. I straightened in the chair, looked at the computer screen, and pulled a stick free from the crumpled packaging. "You've got to promise not to look at me like I'm a crazy person."

"All right."

I put the cigarette between my lips but resisted lighting it. Just the motion and feel of it was almost satisfying enough. "This morning," I mumbled. "I was in the closet—"

Sebastian grinned.

"Shut up."

"I didn't say anything."

I rolled my eyes. "I was in the closet, getting ready to remove some wallpaper in the historical home. I found a false wall."

He perked up and leaned closer to the screen. God, he needed some new hobbies.

"And, uh… a skeleton—"

"Skeleton?" Sebastian protested over me.

I shushed him, as if it really mattered. "A skeleton was there. I swear to God, I saw it. It scared the piss out of me."

Sebastian raised his hands out, palms up. "And?"

"And—what?"

"You found a skeleton. What did you do with it?"

"You're way too calm about this," I said, removing the cigarette from my mouth. "I called the police. A detective showed up, I brought him upstairs, and it was gone."

Sebastian raised an eyebrow. He looked like a dog who'd found a tire and was readying to chase it. "I assume by skeleton, you mean it was not… fresh."

"No. It was old, but I can't give it an age. I prefer dating nautical artifacts, not human remains."

"Any idea who it might have been?"

"He wasn't wearing a name tag, Seb."

"Smartass. You manage a historical home."

I twirled the cigarette and stuck it back in my mouth. "Only the Smith family lived here."

He stared expectantly.

"*Dude*, you need to take up some new interests."

Sebastian frowned.

"I'm not going to presume anything," I continued. "But… there is a rumor… about Captain Smith. His death was controversial, and he never ended up in the family plot."

"Where *did* he end up?"

I shrugged. "There's no evidence that story has any validity to it. He has a headstone out in the Key West cemetery. Some locals also say he was the infamous pirate, One-Eyed Jack, *and* that he haunts the house, so… take the story with a grain of salt."

"Someone didn't want you to have the chance to identify him, perhaps?" Sebastian pointed out.

I realized I was chewing on the filter of the cigarette and took it from my lips. "You think so?"

He shrugged. "Why else would it go missing?"

I tugged on one earring thoughtfully. "Sounds like this could be dangerous."

"I'd talk to the police again, just to be on the safe side."

"Stupid cop thought I was making it up," I grumbled.

"I can ask Calvin to make some calls. Maybe he can scare someone into listening," Sebastian offered.

"I don't need your boyfriend's help," I said, waving a hand at the screen. "Jun has more jurisdiction."

"Is that what you guys call it?"

"What did you want, anyway?" I asked sternly.

Sebastian made a sound under his breath and then smiled. "I recently acquired a tool kit used at sea. I was hoping to catch you before your lunchtime nap and pick your brain about it."

"Lunchtime?" I looked at the clock. "Holy shit, it's really noon?" I shouted.

Sebastian startled. "Uh, yeah. You okay?"

"Oh God. I have to go!"

"Aubs—" Adam called.

"I left Jun at the airport for over two hours!" I jumped out of my chair.

"Aubrey," Adam said again from the doorway.

I spun around, dropped my cigarette, and hunted on the desk for my cell phone. "What?"

"You left him at the airport?" Sebastian repeated.

"My cell's missing," I answered loudly.

"Someone is here to see you, Aubrey," Adam tried.

"Hold on!" I called.

"I think you've been single for too long," Sebastian said thoughtfully.

"Oh my God, oh my God," I groaned. I threw paperwork off my desk as I searched. Jun had probably called a hundred times, wondering where I was, and I'd completely lost track of time—and apparently my phone too!

"There's a guy here," Adam insisted.

"Tell him to wait!" I snapped.

"I'm going to let you go," Sebastian said, and then I heard the Skype call end.

I pushed my chair back and got down under my desk. "I don't have time for this!"

"Hi, Aubrey."

I jumped up and hit my head on the underside. "Ouch! *Fuck*!" I dropped down, cradling my head and hissing. I turned to see legs standing at my desk and a rolling suitcase beside them. I crawled out and looked up.

Jun Tanaka. In the flesh.

My heart skipped a beat. It had been two years since we'd seen each other in person, and I'd been dating his then-partner at the time. It'd been a messy end between me and Matt, and that had been the reason I'd hightailed it to America's wang. I supposed I had Sebastian to thank for even talking to Jun again. If he hadn't needed to get in contact with the FBI around Valentine's for some convoluted mess he was in, Jun wouldn't be standing here now.

I'd have never known Jun had been in love with me for years.

Jun smiled down at me, his entire face alight, and his eyes crinkled in the corners.

Yeah. I definitely had to thank Sebastian for his accidental matchmaking.

"Jun!" I scrambled to my feet.

He held his arms out and leaned down into a hug. The last time I saw Jun, he'd just been a handsome and seemingly straight G-man. Now, after about a month and a half of talking nearly every day, flirting over the phone and on Skype, he was standing *right here*. Still handsome—maybe even more so than two years prior—and I'd come to learn, a very *not* straight G-man.

I'd stressed so much about our first touches. It felt sort of like that excitement and nervousness of meeting an online someone you'd been crushing on, except for the added weirdness that I had a personal history in place with him already. But yeah—first hug. Keep it friendly? Make it intimate? Would touching him *that way* feel right, or would I get a warning bell in my head that he wasn't meant to be anything more than a friend? What if it felt wrong and he wasted all of his paid vacation visiting me for nothing?

Fuck it.

I wrapped my arms around his neck and squeezed tight. Jun was *a lot* taller, like six feet kind of taller. I couldn't press close against him this way, so I slid my arms down, pushed them through his own, and wrapped myself around his chest. Jun's arms settled on my shoulders and he petted my head.

I smiled.

Oh yeah.

This was it.

The perfection my strange life was waiting for.

"I'm so sorry," I said, pulling back and looking up.

Jun loosened his hold, but his hands remained on my shoulders. "It's all right."

"Hell no, it's not. I meant to leave before ten to pick you up, and I got so flustered and sidetracked, now it's noon and—"

"It's okay, Aubrey," he insisted.

Jun's voice was deep. *Really deep.* And when he spoke Japanese? I swear to God, it dropped another octave, if that's even possible. It was a shame he was relatively quiet, because I could literally listen to him talk forever and be into it. A week ago I went online to see if deep voices was some sort of fetish or if I was losing it. Turns out there were studies proving men with deep voices were more often than not the first choice as a potential mate.

So hey, science couldn't cure my narcolepsy, but they did prove that if it were biologically possible, I'd want to make several babies with Jun.

I sighed and looked him over. All my memories of Jun were of him in his "I'm a special agent" suit, so it was surprising to see him in anything but. Not that I expected him to be wearing a tie on vacation, but the tight black pants and fashionable shirt with a low neckline made Jun look like someone out of a magazine. He had some scruff on his usually smooth-shaven face and wore black-framed glasses instead of the usual contacts. Jun's hair was professionally disheveled—the I-rolled-out-of-bed-like-this-and-kept-it look. It was sexy.

"How are—" he started.

"You look really hot," I blurted out.

Jun paused, glanced over my shoulder to where Adam was probably still loitering, then smiled. He reached out and petted my hair again.

"How'd you get here?"

"I rented a car." Jun took his hands off me, and I wanted the warm weight back immediately. "I tried calling but kept getting voicemail."

"Yeah, I think I lost my phone," I said lamely. I glanced at the mess I'd made during my search.

Adam cleared his throat from the doorway and raised his eyebrows when I turned. "So everything's cool?"

"Cool," I said. "Sorry. Ah, Adam this is Jun Tanaka. My... my— yeah." I laughed and put a hand on Jun's arm. "Jun, Adam Love. He runs the gift shop."

Jun inclined his head. "Pleasure."

"Same," Adam said. "Aubs talks about you a lot."

"Not a lot—" I shook my head and looked at Jun. "Want to get lunch?"

CHAPTER THREE

I DIDN'T know what to do with my hands. Put them in my pockets? Seemed standoffish. Crossing them while walking was weird too. I could keep them at my sides and stop freaking out about it—imagine that. But it was the same nervousness as the hug. We weren't officially dating or anything, Jun could be a hard man to read, and he had never been terribly forthcoming with his desires, so I didn't know if I was supposed to hold his hand.

"The radio in the car seemed to only get reception on Cher or Jimmy Buffett songs," Jun was saying.

"My condolences."

He laughed.

I stopped walking. "Hey, hold up for a minute."

Jun paused and looked at me. "Something wrong?"

"I'm just going to ask, because I think you prefer that—being straightforward."

He raised a brow and stared expectantly.

"Is holding hands a yes or no? I'm fine with either," I quickly added. "But for you, I didn't know if…."

Jun immediately reached down and slid his fingers between mine, giving my hand a light squeeze. "Good?"

Awesome, in fact.

We walked toward the boardwalk, which wasn't more than ten minutes from the Smith Home. The whole area was bustling with tourists. Some wore swimsuits and desperately needed more sunscreen, others consulted maps of Old Town in their quest for the art museum or Butterfly Conservatory or just any old bar because it was five o'clock somewhere, right? There were boats docked, and the surface of the water shimmered from the afternoon sun overhead. By sunset the street vendors and performers would be out at Mallory Square and the place would be packed with folks looking to *ooh* and *aah* over the pretty sky.

And I wasn't being sarcastic. It's quite beautiful here in Key West.

I headed toward a white building on the water's edge. The stenciled lettering across the side had faded from the sun long ago, but the name could still barely be made out.

Sea Shack Beer & Grub.

"It's better on the inside," I said. "Well… the food is good, at least. The barbeque shrimp is worth killing over."

Jun smiled and followed me inside.

It was crowded with families at all of the tables, leaving only a handful of open seats at the three-sided bar. There were a few televisions positioned above with some sports being broadcasted, and the farthest wall had a number of open windows, the smell of the ocean coming in on a breeze.

"Bar okay with you?" I asked.

"Sure."

I snatched two stools before an incoming pack of college bros could, and they planted themselves farther away on the side nearest Jun. "So," I said, taking a breath. "Did you have a good flight?"

Jun's smile was both heart-meltingly sweet and ridiculously hot. It was infuriating how he could pull off the naughty-and-nice thing at the same time. He didn't have a big smile; rather, it quirked to one side and he kept his lips pressed closed. It was his eyes. Not to sound lame, but they practically twinkled when he was happy.

"It was fine. I much prefer the skip-and-hop of New York to Florida over the fourteen-hour flights to China and Japan."

Oh right—Jun worked for the FBI's Organized Crime Team and specialized in Asian Criminal Enterprises. He took out serious bad guys like triads and yakuza. He spoke three languages and worked with international organizations to stop underground crime groups. Basically Jun was a superhero. Which, now that I was totally nuts about him, was scary as hell. People shot at him, after all.

"Hello, gentlemen," the bartender said distractedly as she approached. "Get you two a drink?"

"Sapporo on tap," I said.

Jun glanced at me and then her. "Same for me."

"And can we get some barbeque shrimp?" I added.

She nodded, already walking away to grab our drinks.

"I thought you couldn't drink," Jun said, turning in his chair to look at me.

"Yeah, well, one won't kill me. I'm not supposed to mix alcohol with my stimulants. *Which* I forgot to take this morning anyway, so…." I shrugged.

The bartender returned and dropped two paper coasters that had seen better days, then set our full glasses down. "Be back in a few with the food."

Jun thanked her and picked up his beer. "What shall we drink to?"

"Finding my phone so I don't leave you at future airports again?" I asked, picking up my own drink.

He smiled again. "Let's drink to this week and everything that comes with it."

"The good, bad, and ugly?" I asked, clinking my glass against his. "Because you've not seen how much of a hot mess I am first thing in the morning."

"I'm sure you're absolutely gorgeous," Jun murmured before sipping his beer.

Aaaand now I was blushing. Goddamn it. I took several gulps to busy myself.

"So what has you so flustered?" Jun asked.

"Besides you?" I was so smooth.

"It's not because of me," he said, a chuckle woven into his words.

I was so not smooth, apparently. "Nothing important."

Jun arched one perfect brow. "Try me."

"Oh, come on," I whined. "I don't want you looking at me like I'm cuckoo for Cocoa Puffs on the first day you're here."

Jun straightened in his seat. "What's wrong, Aubrey?" He was all serious now, and it was killing the mood.

I frowned and ran my fingers up and down my drink, collecting condensation until I realized it looked like I was lazily jacking the glass off and abruptly stopped. "The 'too long; didn't read' version is this morning there was a human skeleton in the third-floor closet of the historical home, and when I brought a police officer in, it was gone."

Jun gave his beer a thoughtful expression, crossed his long, sexy legs, and said nothing.

"You can't tell me you don't have a smartass remark or two for that claim. I wasn't drinking. I wasn't hallucinating."

"But you saw a skeleton," Jun stated. "I believe you."

I cocked my head to the side. "*Why?*"

"Why shouldn't I?"

"Uh, no one else has, that's all."

Jun picked up his drink and took a sip. "You'd prefer I doubted you?"

"God no."

"Then let's figure out why it was in the closet," Jun concluded.

I waved my hands in protest, knocking over my beer in the act. "Oh shit! Fuck!" I picked up the glass and jumped out of my chair as the Sapporo spilled out across the bar top, my lap, and the floor. "This is sacrilegious!"

Jun stood, grabbed a wad of napkins, and soaked up the spill as the bartender joined us. She took the soiled mess and tossed it out before cleaning the rest up with a rag. I grabbed some of the cheap, tissue-thin napkins and scrubbed at my pants, but the paper just dissolved and shredded into a white mess on my clothes.

Ugh.

"Want a new drink?" Jun asked.

"I'd better not," I said lamely. My cheeks were burning, and I couldn't face him. I was so fucking embarrassed.

Our bartender returned and slapped down baskets of shrimp and a glass of water. "You know you shouldn't drink, Aubs," she said in a chastising tone before walking away.

Jun patted my seat. "Sit down."

I started to, but then one of the dude-bros on Jun's side of the bar called out, "Hey, twink, can I order you a Shirley Temple?"

Now, I wasn't one to take that shit sitting down—so to speak. I'd always stood up for myself, just ask the clown I punched. But I didn't even have a chance to say something snarky and sufficiently pride-bruising before Jun was on his feet and heading over to the testosterone corner.

Whatever he said made the entire group stand with their drinks and take the drunken commotion to another area. Jun sat back down and motioned to my seat again.

I awkwardly sat. "Wow. What did you say to them?"

Jun shook his head and picked up one of the shrimp from the basket.

"Seriously."

He looked at me. "I don't mean to fight your battles. But that behavior is unacceptable."

I shrugged. "It's cool. You know I'd have said something, though, right?"

"Of course." He popped the shrimp in his mouth and murmured, "But sometimes I can't help being the asshole with a badge—these are *really* good."

THE ONE thing I wanted to do after taking Jun out for lunch was bring him home, get naked, do something naughty, and hope like hell that my cataplexy didn't get triggered. I mean, I was all about taking it slow, if that's what Jun wanted, and talking about where we stood as a potential couple, because frankly that was still a gray area for both of us. But after being stood up at the airport and then dealing with my flighty, messy self at the bar, Jun deserved a freaking blowjob.

So where did we end up instead? The Smith Home.

"Jun," I said, trying not to sound like a whiny brat. "My cottage is a lot more inviting. Let's go home. You can unpack and relax…. I can massage your feet."

Jun looked down at me with one raised eyebrow that spoke volumes more than he typically did.

"I'll massage something else," I tried, giving my best suggestive look.

That made him smile, which really wasn't the response I was going for. Jun reached out and petted the back of my head briefly. "You're very cute, Mr. Grant."

Ah, okay, at least he was in a playful mood. Jun always called me Mr. Grant when he flirted. "So? You, me, my place, and maybe let's lose a pair of pants or two along the way?"

"I'd like to see your work first." Jun moved his hand from my hair, pausing briefly at my neck before he dropped it to his side. "And this suspicious closet."

I groaned rather dramatically, took his hand into mine, and dragged him to the gift shop. "All right. But no loitering. In and out, okay?"

"Okay."

I brought him inside and was happy to see a healthy number of tourists moving about the room. I really hadn't wanted to open the house again after this morning's fiasco, but without a body, there wasn't much excuse to keep everything shut down. If the nonprofit board got wind of that and my not-so-rock-solid reasoning behind the locked doors, I'd be shit-canned in a heartbeat. So Adam had opened ticket sales again when Jun and I left for lunch.

"Hey, Aubrey," Adam called from the register.

"Everything okay here?"

Adam nodded. "No one's reported unsightly visitors in the house, at least."

"Hilarious," I said, deadpan. "I'm off the clock, just bringing Jun over to see the place before heading out again."

Adam glanced at Jun. "Sure thing."

I led the way outside and into the gardens. There were a few visitors strolling about the walkways, taking pictures, and reading information plaques about some of the rare and beautiful plants on location.

Jun's hand settled on my lower back, and *holy shit*—I hadn't realized how badly I'd missed that sort of touch from another man. "I'm not so sure your employee likes me."

I pulled my attention away from Jun's hand and glanced up. "Adam?"

"Hmm."

"Why do you say that?"

"Gut feeling."

"What's up? Your cop senses tingling?"

Jun's mouth curved into a small smile, and he started walking along a path toward the towering house ahead. "No."

"He's never even been late, you know. He's always waiting on the porch when I roll into work. Adam's a good guy."

"If he wasn't good, you wouldn't have hired him," Jun said, seeming to agree with me.

"So why do you think he doesn't like you? Adam likes everyone."

"Boyfriend senses."

I stopped, smirked, and put my hands on my hips. "*Ohhh.*"

Jun paused and turned to look at me. "Not that—"

"No, no, I get it," I said, feeling a wicked grin curl my lips. "Mr. Tanaka, are you officially asking me out?"

Jun swallowed, his Adam's apple bobbing. "Not in so many words."

"Why's that?"

"I don't want to make you feel obligated. Especially since I'm here visiting and staying with you…." He shrugged.

"I must be getting old, because that's the hottest thing anyone's ever said to me."

Jun looked away briefly, covering his mouth with a hand to suppress a laugh. "Not looking for a sexy, passionate man these days?"

"Oh, I so am," I corrected. "But a guy who likes to talk about my feelings too? What a turn-on." I took a step closer. "Don't even get me started on men who dust baseboards or know how to balance checkbooks."

Jun glanced from side to side, likely confirming there were no gawking tourists in the vicinity, before he took my hands and pulled me closer. "I do both," he confirmed.

"Yeah? My jeans just got a little tighter."

Jun's eyes crinkled in the corners as he laughed. "You know what other skill I have on my résumé?"

"What's that?"

"I've been known, on more than one occasion, to take scary bugs out of the house."

"Oh shit, you'd best propose to me now, because you're not going anywhere," I said, laughing loud.

Jun kissed my forehead.

"So how about it, Mr. FBI? Want to be my better half?"

Like I said, Jun's pretty quiet. It was kind of cute, because I've seen him in official G-man mode. He was a badass straight out of a Hollywood movie. And flirting? No trouble there, and no issue with PDA either. But actual conversations? It wasn't really his thing. If I waited for him to ask me out, we'd be here until I was eighty.

But I wasn't joking in regard to a guy who cared about my feelings. My last boyfriend—Matt O'Sullivan—had given so few fucks, we were in the negatives by the time I split. I hadn't realized until I was a thousand miles away the toll my self-esteem had taken from that relationship. But Jun gave a crap. He gave many craps. And that was the kind of man you brought home to Ma and Pa.

"I'd like that," Jun said.

"Goodie! Now I have a legitimate excuse to show you my piercings."

"Piercings?"

I made a satisfied noise and let go of him. "Come on. You wanted to see the house."

"That was before I knew you had piercings."

"Yup." God, I was such a little shit sometimes.

"Plural?"

"Uh-huh."

"Like, where?"

I hiked up the porch stairs and opened the door. "I guess you'll have to do a thorough inspection."

Herb was giving his not-so-impressive spiel to a group of visitors when we stepped inside. I waved at him to continue and quietly led Jun up the first set of stairs. We passed by the master bedroom and children's rooms on the second floor before going up the next staircase. The third floor was quiet and empty, which was typical. Tourists never stayed long up here, despite the captain's study being one of the more exciting displays, in my humble opinion.

"Impressive home," Jun said as he reached the landing.

"Thanks. I've put more time and effort into this house than any place I've ever actually lived in." I motioned him over to the closet in question. "So, this is it."

Jun stared at the door, back at the stairs, and then the door again. "Do you mind opening it?"

I nodded and popped the eyehook. It was still empty inside.

I admit a small—*very small*—part of me wanted Skelly to be there again, if for nothing more than to prove I hadn't briefly gone insane that morning. I pointed to the wall at the back. "He was in there."

Jun took a step into the closet. He pulled out his cell phone and turned on the flashlight, looking around.

"Whole lot of nothing, am I right?"

"Yes."

I grunted and cautiously squeezed in beside him. "I'd been peeling old wallpaper and found this lever," I explained, tugging up some of the paper to show Jun. "And the false wall gave way and Skelly fell out."

"Skelly?"

"He was just hanging there like a sad, empty piñata."

"Certainly leaves a lot of unanswered questions," Jun stated, flashing the light here and there, as if hoping to find something in the tiny little nook.

"Adam thought maybe the person was murdered. Because why else would you hide someone? And Sebastian kinda thought the same thing—Skelly was clearly hidden with no intention of being found."

"Sebastian Snow?"

"Yeah."

Jun nodded. "Don't drag him into this."

"I'm not. Just mentioned it in passing."

"That seems to be about all he needs as an excuse to get involved."

"I'm pretty sure even Seb won't fly down to the Keys to sleuth around for a lost skeleton—crazy as he may be."

"Let's keep it that way. I've no interest in making a call to—Winter, was it?—to come fetch his wayward assistant."

Jun knew of Sebastian because his beau, homicide detective Calvin Winter, had been the one asking for FBI intel on a cold case. I didn't think Jun had an issue with either of them, but you know… federal agent versus a metro detective. It was always a whose-dick-is-bigger contest.

Jun leaned into the false wall, shining his flashlight again. "Found your phone."

"What?" I got close and looked inside as Jun reached for it. "How'd the fuck it get in there?"

He handed it over.

I swiped, unlocked the phone, and yeah—four missed calls and half a dozen texts from Jun. I winced and pretended I didn't see them. "Seems okay," I said at length.

I peered back at the wall. The tight spot didn't seem big enough to cram a human into, which said something about how desperate the person who hid the body had been. There was nothing left now but a shitload of dust, which made me sneeze a few times.

"You've got the cutest sneeze," Jun murmured.

"Shut it, mister." I was about to step back, but then something caught my attention. "Jun, shine the light down there."

Jun put the phone's light back on the wall, pointing it down at the bottom of the nook. "Are those words?"

I leaned down as much as I could, blowing dust out of the way. "An *X* on my… heart," I read.

"What's that mean?" Jun asked.

I shook my head, turning to stare at him. "I have no idea."

CHAPTER FOUR

PATSY CLINE puts me to sleep.

I like her voice, but every time I hear any of her songs, insta-nap.

I leaned over and hit the radio button, trying another preprogrammed station in Jun's rental car. Hello, Rihanna, my gorgeous queen. "S&M." Sex was in the air. Good song, that one.

Jun glanced at me.

"Patsy is like warm milk at bedtime," I protested.

"It was better than this. This song is awful."

I gasped. "Take it back!"

"What?"

"I love this song. You should see me dancing to it after I've had a few."

His mouth quirked. "I won't get between you and your pop divas."

Jun's cool and chic appearance fooled a lot of people. He was a bit of a bad boy deep down. He listened solely to the hardest rock and metal and old-school punk that could be scrounged up. I was talking the kind of music where you could barely understand the lyrics and someone was going to give themselves a neck injury from thrashing. Jun would probably be right at home in a mosh pit.

I only knew he was *so not* a Rihanna fan because a few years back he had gone out to a bar with me and Matt after work. Matt had spent the entire time flirting with some younger guys there—and fuck, it still hurt thinking about that. About how stupid and unwanted that made me feel, and Jun had seen it all. He sat with me all night, doing his best to chat, which was where I also learned he wasn't a chatter, and he ended up bonding with me over our extremely diverse musical tastes.

"You okay?" Jun asked, glancing away from the road once or twice.

"Yeah," I said quickly and a bit too loudly. "I was thinking about the time you nearly blew out my eardrums with Five Finger Death Punch."

"I knew you were lying when you said you liked them."

"I was trying to impress you." I reached over and put my hand on Jun's thigh. It was solid muscle and felt *right* to touch. "Did it work?"

He only smiled in response.

After Jun and I found the message in the closet, I was done. No more crazy, creepy shit for me, thank you very much. I'd put Adam in charge of closing up for the night, grabbed my belongings, and we left. The only thing I wanted to do for the next week and a half was relax on the beach, pretend to be a tourist, and do a whole lot of naked lounging with Jun. A vanishing skeleton and mystery message were not going to ruin my vacation.

So help me if something came between me and sexy Mr. Tanaka over the next ten days. I might be tiny, but I would fuck someone's shit up.

"Left or right?" Jun asked at the next intersection.

"Left here," I said. I sat up a bit and pointed to a cottage coming up. "That blue one is me. This is my parking spot too."

Jun pulled up on the side of the road. "Where's this pink Vespa I've heard so much about?" he asked, taking the keys from the ignition.

"Oh, the Princess?" I asked, smirking. "Backyard."

Jun laughed as he climbed out of the driver's seat and went around back to fetch his suitcase.

I got out and walked to the front door, unlocked it, and held it open. "Welcome to Chez Grant. Come for the home cooking—stay for the sweet ass."

"Does everyone get that offer?" Jun asked as he stepped inside.

"Only crime-fighting linguists."

"Sounds like a short list."

I shut the door and turned to look up at him. "You'd be surprised. I think I can squeeze you in for brunches every other Wednesday. What do you say? Omelets from scratch, followed by your front and my back?"

Jun set his laptop bag beside the rolling suitcase and approached me. I backed up against the door and loved how he towered over me. I could feel the heat of his body and the tension rippling in his muscles. So much self-control. Maybe too much.

"Although I think my tables are reserved now," I whispered.

"Last name, Tanaka. Want me to spell that?"

"I think I got it."

Jun's gaze wandered briefly, and it felt like he was stripping me with his eyes. My breath was coming shallow and quick, and my dick had most definitely perked up, thinking it was go time.

No reason to stand at attention. He hasn't even touched you yet!

"Let's be certain," Jun said, voice dropping so deep, it was like he was caressing my balls with it. He got as close as he could without our bodies actually touching, and I could feel myself starting to vibrate as I held back from grabbing him. Jun gently pressed his index finger to my throat and drew what felt like a *T*.

"T," he stated.

He went a bit lower, just under my collarbones.

"A," I said.

Jun dragged his finger down and across to my nipple, where it bumped a barbell piercing. His mouth did that lopsided smile when I let out a sudden breath. "N," he said as he drew the letter.

I swallowed.

Jun slowly brought his hand down to the middle of my stomach and pressed another shape against my body.

"A," I whispered.

Jun smiled a bit more boldly. He slid his index finger down to my belly, then paused at another piercing. "K," he said as he gave the ring a little nudge, and what was never an erotic piercing for me suddenly made my entire body ache. Jun raised his eyes, stared hard at me, and brought his finger down against my straining cock, drawing a shape against it.

"*Ahh*," I groaned, tilting my head back against the door.

Jun removed his hand.

"Going to spell and run?" I mumbled. I started to move from the door and staggered.

Jun grabbed me. "You okay?"

"I'm fine," I insisted, moving out of his hold.

"There's no reason to rush," Jun confirmed.

"Except that I've got a chub, which, when you're wearing skinny jeans…." I straightened my posture and pointed to the affliction I was suffering from.

Jun was amused. That bastard. He unzipped the front of his suitcase and removed a pair of black house slippers. He toed off his expensive-looking shoes, briefly flashed his bright, rainbow-striped socks, and put the slippers on.

I glanced at my torn, scuffed-up Chucks. I walked a narrow line of caring very much about my looks—let's admit it, my hair, piercings, and back tattoo make me look fierce—while also appearing like I've forgotten how to adult, considering my questionable wardrobe. Cheap, teenage-style clothes mostly, and I wouldn't be surprised if these Cons were from 1992.

"What's with the socks?" I asked.

"My sister buys me a pair of silly socks every year. I have a lot."

"Aww," I cooed. "That's cute."

Jun cleared his throat.

I walked into the living room. "So. Downstairs."

The cottage was probably bigger than what I needed, considering I lived by myself, but it was really quite gorgeous and I was used to rent rates that bleed you, coming from New York, so I kept it. Each room was painted in bright, beachy colors seen all over the island—blues, greens, and pinks, with a few eclectic pieces of local art on the walls. The living room had the basic essentials—television, couch, and a bookshelf full of romance novels and cookbooks.

I know, right? And my appointment book is suddenly *always full* whenever I find a romance novel about a chef and a cop.

I walked to the open doorway of the kitchen and flipped on the light for Jun to see. Nothing super impressive, but my old place in Brooklyn had exactly half a counter, and here I had several counter spaces *and* a dishwasher.

"There's a laundry room by the back door," I began before leading Jun to a spiral staircase. "My bed and bathroom are in the loft. You can bring your suitcase if you want."

I went up ahead of him to make sure, in my rush to get to work earlier than usual that morning, I hadn't left dirty socks or briefs lying around. Not like Jun hadn't seen another man's underwear in his lifetime; he was forty-one and not a virgin. But still. I wanted to go a full twenty-four hours before he saw what a shitty housekeeper I was.

Lo and behold, there was a pair lying on the floor, which I quickly tossed in the hamper. There were also several shirts left on the bedspread from when I was trying to pick out what would make me look the cutest, because naturally I'd wanted to impress Jun that morning. Then, of course, I realized I'd spent way too long hemming and hawing, was late, and left wearing an *X-Files*-themed shirt. Monster of the week wasn't the look I had been going for, but c'est la vie.

I turned as Jun reached the top. "Not bad, right?"

"Not at all." He pushed his suitcase to the banister that overlooked the ground floor.

I picked up the T-shirts and went to the closet to hang them. "I know it's lame," I began, shutting the door and looking at Jun, "but would you mind if I took a quick nap? I'm supposed to take it at one, but better late than never."

"It's not lame," he answered. "Go right ahead. How long do you need? An hour?"

"Oh no, twenty minutes," I said. I flopped on the bed and rolled to my side. "Any longer makes me groggy." I fished my cell out of my pocket and set the alarm before putting it on the nightstand. I looked back at Jun and patted the bed in invitation. Exhaustion was already weighing me down. It took me under a minute to fall into a deep sleep— but at least I'd felt Jun slide his arm around my waist before I was off to never-never land.

NARCOLEPTICS DREAM a lot. That's not surprising, since even though I crashed for twenty minutes and REM sleep doesn't start for ninety in a normal person, I fall into it almost immediately. What a lot of people didn't know was the surprising number of nightmares we tended to have.

I remembered a lot of my dreams, and this one hadn't started out scary at all. I was walking down Duval Street with Cher—I think because Jun had mentioned her being on the radio and that nugget lodged itself into my brain. We were looking for a rake, but when we couldn't find one anywhere, that's when the panic started seeping in and turning the dream into a nightmare. We needed a rake to stop the skeleton in the closet.

And I know—what the fuck kind of logic was this? Cher + rake = certain victory. But a dream was a dream, and in that moment, I knew if we didn't find a rake, we were so up the creek without a paddle.

Cher and I never saw the skeleton, though. I'd managed to wake myself up before my nightmare had the chance to scare the piss out of me, but coming back to the real world was sluggish and... *disjointed*. I opened my eyes, but the rest of me was, to put it simply, still asleep. Sleep paralysis. Typically when people fell asleep, our bodies paralyzed themselves so we didn't act out dreams and hurt ourselves. But sometimes when I woke, my body hadn't always received the message.

It's difficult to explain. Sometimes, in the moment, I knew what it was, but sometimes I didn't. And every time, no matter what, it was goddamn terrifying. My mind was going a million miles a minute and couldn't understand why the rest of me wasn't responding. I typically had hallucinations too. Nuts, right? Once, I hallucinated an alarm clock was creeping across the room to kill me. But that was tame compared to what I woke to this time.

Skelly was staring at me from the side of the bed. Only the top half of him, slumped forward like how he'd been in the wall. He lurched suddenly and grabbed the edge of the bed to pull himself up.

I tried to shout. I tried to kick and thrash.

Tried and tried and, Jesus Christ, he was coming! Right *there*, touching my leg and—

I bolted upright in bed suddenly, gasping for air, the dying end of a scream coming out of me.

"Aubrey?" Jun was there beside me. He petted the back of my head with sure, gentle strokes. "Are you all right?"

My chest heaved as I caught my breath. "N-no, what? I—bad dream." I turned and stared at Jun. "Sleep paralysis," I corrected as the fog in my mind began to clear. "It's scary."

Jun frowned. He moved his hand around to cup my cheek. "Can I get you anything?"

"Just you," I said. It came out like a reflex. I didn't even realize I'd said it until it was too late.

But he smiled. Big. The twinkle in his dark eyes returned. Jun leaned forward, closing the space between us. His mouth was only an inch or two away from mine.

Do it. Kiss him.

We *were* officially dating, after all.

I tilted my mouth to meet his.

And then my alarm cockblocked me—Nicki Minaj telling haters what they could blow.

I WAS a romantic at heart.

I didn't want *a* kiss; I wanted *the* kiss. So I didn't push when the moment between us had been lost. Another would present itself, and it'd be the best goddamn kiss I've had in my entire adult life.

Neither of us had been particularly hungry for a full meal around dinner, so I made a plate of bruschetta with tomato and basil, and we parked ourselves in front of the television. Jun had a glass of wine. I stuck with water.

I was shaky with watching movies. I never lasted through the entire thing, ending up micronapping through the important bits and waking for the boring ones, so I stuck to short television episodes. Under thirty minutes was about all I could take with passive activity. Except this time I wasn't home alone and bored with the same three shows I never strayed from. Jun was right beside me, and it was pretty fantastic.

I really liked him. He made my stomach do summersaults.

So instead of getting up after two episodes and three nap attacks to do something else, I stayed right there beside him. Jun wrapped his arm around my shoulders and let me lounge in and out of consciousness against his chest. Everything about him was good. Hell, Jun even *smelled* right, if that made a lick of sense.

I opened my eyes when the room went quiet. Jun was flipping through Netflix. "Oh, that," I said suddenly, making him pause.

"Since when do you like horror movies?"

"You'll protect me."

"This is in Japanese, Aubrey."

"Subtitles?" I tilted my head from lying against him to see him staring at me. "What? Maybe I'd like to pick up a few words."

"Why's that?"

My heart did a little flutter. "Because you speak it."

He smiled.

"And because you sound so freaking hot doing so."

Jun slid his fingers through my hair and spoke something in Japanese in his deep, powerful voice.

Gay baby-making mode, activate!

"Oh my God, you tease," I said, sitting up to look at him better. "What'd you say?"

He kept a straight face. "Where's the toilet."

"What? You did not!"

"Sure I did. *Toire* means toilet."

I smacked his arm lightly. "You're an ass!"

Jun chuckled. "Sorry."

I got up on my knees and swung one leg over Jun, settling on his lap. I slid my arms over his shoulders and rested them on the back of the couch. He dropped the remote to the cushion and put his hands on my hips. I curled one hand into his stylish hair. I liked guys with hair long enough to grip, and judging by the quiet gasp Jun made, he enjoyed being on the receiving end of that. I gave the handful a tug, just to test the waters, and his lips parted.

Now that was an invitation if there ever was one.

But Jun's hands grabbed the bottom of my T-shirt before I had a chance to claim his mouth, and he pushed the clothing up. His hands on my bare skin were like fire. He drew the shirt up to my nipples and then dragged his fingertips across the piercings.

I made a groan that sounded every bit of the two years I hadn't been getting any. "*Jesus*," I said, drawing it out into syllables that didn't exist.

Jun flicked each of them again. "I like these," he whispered.

Good. They were totally worth every penny.

He didn't do anything else after that, just moved his palms up and down my sides. Jun had sort of hinted over our daily phone calls that he wasn't exactly an instigator in bed, but he never came out and said it. I'd been blunt about holding hands and us dating, because I suspected that if I was straightforward with Jun, he'd act. It really boiled down to that he simply never made the first move.

And here was the thing I was beginning to suspect about Jun. Like me, he was probably a little nervous about our first time together, but I didn't think there was any sort of wall that needed to be broken down with him. He could flirt and tease and show affection, no problem. I was pretty sure he just got off on being told what to do in bed. Whether he topped or I did wasn't important; being ordered was what he liked. Jun was always in command at work, so maybe he found it relaxing when, at home, someone else took the lead.

And it was new territory to me, but hey, I was more than happy to expand my horizons. The idea of telling a hotshot FBI agent what to do was sort of turning me on anyway.

"Jun?"

"Hmm?"

"Lick my nipples."

His eyes widened slightly behind his glasses, and I caught a tiny intake of air. Oh yeah—that was *so* what he wanted. Jun took my hips again and leaned forward. His pink tongue slipped from between his lips, and then there it was, wet and warm, lavishing my piercings. He kissed and licked and used his tongue to toy with the barbell. I gripped the back of his head with both hands to keep Jun from moving away. He groaned in response and slid his hands lower, moving around to my back.

"Touch my ass," I ordered, although I sort of lost the commanding tone because whatever the fuck he was doing with his tongue was going to make me shoot in about ten seconds.

Jun obeyed, his hands moving to hold my cheeks, kneading through my jeans.

Yeah, I could get into this real fast.

I tipped Jun's head back by tugging on his hair. He looked up at me, breathing fast.

Fuck.

I leaned down to kiss him, to have that talented tongue in my mouth, to feel the rasp of his stubble against my own soft skin—

My phone rang obnoxiously from the coffee table, shattering the silence and whispered breaths between us. Jun leaned back against the couch cushion. He let go of my ass and looked up at me, not angry or annoyed, just... like he had all the time and patience in the world.

"Don't lose that train of thought," I said as I scrambled off his lap, tugging my T-shirt down and half-tripping into the table. I heard him laugh quietly as I grabbed the phone and swiped to accept the incoming call. "Hello?"

"Mr. Grant?"

"Speaking."

"This is Joe Hernandez with Island Security."

"Oh no," I said with a sigh.

"Afraid so."

I looked over my shoulder at Jun. "You've gotta be kidding," I muttered. "What sensor went off this time?"

"First floor," Joe answered. "I know it's after-hours. I can send a police cruiser by the home, if you'd prefer."

"No, no," I said, heaving myself to my feet. "They hate wasting their time doing drive-bys. I'll go check."

"Very good. Give us a call back if you need further assistance."

I said goodbye, hung up, and looked back at Jun. "Will you hate me if I said our fun has to wait?"

He got to his feet. "What's wrong?"

"The motion sensors at the Smith Home are going off."

"IT'S REALLY nothing to worry about," I told Jun for, like, the hundredth time as I unlocked the gate outside the property.

Jun had insisted on coming, maybe because it sounded suspicious or dangerous to him, but the security company and I had been playing this game for a while. I'd had the old detectors uninstalled shortly after accepting the job, because they seemed to always be malfunctioning, and had Island Security take over. Lo and behold, the same thing happened with their equipment. The motion sensors inside went off at random. Sometimes not for months at a time, and other times like once a week. Once, last October, they went off three times in the same night. That had been a real pain.

The police had been called to check the historic property every time, but it was like a running joke on the island. Everyone knew the house was secure. When I became property manager, I took the responsibility of confirming everything was safe, no matter the hour. I'd regretted how much I'd insisted upon the duty once I realized the new gear didn't function any better than the old.

But hey—life, right? Take it in stride.

The one thing I could really do without were the rumors that spread because of this. One technological oopsie and the Conchs—island locals— waved their finger at me, saying, "See, I told you the place is haunted!"

It *wasn't*. Perhaps it was faulty wiring. Or....

I went up the porch steps, stopped to fish out my house keys, and unlocked the hurricane door. "This happens all the time."

"This is really a job for the police, Aubrey," Jun said firmly.

"I know, but things work differently down here." I stood and glanced up to offer a smile. "Relax."

He frowned.

I pushed the heavy door open and stepped into the pitch-black house. I turned on the little desk lamp beside the door to illuminate the security panel before punching in my code and silencing the chirping alarm.

I will admit, at night the Smith Home was… different. Duval was only a block away, and even with the bands playing and loud drunks hanging out in the bars, inside the home it was like nothing could penetrate the walls. A little bit creepy—like, *itty bitty*. Just don't tell anyone I said that.

"Now what?" Jun asked.

"I walk through the house to confirm it's all good and then go home."

"Aubrey," Jun said again in his *not happy* tone. "I don't want you doing this alone anymore. It's night, there are valuables in here, and what if someone had actually broken in and you didn't suspect danger?"

"Jun—"

"I'm serious." His face was cast in partial shadow, but he was giving me his angry cop expression—something I hadn't seen since New York. I certainly didn't enjoy being on the receiving end of it either.

"You know I'm not a helpless little wimp, yeah?" I went to the stairs and started up.

"I never said you were."

I groaned and waved my hands. "I don't tell you how to do your job, do I?"

"It's not the same. This is a matter of personal safety."

"So I'll buy some mace," I replied in a half-assed attempt to get Jun to drop it.

"Aubrey," he said again.

"Oh my God. Jun. Chill out, okay?" I asked, pausing to turn and look down at him. "It's fine. Everything's *fine*. Just stay here and let me do my job so we can go home." I resisted the bad habit of rolling my eyes and finished going up.

I'd walked the halls of the Smith Home a million and one times, so typically I didn't bother with lights until I got to the third floor and then worked my way down. Jun's paranoia wasn't enough to make me deviate from how I'd conducted myself every time the sensors picked up motion that wasn't there. I had no reason to suspect some psycho robber/killer/gang boss or whatever Jun felt was hiding in the shadows was, in fact, there at all.

There hadn't been a cause for alarm in the past, and besides Skelly's World Famous Disappearing Act, I never expected there to be an issue in the house again. But remember what folks said to me?

"Mr. Aubrey Grant, what a strange life you live."

Ain't it the truth.

I tripped on something in the middle of the hall on the second floor, went head over heels, and landed on the other side. I swore a stream of obscenities colorful enough to make my grandmother roll in her grave a dozen times over.

"What was that?" Jun called from downstairs. "Aubrey?"

"I'm fine!" I answered. "Just tripped."

When I pried my cell phone free from my butt pocket and turned on the flashlight, I realized I was going to have to get used to bodies and add them to the list of strange and unusual circumstances I'd been a part of.

Because there was a dead man in the middle of the hall, a wooden marlinespike protruding from his chest.

CHAPTER FIVE

THE LIGHT illuminating the figure shook wildly, and I realized that was because of me. I fumbled with the phone and dropped it. The rubber case hit the wooden floor with a thud and bounced once onto its back, engulfing me in darkness again.

I immediately slumped to the floor. Hello, cataplexy! I'm not sure how long it had me down for the count—it's usually less than a minute—but sitting up was a struggle, and I felt disoriented and sleepy.

Ugh.

What was I doing…? Oh—*the body*.

My blood started pounding in my ears, and I felt light-headed. If I jerked too quickly for the light, I was pretty certain I'd throw up.

Fuck me sideways. What was going on? Who the hell was *this* guy?

I slowly picked up the phone again and flashed the light in the body's direction. The marlinespike was still sticking out of his chest, and I swallowed the bile trying to race up my throat. Okay. So. We could probably assume he didn't die here alone or by his own hand. And was that Captain Smith's spike? Oh, so not cool! The integrity of the—*fuck*, focus.

I took a breath and could smell the blood in the air. I gagged and turned my head away.

Smith's marlinespike had a dull point. No way he could have driven that into himself. Which meant…. Yeah. Great. Someone else killed him. Jun was right, and now I had to apologize for telling him to chill.

But how'd these criminals get inside? The hurricane and house doors were locked, and I was sure the back door was secure too. And even if it wasn't, the outside alarm would have gone off if the doors had been opened. They hadn't. So what did they do, scale the freaking house?

The parlor window.

Fuckity fucknutter!

I opened my mouth to call for Jun because I wasn't sure I could get up and walk around the dead guy by myself, but then I heard a creak from one of the children's rooms on my left. My entire body tensed.

No reason to freak out. It was an old house. It creaked and groaned and settled all the time.

No reason at all—other than a second person had been in here at one point to do the killing. And they might still be around. No. Freaking. Biggie.

I stared hard at the marlinespike and swallowed the lump in my throat. I tore my gaze away after a moment and slowly raised my phone to point the light at the bedroom doorway.

Captain Smith, silhouetted by the darkness inside the room, stared back at me.

And then I screamed.

Screamed high-pitched bloody murder, because Captain Smith had been dead since 1871, and there I was, looking at the guy! He was as real as could be. The clothes, the beard—a spitting image of the family portraits. He even had the eye patch from a misfortune at sea in 1861, where he lost his left eye.

"Jun!" I screamed, then collapsed onto my back again.

The thing about cataplexy was, it looked like I was unconscious, but I wasn't. I was aware of everything going on around me. I could hear and understand—I just couldn't respond. I couldn't move my body because it was like someone pulled the power plug. My cataplexy was why I took life in stride, because if I allowed myself to become overwhelmed with emotions, good or bad, it triggered my attacks. So yeah, I was fairly chill and easygoing.

Except now.

Because who in their right mind could be cool about coming face-to-face with the ghost of a long-since-dead sea captain?

I heard feet pounding—a door—more feet—

"Aubrey!" Jun's hands were on me, hoisting me up to a sitting position, but he had to hold me in place. "Aubrey, hey, come on. Wake up."

I'm awake, just give me a second.

His hand touched my cheek, petting gently before it began roaming the rest of me.

Oh God, did Jun think I'd been hurt? Come on, get with the program, body!

"'M fine," I slurred. I slowly opened my eyes and blinked.

Jun's face was in front of mine. He knelt in the hallway, one hand holding my back and the other supporting my head. "Are you awake?"

"Cata—plexy. I'm awake."

Jun knew the difference. He'd done his homework on narcolepsy years ago when we'd first met. But I guess in the dark and not knowing the circumstances of me on the floor, he could have suspected a number of things besides cataplexy.

Jun let go of my head when it stopped lolling back. He looked over his shoulder at Most Definitely Had to Be Dead Man, and then back at me. "What happened?"

"I dunno." I rubbed my eyes, trying to shake off the lethargic feelings. "There was—I tripped over him," I said, pointing at the body. "And then, I saw a ghost."

"What?"

"It was Captain Smith." My eyes widened and I grabbed Jun's hands firmly. "I saw him! In the doorway to the children's room!"

Jun looked over his shoulder at the doorway, but it was empty. "Stay here," he ordered, getting to his feet.

"Wait, Jun! He—he killed this guy, don't go in there!"

Could ghosts stab someone to death with an antique marlinespike? Maybe. I didn't think there were any afterlife rules against it, anyway.

Jun ignored me, because *duh*. He used the flashlight on his cell to light the way to the bedroom. He looked around the corner, scanning the room with his light before going in. He came back out before I could struggle to my feet.

"Where is he?" I asked.

"It's empty," Jun confirmed. "You didn't see where he went?"

I shook my head. "I collapsed. I was scared to death," I said, sort of surprised to so freely admit that was the case.

Jun immediately joined my side once more to help me stand before giving me a tight hug. Warm, safe, strong. Could I just stay attached to him for a while? Like a remora on a shark? Not forever, just until I wasn't shaking anymore.

"If it was a ghost, he could be anywhere," I said.

"I thought you didn't believe in ghosts?"

"It was Captain Smith!" I protested, looking up. "The clothes were historically accurate! The beard, the eye patch. Jun, I've spent two years dedicated to the man's legacy—I know what he looks like!"

Jun nodded. "Okay. But the fact is, ghosts don't kill." He gently let go of me. A few passing cars outside caused dim lights to dance through the hall. I watched Jun press his fingers to the dead man's neck. He tilted his head, studying the body and the pool of blood.

"He is… *dead*, yeah?" I asked.

"Yes. Did you touch him at all?"

"I didn't see him. I didn't turn the lights on. I just tripped over him. But that's my marlinespike, I think."

"I need to check the rest of the house," Jun replied as he stood straight again.

I fiercely shook my head. "Don't."

Jun took my hand and gave it a squeeze. "Stay here."

He let go and then moved past me to check the master bedroom on the right before heading upstairs to the third floor. I listened to Jun's steps as he walked overhead, searching the captain's study and confirming the house was empty of any intruders.

"Someone's been up here," he called down to me.

"How can you tell?" I asked, not moving from my spot and nervously looking about the dark hall.

"The rope barriers in the study have been knocked down."

"That's where the marlinespike is kept!" I shouted back.

Even though Jun had confirmed the second floor was empty, that didn't convince my heart to stop pounding away, and I briefly thought I was going to pass out all dramatically like a Southern belle. There *had* been a man—a ghost—Captain Smith.

So where had he gone? He could have ghost-poofed. I didn't know what that actually meant, but ghosts, like… vanish and appear wherever they want, don't they? Fuck.

Jun was walking back down the stairs. "We need to call the police."

"Did you open a door?" I asked, looking up.

"Which door?"

"I remember a door," I said, sort of distracted as I pulled the sound from my memory. When I screamed and collapsed, there had been running, and I thought it was Jun coming to my rescue, but then there'd been the sound of a door….

"I didn't open anything."

I took a step forward but halted at the body. No berth was wide enough. Another car drove by and lit up the pool of blood. There was so much. It was so dark, like a thick red wine.

The bruschetta was going to come back up.

Jun noticed, took my hand, and tugged me along, all but forcing me down the hallway and away from the stench of blood and death.

"Maybe I heard this," I said. I made Jun stop at the stairs and pointed to the back balcony doors.

Jun pulled me to stand behind him and approached the door. He used his knuckles to press down on the handle, and the door easily swung open. "Should it be locked?"

"Yup."

I grabbed the back of his shirt and peered around him. The balcony was empty, save for a lone rocking chair. During the day, it offered a gorgeous view of the garden, but at night there were only the spooky shapes of towering palm trees swaying in the cool air.

"Come on," Jun said, his tone firm and not at all afraid. "Let's go to the gift shop and phone the police."

I SAT on the register counter, legs dangling over the side. I kept my head down and focused on a yoga breathing exercise—which was about as far into yoga as I'd ever gotten. The mat might be cushy, but a sleep attack in the middle of a downward-facing dog still hurt.

"Aubrey."

I glanced up. Jun was holding out a coffee cup he must have found on my desk. "Hard liquor?" I asked.

His mouth quirked. "Water. You're still pale."

I murmured a thank-you and took the mug, realizing belatedly the rather erotic artwork it featured.

Jun leaned back against the counter beside me, crossing his arms. "*Tako to ama.*"

"Huh?"

He nodded at the mug. "That woodblock art. It's called *Tako to ama.*"

I loved octopuses. Maybe that's weird? I thought they were just the coolest sea creatures ever. I wished I could go scuba diving and see one under the waves, but—narcolepsy. Not safe. So I collected octopus-related items instead. And the mug in question depicted Japanese artwork from the 1800s—a young woman diver having a sexual encounter with two octopuses.

"You're familiar with this?"

"Sure. Hokusai was a brilliant artist. He created *The Great Wave.*"

I turned the cup around absently. "I have to hide this whenever any of the board members come by for a visit."

Jun turned his head, staring at the front door. "I suppose cunnilingus and cephalopods aren't for everyone."

I snorted and choked on a mouthful of water before spitting half of it out.

Jun laughed.

I smacked my chest several times, coughing after I managed to swallow what was left. "Don't do that!"

He looked at me, smiled, and stroked my back gently. "Feel better?"

"No, but I'll live." I set the mug beside me. "I'm sorry."

"For what?"

"Telling you to chill, when you turned out to be right. Nothing like this has ever happened before."

Jun put his hand on my neck and dragged his fingers through the ends of my hair. "I don't want to be overbearing." He met my gaze. "I care about you. And—" He sighed. "I've seen a lot. That's all."

"I get it." And I'd be an ass if I didn't cut Jun a bit of slack. He dealt day in and day out with people who murdered, kidnapped, smuggled drugs and other humans—I think he deserved to be protective, even if it annoyed me in the moment.

Two police cruisers rolled up to the gift shop, their blue and red lights illuminating the street and making the shop look like a rave party. Jun left me on the counter, unlocked the door, and greeted two uniformed officers and one in plain clothes. Big surprise, that was my buddy Tillman. At least Jun was still carrying his badge, which he promptly showed the officers, although he was quick to add he was on vacation and just happened to be here. Maybe Tillman would take this a bit more seriously if he thought a Fed would make some phone calls if they were unsatisfied.

I bet Jun would do it too. Sexy badass that he was.

"Agent Tanaka," Tillman repeated. He squared his shoulders, but no matter how big he tried to appear, he still had to tilt his head to look up at Jun. "I responded to Mr. Grant's call earlier today about a skeleton found on the property. So if that—"

"Island Security called me," I said from where I still kept my ass parked. "About eight thirty. The motion detector on the first floor sent an alarm, so I came to turn it off."

Jun nodded. "An intruder was found dead on the second floor. Aubrey says a second subject was seen, but escaped before they could be apprehended."

I winced. A subject was seen, yes. But could a ghost be handcuffed? An hour ago I was a Negative Nancy on the idea of an afterlife, but I saw *Captain fucking Smith*! How else could that be explained but by the supernatural?

I hopped down from the counter and took a step before a powerful wave of exhaustion hit me. Oh Jesus. I needed a nap. Just a quick one.

I WOKE up on the floor.

Nothing new there. I couldn't recall the number of different floors I'd napped on over the years.

"Are you awake?" Jun asked from somewhere nearby.

I sat up, nodded, and rubbed my eyes.

"He drops like a ragdoll," an unfamiliar voice stated. One of the cops, I guessed.

"He's narcoleptic," Jun replied. He crouched at my side, taking my hand. "Want to stand?"

"Hmm, yeah." I got to my feet with his help and looked around. Tillman and one of the other officers were gone. "How long was I sleeping?"

"A few minutes," Jun answered. "Tillman and Officer Lane are checking the house."

"I need to go over there." I turned, but my knees went a bit Jell-O for a second, and I stumbled.

Jun grabbed me again before I could fall sideways into a display of stupid cup coasters. "You need to go to bed."

"Okay, *dad*," I scoffed. I waved Jun away when I noticed the remaining officer staring. I got stared at enough, and Jun babying me wouldn't make it better. I tugged at my clothes, trying to put myself in order. "I can't go until I know what's happening. It's my job."

"Tillman asked that you folks wait here," the remaining officer said.

I turned to glare at him. "And your name is?"

"Officer Barney."

"Barney. I manage this property, and I need to be able to assure the nonprofit committee that keeps the doors open and my employees paid that there has been no damage to the house or any of its artifacts."

"You can bring that up with Tillman, Mr. Grant."

My left eyelid twitched. I looked up at Jun and whispered, "Pull jurisdiction."

"What?"

I waved my hands at him. "Get all in their face with the FBI thing."

"This doesn't fall under any sort of FBI jurisdiction, Aubrey," Jun said calmly. "Local police can handle this. Besides, did you want me working on our vacation?"

My shoulders slumped. "No," I muttered. I walked to the window nearby and cupped my hands around my eyes while looking out. Every light in the house seemed to be on, and an ambulance was pulling up outside the gate. "I'm waiting in the garden for Tillman," I said. I made a dash for the door that led outside and escaped before Barney could get the "—ant" part of my name out.

I ran down the winding path to the Smith Home, Chucks squishing and sliding on fallen sapodilla fruits. A few late-night tourists, likely in between bars, were watching the house curiously from the other side of the picket fence. Tillman was coming out of the front door to speak with the EMTs. I stopped running at the steps, not going up as he gave me a glare, like "I dare you, shrimp." Although I glared back, hoping it came across as "Eat my shorts."

I had to give it to Tillman. At least when he *was* handed a body, the man was quick to call in reinforcements. Before I knew it, the house was swarming with crime-scene photographers, more cops, and the county medical examiner, who was standing by to take the dead intruder away. Of course, that was frankly… awful for business, but at least it was late at night. And those around to see the mess of police cruisers were at least on the far side of not sober, so… maybe they'd forget any of this ever happened?

As if.

I was left sitting on the porch steps for a while, holding my head in my hands. Jun had, of course, followed me out and had been patiently waiting with me the entire time. He had his hand resting on the top of my head, absently combing his fingers through my hair. It was nice. Comforting. I liked how he didn't hesitate with public affection.

"What time is it?" I finally murmured.

A pause. Then Jun said, "Quarter to eleven."

I groaned and whined loudly. "I'm so tired!"

Jun stepped closer, feet against the bottom step so I could lean my forehead against his thigh. "When do you go to bed?"

"Ten." Yes, I had a bedtime. My doctor recommended I keep a strict sleep schedule to ward off the daytime sleepiness.

"They look to be wrapping up," Jun said. "We'll go home soon."

We'll go home. I… liked how that sounded. And not just because I was ready to crash.

Jun prodded my shoulder as I was dozing against him, and I sat up straight, blinking. "What?"

"Tillman."

I looked over my shoulder as said cop walked out the front door and across the porch. I got to my feet. "So?"

"Did you know the deceased?" Tillman asked in return, coming down the steps.

I shook my head. "No. I mean, I didn't get a good look at his face because I never turned the lights on. I had a flashlight, but I was… sidetracked by the marlinespike in his chest." Probably wasn't the right time to mention that I fully expected to have the murder weapon back in the possession of the museum.

"How well did you know Lou Cassidy?"

"Cassidy?" I scrunched my face up and then pointed across the street. "The pirate museum guy?"

"That's the one."

"Holy shit, was that him?" I shouted.

"What was your relationship?" Tillman asked.

I shook my head. "I wasn't aware I had a relationship with him. He worked at Key Pirates Museum. They're across the street from us, a few doors down from the Custom House."

"How often did he tour this home?"

"I don't know… every few months he came by," I said, thinking hard. "He's one of the Conchs that insisted Smith was a pirate. Whenever he visited, he'd ask me about loaning some of our artifacts to them. He wanted to set up a display on Smith, portraying him as One-Eyed Jack."

"What did you tell him?"

"I told him no," I said firmly. "I told him that there's no historical evidence to back up the belief that Smith was a pirate. By all accounts he was a prosperous wrecker and investor. He didn't make his fortune in any devious way, so I absolutely wouldn't loan my hard work and research to a museum that would paint him as a villain."

"Did you ever argue about it?" Tillman asked.

"Argue?" I echoed.

Jun held up a hand. "I don't appreciate where you're directing this line of inquiry, Detective. I've been at Aubrey's side all day. To insinuate this fellow's death was at all due to him doesn't sit well with me."

"Just making sure I understand the situation, Agent Tanaka," Tillman said in a clipped tone.

"Look," I said, getting in between them, because if there was one person Tillman clearly disliked more than me, it was Jun. "Cassidy was a jerk about it. He insulted the work I'd done on the house, but—"

"Aubrey," Jun said firmly.

"I didn't hurt anyone," I protested. "That's insane to even suggest!" I looked up at Tillman. "What about a second person? The balcony door on the second floor was unlocked. Is there evidence someone else was here?"

"We're still looking," Tillman answered. "We'll need access to your security footage."

"Fine," I said. "Take all of it. Be my guest. Can I go inside and check the antiques for damage? Jun said there appeared to be some kind of scuffle on the third floor. I need to—"

"When the house is no longer an active crime scene, you'll be able to resume your work, Mr. Grant."

"What? *No*, I need to go in now," I insisted.

"I'm afraid I can't allow that," Tillman said with a tone of finality. "We'll be sure to lock the place up. Good night."

"What the fu—!"

"Aubrey," Jun said, interrupting me from swearing at a cop who'd probably need that one tiny insult as an excuse to throw my ass in jail. He took my hand in his own and gave it a squeeze. "Come on."

I WAS an angry little camper.

I fumed like a twelve-year-old brat the entire way back to my cottage and didn't get out of the car when Jun parked and turned it off. He walked around to the passenger side and opened the door, holding his hand out for mine. I waited a good minute before shoving off the seat belt and climbing out.

Jun shut the front door after we got inside. "Let's go to bed."

"I have to make some phone calls," I snapped. I wasn't mad at him. I was mad at Tillman. And dead Cassidy. And Skelly. And Ghost Smith. And—God, I was just *angry*! Why was all of this bullshit happening? Why now, when all I wanted was to spend a week and a half with Jun before he went back to New York and God only knew when we'd see each other again?

Jun came up behind me, put his hands on my shoulders, and dug into the knotted muscles. "It's after eleven," he said, voice still calm. "You don't need to be waking up staff tonight when there's nothing that can be done. Call first thing in the morning, once you've gotten some rest."

Read: Once you've come down from that twelve out of ten on the rage scale.

I shrugged his hands off and marched into the kitchen, where I began rummaging through the cupboards. I had Jolly Ranchers and Starbursts in there somewhere, and I needed to stuff those bags in my face right now.

"What're you looking for?" Jun asked.

"Candy. Before I light up because I'm really stressed out!" I didn't mean to yell, but I'd found my breaking point that night, and it was dealing with murder. I just—nope. Nope, nope, a thousand times, nope. *Hashtag nope*.

I heard Jun's quiet steps go upstairs, and I realized I'd probably pissed him off. He hadn't done anything wrong, and here I was, shouting at him like it was his fault I couldn't find my sugar and artificial color, Red #40. I slammed the upper cupboards shut and started pawing through the bottom ones, full of dry foods and pots and pans. Maybe I'd eaten them all and forgot to replenish stock.

Uuugh.

I stood and went to the fridge to read the grocery list I kept held in place with a Cthulhu magnet. Soy milk, scallops, celery, potatoes, candy— crap. I sighed and thumped my forehead against the fridge. I could hear Jun coming back down the spiral staircase and entering the kitchen. Then I smelled tobacco under my nose and looked to the side.

Jun was holding a cigarette out.

"I haven't had one for a month," I protested weakly, taking it.

"I won't say anything."

Fuck it. One wouldn't kill me.

Well. I said that back when I was sixteen, too, and here I was, thirty-eight and trying to quit. It'd kill me eventually.

"Just one. And I need to pick up some candy tomorrow."

"All right."

I put the cigarette to my lips, and Jun held a lighter out, cupping a hand around the flame as he lit the end for me. Sweet, delicious nicotine. I missed you so much!

"Better?"

I nodded and blew the smoke out to one side. "Better," I reluctantly agreed. I went to the sink to use it as an ashtray, since in my bold attempt to quit, I'd thrown all of mine out. "Why do you have cigarettes? I thought you quit years ago."

Jun moved to stand in front of me. "I always keep a pack around."

"For emergencies?"

"You never know."

I snorted and brought the cigarette to my lips again. "Thanks."

"Sure."

I didn't say anything for a few minutes. I tried to not think of anything but inhale, exhale, and tap the ash. I was like Joe Pesci when I was agitated. Not a pretty scene, and I definitely didn't want Jun to remember my kitchen freak-out as one of the highlights of his trip.

I looked up. Jun was staring. "How did I land someone like you?" I asked. It was more of an internal thought, but it sort of slipped out. Once, Jun had been nothing to me but my boyfriend's partner. And now.... Now he was everything to me.

"That's what I've been asking myself all day," Jun answered. He put his hands on either side of the sink, keeping me pinned where I was.

"Ever think that sometimes we have to get royally screwed over so we can appreciate life better?"

"How do you mean?"

"Matt was a shitty boyfriend," I stated.

Jun nodded but didn't say anything. Maybe out of respect for the fact that they'd worked together for several years.

"And I fell for that hardass, bad-boy vibe," I continued. "Even when he treated me poorly, I just took it because he was this guy who was big and strong and so much cooler than me. When he cheated, I thought—you know, he must have had a reason. So there had to be something wrong with me."

"There's nothing wrong with you," Jun answered, his voice barely above a whisper.

I stared at my nearly finished cigarette. "When I met you, the voice of reason that kept Matt from putting his foot in his mouth, I think that's when I started liking you. You were always so calm and collected. I enjoyed hanging out with you. I should have recognized back then that you were so obviously the better choice, but… maybe I would have never learned how you felt if Matt hadn't been the way he was." I reached awkwardly around Jun's arms to tap ash off the cigarette. "Would you have ever called me on your own? If Sebastian never reached out to the FBI?"

Jun's gaze sort of wandered. "I'm not sure."

I took another drag from the cigarette.

Jun looked at me again. "I was in love with you for a long time, even after you moved. It felt like a part of me left with you."

Jesus Christ. My hand with the cigarette shook a little.

"It would have hurt if you didn't want to renew our friendship. But I… think I couldn't bear having my heart broken again, having you in my life once more and still keeping at arm's length."

"But you *did* call," I said, managing to not have my voice crack as I spoke.

Jun smiled a little. "Because you'd given my name to Sebastian, not Matt's. I thought… you remembered me for a reason."

"I'm glad you did," I insisted. "*Duh*, right?"

Jun's eyes crinkled in the corners. "Duh," he agreed.

I put my free hand on his slender hip. "Dating the wrong guy taught me a lot. And I can be dense. I need hands-on learning activities."

Jun chuckled. He reached for my cigarette and took the last drag. He dropped the butt into the sink and exhaled slowly. "I love you very much. And I'm honored you've given me a chance to earn hearing those words from you."

My throat tightened. How the hell did Jun get away with saying things like that and still come off as cool and suave and utterly sincere? I reached up with both hands and put them around the back of his neck. I pulled Jun down to me.

Our mouths touched.

Simple, sweet, and with just a bite of nicotine.

CHAPTER SIX

THERE HADN'T been sex.

In fact, I was lucky I'd even managed to make it upstairs after the cigarette and kiss, because I was so tired, I thought I'd puke and pass out. It was the kind of fatigue that made your skin hurt. Totally brutal, but somehow I'd navigated the stairs, changed into pajamas, and even remained vertical long enough to take a leak.

Anyway, I slept like I was dead. But the life of a narcoleptic was both too much sleep and never enough, and all good things came to an end.

I customized my alarms because life was all about the little pleasures. Nicki owned all of my scheduled nap wake-ups, and until recently Taylor had always started my mornings off. But I found her voice, lovely as it was, didn't keep me awake at six, so now it was my longtime go-to girl, Britney.

Because Britney. Need I say more? Didn't think so.

I raised my head from the pillow and stared at my phone before grunting and dropping back down. "Too early...."

"Turn it off," Jun murmured from behind me.

I reached out, blindly groping for the phone before silencing the alarm.

Jun sighed, rolled over, and pressed against my back. He slid an arm around me, and his breath warmed the back of my neck. I touched his arm briefly, and holy shit! He wasn't even flexing and it was like a rock.

"Good lord," I muttered, voice raspy. "You are deceptively jacked."

Jun gave a sleepy laugh and tightened his embrace. His cock pressed against me, sliding into place between my cheeks with only our thin cotton pants separating us. He was hard and ready to go if I gave the word. Nice to know everything downstairs was in perfect working order.

"Time to get up," I said against the pillow, words a bit slurred.

"Yeah?" he asked, making no attempt to move.

"I don't want to mess up my schedule. Six o'clock, time to go."

Jun hummed and loosened his hold on me. He slid his hand along the slight curve of my body and rested it briefly on my hip before letting go entirely. "I'll start a pot of coffee," he said, sitting up.

"Oh, wait, it's decaf," I replied, turning to watch him.

Jun put his glasses on and gave me a critical look.

"I bought some regular grounds for you. In the cupboard above the coffeepot, on the left."

He leaned over and kissed me so gently, it was like a whisper, then went into the bathroom. Jun came out a moment later, looking far more refreshed and alert than I ever hoped to be in the morning. I sat up in bed so I could lean over and watch him go downstairs. Jun was fucking ripped and I'd been too tired the night before to even notice. He wasn't a bulky guy, just 100 percent lean muscle.

Jun walking around shirtless was going to give me a case of the vapors.

By the time I'd stumbled out of bed and brushed my teeth, I could smell coffee perking in the kitchen. I yanked a ratty T-shirt on, took my phone, and made the morning commute down the stairs that I hadn't considered a hazard when I first was looking to rent the place. But two years later, I hated myself every time I had to navigate them half-awake.

Aubrey Grant, age thirty-eight, killed by a set of stairs. In his defense, they really brought the look of the cottage together.

Jun held out a cup when I entered the kitchen. "I made yours first."

"Aww, you're a gentleman." I thanked him and took the mug.

I missed normal coffee, but I had to be strict about what I ate, just like when and for how long I slept. When there was no cure for a disease, the best you could hope for was management. My doctor advised staying away from stimulants like coffee and energy drinks and taking a prescription instead.

Jun put a new filter into the machine and started a pot for himself. "Why drink decaf?"

"Psychological, I guess," I said before sipping my coffee. "What do you want for breakfast?"

He leaned against the opposite counter and crossed his arms. I was pretty sure only my libido was awake so far, because he was talking and I zoned out, thinking mostly about licking his chest. I bet Jun tasted good.

Mmm....

"Aubrey?"

I startled and looked up. "What?"

He raised an eyebrow. "Were you listening?"

I set my mug on the counter before hoisting myself up. "I admit I wasn't." I took another sip of coffee. "I was preoccupied."

"With?"

I smirked. "Sexual fantasies." I motioned Jun over with a little "come hither" wave.

His crossed arms relaxed to his sides, and Jun pushed away to come stand in front of me. He put his hands on my knees, slowly spread my legs, and moved to stand between them. He stared at me again, awaiting further instruction.

I slid forward, wrapped my legs around his waist, and locked my ankles together. "What do you want?"

Jun swallowed. "You," he whispered. "Any way you'll let me."

In that one moment, there was nothing. Nothing in the entire world but him and me.

"I want your mouth," I said. "And I want it to be fucking filthy."

An intake of air.

Dilated pupils.

And then Jun crushed his lips against mine, pushed his tongue into my mouth, and shoved me farther back on the counter. He bit my lip, then moved down to suck on my neck, and it was like a direct on-switch for my dick. I gripped him hard, pressing Jun against me, encouraging him to leave a mark because fuck if I gave a single shit what people thought when they saw a deep purple hickey.

He let up with a gasp, licking the column of my neck before kissing my mouth like a man who'd been dying of thirst and finally came upon an oasis. Jun's taste was pure passion. Just male and heat and a clever tongue that was going to make me shoot before I'd even had a full minute of playtime.

I managed to push him back, breaking the kiss. "Too fast."

"Sorry." His hands left my body.

"N-no, I mean, make it last a bit longer," I said. I took Jun's hands and put them back on my chest.

"Oh." He laughed, breathless.

I grabbed a fistful of his hair, and he gasped again. "Suck me."

"Yes," Jun said obediently, a tremble in his voice. He slid his thumbs into the waistline of my pants and tugged them down with a bit of shifting about on my part.

My cock jutted straight up as it was freed from my pajamas. The head was already oozing precum from just a few heavy kisses, so if there was any doubt regarding whether I was digging the control I had over Jun in bedroom matters, that flew wherever my pants had gone. Jun took his glasses off and set them on the counter before he planted his hands on either side of me and leaned down.

"Kiss it," I ordered.

Jun's hot lips pressed against the head, kissing over and over as he worked down the length to my balls.

I swore quietly. "You speak three languages, and I bet give the best head in the world too," I murmured, watching Jun. "What can't that tongue do?"

Jun's breath was hot against my balls, and that goddamn glorious tongue snuck out to give each a good lick.

I hummed in the back of my throat and reached down to hold the base of my cock. I tapped it against Jun's cheek and left a glistening spot of spit and precum. "Show me how much you can take."

Jun groaned like he was coming apart at the seams, and I reveled in it. Jun deep-throated me, his knuckles turning white and his biceps flexing as he gripped the counter. I loved that this handsome, strapping, dangerous man had my cock stuffed down his throat because I'd ordered him to.

"Fuck," I moaned, one hand still holding a fistful of hair. "I bet you could come right now, just from getting me off, right?"

Jun let up a bit on my cock, managing a strangled whimper as he sucked the head and swirled his tongue around the crown.

"Oh God!" I gripped his head in both hands, leaning over as Jun stroked my orgasm closer with each swipe of his tongue. My breath came out hard and erratic, and my stomach clenched. "Jun—Jun, *yes*! I'm close! *Fuck*, I want you to come right now!"

I felt his body tense and shudder just then. And that revelation— that I really had managed to get Jun off by more or less telling him to— made the floodgates open. The first spurt erupted in Jun's mouth before I could find my voice to warn him. The second hit his lips and cheek as he pulled off, and a weak third dribbled down his chin.

My hands slid from Jun's head and my arms hung limp at my sides. My head thumped back against the cupboard door. "Jesus."

Jun stood straight, wiping my cum from his face with a thumb and licking it clean.

Holy every-expletive-known-to-man.

I tried to say something, but it came out like a half-assed grunt.

"Filthy enough?" Jun asked.

I started laughing. I'd shot my load on his face, he was licking it off, and had to ask if it was filthy enough? "What do you think?"

Jun smiled.

I slowly sat up, gripping his biceps. "I think we work pretty well together."

He nodded and curled a hand around my cheek and jaw. Jun leaned close and kissed me, sharing the taste of myself. "I've waited a long time to do that," he whispered.

"You know what they say about delayed gratification."

Jun chuckled. "Three years of wanting to blow you is pushing it, and I'm a patient man."

"I plan to test every ounce of patience you have," I murmured. "I'll make you putty in my hands."

Jun's lips parted, and he kissed me a bit harder, our tongues twining together briefly before he finally pulled back. "I should shower."

"I should clean the counter."

He laughed and went to fetch my discarded pants.

I hopped down, taking the offered clothing. "I'll start breakfast while you clean up."

"Okay." He combed his fingers through my hair and left the kitchen.

I stood still, listening as Jun's footsteps vanished up the stairs, and I was left alone in the kitchen to fan my face with a pot holder. Nothing like a morning romp to get the blood pumping.

I scrubbed the counter clean of sweat and any wayward cum shots while eyeing my phone in its bright pink case sitting beside my now-cold coffee.

Damn it.

I called the housecleaner and kept last night's news vague—the Smith Home was closed for a few days, no need to come by. Then I called Herb and the two other part-time tour guides. I was a little more honest with them—the house was closed by the police for a few days because of intruder activity last night, and someone had been hurt. Frankly, I think they were all happy to have a few extra days off during the busy season.

Adam was the only employee I leveled with.

"A murder?" he shouted.

"Yeah." I propped the phone between my ear and shoulder so I could rummage through the fridge. "The motion detector went off last night, but when Jun and I got there, someone had actually broken in."

"And died," Adam concluded.

"It was Lou Cassidy."

"The pirate guy?"

"That's him."

"Oh my God. This is…. I thought this kind of stuff didn't happen down here. Awful…," he murmured, voice quieting on the other end.

I pulled out a few containers of berries and a big avocado from the fridge. "Whoever else had been in the house stabbed him in the chest with Smith's marlinespike."

"Holy…," Adam said, sort of breathless. "God. I… I just bumped into him at the grocery store the other day. He's *really* dead?"

"Really," I said. "I'm sorry. I know this is not the sort of phone call you want early in the morning."

"No, no," he said. "You're okay, though, right?"

"Me? Sure."

"It's just—you found him."

"Don't remind me," I answered, dropping the food on the counter. I grabbed a knife and began cutting the avocado. "Jun was there to scrape me off the floor."

"Yeah," Adam answered, and he sounded a little—I don't know—unimpressed? Maybe Jun was right about him being jealous. That would be like a May/December romance, with me being the old guy, though, wouldn't it? Yuck, no thanks.

"Anyway—"

"How long is the house closed?" Adam asked.

"I'm not sure. I'm hoping only a day or two, but I need to talk to the board and the police to confirm what's happening. I'll give you an update when I have a bit more to go on."

"Sure. Hey, Aubs?"

"Yeah?"

"If you need anything, don't hesitate to call me."

I set the cut avocado down. "What could I need?"

"I just mean, you know, in a week and a half, I'll still be here."

Ah-ha. Okay. Jun was good. I had to put an end to this before it got serious. And I had to be nice about it, because I certainly didn't want Adam quitting on me and I really did like him. But friends only, please and thank you. Adam really needed to focus on kids within his own decade.

"That's really sweet, Adam. I appreciate it, but I need you to know that… Jun and I… it's an official thing now."

"Oh."

And here I'd been thinking for months that Adam was just a naïve straight boy who moved to the Keys to find himself after college. Forget broken gaydar—apparently I never had any to start with.

"Right," I stated.

"That was fast."

"It was a long time coming," I clarified.

Adam cleared his throat. "Give me a ring when we're supposed to be at work again."

"Will do."

"Bye." He hung up before I had the chance to respond. I felt a little bad, but I didn't want him to get any more invested in whatever feelings he had for me. It would only make it that much harder to let go of them.

I heard Jun walking around upstairs again, so I decided to make my last call—to the nonprofit board—after breakfast. Yes, I was putting off what I didn't want to do, thanks for checking.

Calling the board meant getting the receptionist, Liz Blake, who always patched me through to Mr. Horner, since they were a couple, but only in Horner's wildest dreams was he in charge. Then I'd have to convince Horner to put me on with Ms. Price, the president, but Bob Ricci would always intercept the call, claiming Price was busy and he'd take a message. It was always a mess. It'd take me an hour to reach the president, and then it was a crapshoot whether she'd pick up or was out to the world's longest lunch meeting.

Mostly, I ran the Smith Home on my own.

I toasted some bread and put it on plates before setting a dollop of cottage cheese on top of each slice. I added drizzled honey, raspberries, blackberries, all of the avocado, and a sprinkle of sea salt. A healthy and gorgeous breakfast, perfect for wooing my new man with.

Jun stepped into the kitchen as I swallowed my prescription stimulant with some lukewarm water from the tap. I froze, watching him retrieve the glasses he'd left on the counter. God. How did he look so hot all the time? I mean, seriously. I'd just had an incredible orgasm, so my dick was more or less behaving itself, and he *still* looked good enough to eat my breakfast off. He wasn't even wearing anything super fashionable today, just dark jeans and what looked like a homemade Dead Kennedys T-shirt. His thighs looked great in that tight material, though. And short sleeves on a man who had muscles to show off was always A-OK in my book.

"Something wrong?" Jun asked.

"Adam likes me," I blurted. "Er—you were right."

He nodded. "Figured."

"I can't believe I never got any hints," I said, shaking my head.

"What did he say?"

"Nothing, really. Just, in ten days you'd be gone and he'd still be here for me."

Jun's expression seemed to harden from the way his eyes narrowed. "If you'd rather not…. I know long distance for some people is—"

"Hey, hey, hey," I interrupted, waving a hand. "Don't even go there. We can totally do a thousand miles. Right?"

"Yes."

"Then don't let what he said get to you." I took Jun's hips and stood on my toes to kiss him. "I told him we were official."

"Did you?"

"As official as pumpkin spice in autumn."

Jun's mouth tilted to the side. "That's quite a serious commitment, Mr. Grant."

"I figured you'd be game, Mr. Tanaka," I teased back.

He laughed and gave me a brief hug before letting go and nodding at the food. "What's this?"

"Avocado toast," I said, picking up a plate and holding it out. "And some other goodies."

"Thank you."

"Of course."

Jun helped himself to the untouched coffee, and we walked with our breakfasts to the couch.

I took a big bite of the toast after plopping down beside him. "Man, I forgot how hungry sex makes me."

He chuckled. "It's certainly been a while for both of us."

I hummed in agreement, taking another bite. "I need to talk to the police and see when they're going to be finished at the home. Do you think it'll take long?"

"Always depends."

"Hmm… besides that, I'm all yours. What would you like to do today?" I turned sideways to look at Jun and tucked a leg under myself. "We've got a lot of historical homes and museums, although don't feel obligated just because I enjoy them. Oh, maybe we can go to Mallory Square at sunset, or do some shopping—" I paused when my eyelids drooped, and then I was out.

JUN'S HAND was planted in the middle of my chest. I blinked at it and slowly raised my head. He was eating his breakfast—calm as you please—holding me up from napping in my toast or crumbling into his lap. He glanced at me. "Awake?"

"Yeah."

He let go.

I rubbed my eyes. "How long?"

He looked at his watch. "A minute or two. Feel better?"

I nodded. Silly as it might sound, a two-minute nap did usually leave me feeling alert and refreshed, if only for a little while. I picked up my toast and started eating again. "Thanks," I added. "I mean, for knowing how narcolepsy works and not freaking out whenever stuff like this happens."

"It'd make for a trying relationship if I got upset over every micronap, or took your sleepiness as some sort of insult," Jun stated.

"That'd suck," I answered.

Jun reached out and gave one of my gauged ears a light tug. "Let's go shopping today," he answered, like I hadn't just been fast asleep a second prior.

My cell rang from the kitchen.

"Crap." I stood, stubbed my toe against the foot of the coffee table, and hobbled into the other room. I looked at the ID and groaned before accepting the call from the board's office. "Good morning," I said as pleasantly as possible. I turned and wandered back into the living room.

"Aubrey, what the hell is going on down there?" Bob Ricci thundered.

The real reason the nonprofit board left me alone so much to run the house was because, while I was in Key West, they were up in Marathon, and none of them wanted to drive an hour each way and chance bad traffic on Seven Mile Bridge just to be a warm body as I dealt with the boring, day-to-day transactions. I mean really, they were only concerned with whether I was making money and wanting to spend money.

I pulled the phone away from my ear at Bob's shout. "I'm afraid you'll need to be more specific," I answered. Bob and I had this ongoing thing of, how did I put this… *hating each other*. So for all I knew, he could have been really angry about the conch-blowing contest that happened the other week. How should I know?

"I received a call from Detective Burt Tillman this morning."

"Uh-huh," I responded.

Jun watched me from the couch.

"Did you have any intention of notifying the board about a homicide investigation, or were you hoping to sweep that under the welcome mat?"

I felt myself bristle. "I certainly did intend to tell you. But the fact was, it was after eleven when I'd left the Smith Home, and I don't have any of the board's home phone numbers. And waking you in the middle of the night wouldn't have helped the situation," I continued. "I was about to call in a matter of moments. You see, I typically get the best results when your office is open and someone is actually there to pick up the phone."

"How did this all start?"

"Er—I suppose when Lou Cassidy had it in his mind to break in?"

"Tillman mentioned a second body."

"Oh. The skeleton."

"What skeleton?"

"Tillman didn't pursue my claim because when I called the police and he came to investigate, there was nothing there."

"He said you were hysterical."

"I doubt he said that," I replied calmly. I took a deep breath and mentally reminded myself over and over that Bob *always* tried to get a rise out of me. Anything as an excuse to go to Price and get me fired.

"Explain to me why you failed to report this… this *skeleton* to the board," Bob demanded.

"Because I had nothing to say about it. It was gone. Like, up and vanished. I can't explain it."

"Are you on drugs?"

"Only legal ones." I sat on the couch, ignoring the look Jun was giving me now. "I was stripping wallpaper in the third-floor closet—"

"Who gave you the authority to do that?"

"Uhm… you guys. As part of the ongoing restoration I'm doing on the walls. The home wasn't originally wallpapered, so I was removing it."

"You have to get approval from the board to make any drastic alterations to the house, Aubrey!" Bob was all but shouting again. "This is totally unacceptable!"

"Are you serious?" I asked, not noticing at what point I'd stood again. "I practically handed you guys a bible of everything I was doing to the walls. Do you want me to call every time I sweep the floors too? How about when I have the outside windows washed? God forbid, because some of the dirt might be old!"

"Now you're pissing me off!" he exclaimed, totally losing his cool.

"Feeling's mutual!"

"You are not allowed to touch that closet," Bob said. "And I forbid you from entering that home for the foreseeable future. I'll be speaking to Price about your termination."

"Go to hell, *Bob*!" I hollered before ending the call. I turned and threw the phone at the couch, watching it wedge itself between the bottom and back cushions.

Jun calmly stood, took my upper arm, and led me several steps away from the couch.

"He's trying to get me fired!" I said, and I was sort of horrified that my throat had gotten tight and my eyes were watering. I complained about the job, sure, like any person would, but I loved working at the Smith Home. The blood, sweat, and tears I had invested into making it one of Old Town's top attractions could never be returned to me.

Jun stared down at me, rubbing my shoulders and not saying a word.

"That stupid son of a bitch is going to tell Price to fire me because of wallpaper! Fucking *wallpaper*!"

"Aubrey."

"No! This vacation has been a train wreck! There was a skeleton in a closet, I forgot you at the airport, someone was murdered, and now I'm going to lose the job I love because I didn't bold, highlight, underline, and asterisk that I may or may not need to remove historically inaccurate wallpaper in a supply closet that no one but me and the cleaning lady will ever see!" And then a dam broke and I started sobbing.

This was not the weird shit in life that I took with a shrug and some lighthearted humor.

This was just mean and unfair.

Jun wrapped his arms around me and pressed me against his chest. He petted the back of my head gently. "Shh…. Tension runs high when these sorts of tragic events occur, especially if you're not someone who handles it for a living."

"What do I do if I lose my job?"

"Find another one."

"But—"

"You're smart and kind, and I'm sure plenty of people around here can appreciate the work you've done on the Smith Home." Jun tilted my chin up and wiped my face. "Please don't cry."

"I hate Bob so much."

"I couldn't tell."

I sniffed and hiccupped. "I should try to get through to the president of the board and explain my side of the story."

"Let's wait until you've calmed down a little."

"She's a reasonable person," I said, hoping I didn't sound like I was babbling insanely.

"Then I'm sure she'll want to talk to you instead of blindly accepting the opinion of a dumbass."

I laughed and cried a bit at the same time. "I'm so sorry. I'm getting snot all over your cool shirt. I swear I'm not usually a crier."

"It's okay." Jun kissed my forehead.

My phone started ringing from somewhere inside the couch.

Jun shook his head when I moved to go get it. "Ignore it."

I FELT better after a hot shower.

Jun was right. Calling Ms. Price while I was upset and in hysterics wasn't going to win me any brownie points. I needed to calm down, collect myself, and handle the situation like an adult. So I relaxed under the scalding water and listened to music as I got dressed. And this time I took a few extra minutes to actually wear something cute that wasn't stained with coffee or *spilled Sapporo*. Purple skinny jeans—and I mean business in purple pants—an adorable T-shirt that had a narwhal on it proclaiming: I'm gay!, and I took out my plugs and replaced them with rainbow tentacle-shaped earrings, because *obviously*.

"Okay," I said, coming down the spiral stairs. "Fuck it. Let's go enjoy our vacation."

Jun had been watching television but smiled and turned it off as I got to the landing. He stood. "You look cute."

Mission accomplished.

"Thanks," I said, feeling my chest puff out a bit. Jun-compliments did funny things to my heart and stomach. If it were anyone else, I'd consider seeing a doctor for some rare, dual gut and arrhythmia condition, but Jun?

Nah.

I thought I was just experiencing... that thing before it becomes *the thing*. You know? The feelings before the L-word. English totally sucked sometimes. What could I say about Jun at this stage? I was in "like" with him? A lot? So lame.

"Let me dig out my phone, and we can skedaddle." I went to the couch and tugged the back cushions free to retrieve the cell, then checked the call I'd ignored.

Voicemail.

I tried to verify the number, but it came up as Blocked ID. I guess that happens—probably some "you've been preapproved for a credit card" company calling from a big corporate line or something. I chose the voicemail and brought the phone to my ear.

It buzzed and crackled on the other end for several seconds, like it was a bad connection. Then I made out a distorted, deep, creepy voice saying, "Aubrey. Don't go back inside."

CHAPTER SEVEN

"JUST LISTEN to it," I insisted, holding my phone up.

Jun was driving, and I was riding shotgun while being the most irritating passenger he'd likely ever had. "Whatever it is, it's not a ghost," he replied.

"Shh! Listen!" I barked. I put the phone on speaker and played the voicemail.

"Aubrey. Don't go back inside," the disturbing voice said.

"That could be anyone," Jun pointed out.

"It's a blocked number."

"It's easy to block a number on a smartphone when you make outgoing calls."

He was being too calm and rational. Or I was being too loony. Maybe a bit of both?

"Logically," I began, waving my hands as I spoke, "I know it's not a ghost. Ghosts don't make telephone calls. If they did, everyone and their brother would be getting rings from late Aunt Gertrude complaining that they weren't feeding her beloved Mittens the right wet food."

Jun snorted. "A reality like that would require Victor Bayne on speed dial."

"Oh my God, you didn't just say that."

Jun glanced at me.

I smirked. "I have all the books."

"So do I."

"Anyway, something *is* going on that I can't explain," I continued after a beat.

Jun drove past the Smith Home and turned left toward the Custom House.

"Jun, Duval is the other way."

He parked outside of Key Pirates Museum before turning off the car. "Come on."

"Wait, what're we—Jun?" I scrambled out after him.

He paid for a parking ticket at a nearby machine, returned to place it on the dash of the car, then met me on the passenger side. "I agree with you," he stated.

"Agree with what exactly?"

"All of it. That something weird is going on and you've somehow gotten caught in the middle."

A shiver crept along my spine, like an angry spirit had whispered secrets against my skin. I swallowed. "So what do we do?"

Because if anyone knew the next step, it would be an FBI agent, right?

Jun shook his head. "Not sure."

My shoulders slumped.

He motioned with a nod for me to follow as he walked toward the museum. His pace was deliberately slow. "We need to consider what we know."

"Are we crime solving?" I whispered harshly.

Jun stopped. "No." A smile crossed his face. Quick. There and gone. "Yesterday morning you found an old skeleton while removing wallpaper."

"Right."

"Twenty minutes later, despite a locked house, it disappeared."

"Yes. But the parlor window is broken. I figured out how to open it from the outside. So a possible exit."

"And a possible entrance into the house last night," Jun added.

I nodded. "Whatever happened between Lou Cassidy and the… the… Smith-lookalike, it must have begun in the captain's study, because the marlinespike was used as a weapon."

Jun put his hands on his hips, surveying the flocks of tourists around us as he listened to me. "Cassidy was, for all intents and purposes, a business rival."

"I guess so," I said, frowning.

"He wanted to turn the Smith you'd built up as a successful businessman into a pirate in the public's eye?"

"Right."

"Who knows about the skeleton?" Jun asked.

"Besides everyone?" I said. "You, me, Adam, Herb, Tillman, the board…."

"And who knows about Cassidy?"

"The same, pretty much, plus all the cops."

Jun put his hand on the back of my head, petting. I loved when he did that. It seemed to soothe him and made me feel special. "We've overlooked one incident."

"What's that?"

Jun glanced down. "In the closet. The message written at the bottom of the nook."

"An *X* on my heart," I whispered. "And only you and I know about that."

"Maybe someone else," Jun said. "Considering how quickly the skeleton vanished, someone knew exactly where to look and felt it imperative you not uncover the identity."

"Do you think someone's been watching me?" I asked. The cottage cheese and avocado from breakfast rolled around in my stomach.

Jun didn't exactly answer that question. "Someone's been watching you more closely than what I deem comfortable."

I felt like I had creepy-crawlies all over my body and scratched nervously at my chest.

"You said something last night about Smith," Jun said. He dropped his hand from my hair and slid his fingers through mine as he started walking toward the colorfully painted museum storefront. "Him being a wrecker?"

"Yeah."

"What's a wrecker?"

And just like that, I got on my little historian pedestal. "Wrecking was a prosperous job down here in the Keys. Because of all the reefs and shallow water, visiting merchants and other vessels would become stranded, and wreckers would sail out to help either save the ship or, if the ship was doomed to sink, at least get the cargo safely to shore."

"But for a price?" Jun asked.

I swung his arm lazily. "There's always a price. An ambulance will come to your rescue, but you'd better believe you're getting a bill for it. Some wreckers—like Smith—were honest men. Some were no better than pirates with a different job title. They'd sabotage incoming ships and basically hold the captains for ransom."

Jun stopped outside the door. "To play devil's advocate—"

"How do I know Smith was a fair man?"

He nodded, looking expectant.

"Court records. If a captain didn't agree with the fee a wrecker charged, they could dispute it in court. Smith usually won, and compared to his fellow businessmen, he went to court far less than they."

Jun let go of my hand and opened the door. "Learn something new every day."

Inside Key Pirates, the lights were low and the walls were painted with fabulous depictions of ships at sea. Overhead speakers looped tracks of waves crashing into rocks, the sound of men working aboard a ship, and the stereotypical "arghs" and "ye be walkin' the planks." The gift shop was loaded with people, and the register was dinging away with sale after sale.

Pirates sell, what could I say?

Although, I was sort of surprised they were open, what with Cassidy being… currently dead and all. But it wasn't like he was the owner. He worked as one of the pay-me-to-talk personal guides. And during March in a town dependent on tourism, I couldn't blame them for keeping the doors open. I wondered if any of the employees knew. Someone had to.

"Welcome to Key Pirates!" a chipper woman said as Jun approached the counter. "Prepare yourself for swashbuckling and adventure!"

Jesus. How many times a day did she have to say that?

Jun smiled politely and pulled out his wallet to purchase tickets.

"On Thursdays, all children twelve and under are half-price."

I slid up beside Jun. "No kids."

She looked down and recognized me. "Oh hey, Mr. Grant! You work at the Smith Home, don't you?" she asked, jutting her thumb backward to indicate the direction of the house.

"That'd be me."

"We always appreciate our local customers. Glen has you on his discounts list!"

"He does?" Glen was the owner. I really didn't know anything about him. I think we'd talked all of one time at a gallery opening two years ago at the art museum. Glen never gave me shit about Smith and the pirate rumors that clung to his name. That was solely Cassidy.

She motioned between me and Jun. "You guys visiting together? We don't usually extend the discount to the entire party, but I can make an exception today," she finished, offering Jun her biggest and whitest smile. "That'll be sixteen dollars for two adults."

Jun handed her a credit card.

I nudged him in the ribs with an elbow. "Someone likes you," I murmured.

"We have something in common, then," he stated, smiling back at the woman as he took his card and signed a receipt. Jun accepted the tickets she handed over.

"What's that?" I asked, following him toward the door leading to the next room.

"We both like cock."

Jun had to steady me when I started laughing and my knees got weak.

It'd been a while since I'd visited Key Pirates, but it was still an admittedly impressive museum. The well-researched parts, anyway. The huge room displayed countless treasures and artifacts recovered from two of the most famous shipwrecks in the area, the *Nuestra Señora de Atocha* and *Santa Margarita* of 1622. The Spanish galleons were special warships, designed to sail in convoys that protected merchant ships going to and from the New World and Spain. The *Atocha* and *Margarita* met tragic fates off the Florida Keys when they tried for Europe during the height of hurricane season. The galleons had been carrying somewhere around what would now be worth over 400 million in treasure—all lost at sea.

At the time, the Spanish had tried to recover their treasure, and I think had successfully located around half of what was once in the hulls of the *Margarita*, but the *Atocha* sank in fifty-five feet of water, and late October hurricanes caused the treasure to be further scattered across the ocean floor. The galleons typically held the most impressive cargo, like gold, silver, and precious stones, while merchant ships hauled agricultural products. So yeah, several ships in the convoy had been lost, but treasure hunters only really cared about the *Atocha*. After all, it had once been carrying over 200,000 pieces of eight silver coins. The sister ships had been discovered in the 1980s, and since then, much of their treasures had been lifted from the ocean floor.

But there was still more, according to the original ship manifests, that had yet to be found. Not including possessions belonging to wealthy passengers lost at sea.

That left for a hell of a lot of uncounted riches.

This part I liked. Real history, with facts and evidence and tangible items recovered and restored. The shit in the next room—the dumb pirate crap Cassidy had been trying to put together? No. Just no.

I grabbed Jun's hand and dragged him to a display featuring one of the recovered coins. "Look at this! Minted in the New World. Mexico—you can tell by the reserve stamp of the cross. Grade One *Atocha* coins can fetch upward of ten grand. Pretty cool, huh?"

"Very interesting," he agreed. "But these aren't pirate treasures, right?"

"No, sunken treasure belonging to King Philip IV."

"Then why is it in Key Pirates?"

"This place used to be called Key Treasures," I explained. "Then Cassidy was hired, and I don't know what he did to convince the owner, but Glen changed the name to Pirates and has been letting Cassidy expand and create pirate displays." I shrugged and let go of Jun's hand to slide my arm around his waist. "Maybe Glen will drop this pirate stuff now."

"Seems to me that Cassidy had to be onto something," Jun said as he walked with me to the display of an emerald ring that was worth so much, I could buy a New York City penthouse with the sale.

"What do you mean?"

"He must have had a reason for finding a connection between Smith and pirates. You know?"

I looked up. "Yeah, but who are you going to believe, him or me?"

"You, of course."

"Damn right."

"Still leaves for unanswered questions," Jun said quietly.

"Smith lost an eye at sea," I stated. "Maybe that's how the rumor was born. Eye patches and peg legs are all anyone thinks when you say *pirate*."

"Aubrey Grant?" someone piped up.

Jun and I both turned around. Was that Glen? I thought it was Glen. He was an older guy, maybe in his midfifties, with salt-and-pepper hair and a bit of a gut. I let go of Jun. "Hi, Glen."

"I haven't seen you around here for some time." Glen hurried over and shook my hand.

"I suppose not. I, uhm—hey, Glen? About Lou Cassidy…."

Glen's eyes widened. "Oh God. You haven't heard."

"No, I—"

Glen looked at Jun as he took my shoulder. "We'll only be a minute."

"*Glen!*" I protested, but he'd already started dragging me across the show floor and through another door.

"Aubrey, I'm so sorry to say this," Glen stated upon shutting the door and turning to stare at me. "It's about Lou."

"He's dead," I stated.

"*Yes!*" Glen hissed. "The police said he was—oh, Aubrey, I'm so ashamed. I thought Lou was a good man. He's really done a lot for my museum over the last year. I was going to come see you in person."

"For what?" I asked, crossing my arms.

"To apologize, on Lou's behalf. Breaking and entering?" Glen put a hand to his belly like he had indigestion. "I'm so sorry."

"It's all right," I insisted. "Honestly. And I know we've never been buddy-buddy," I continued, making a quick motion between us. "But between businessmen, I appreciate this."

Glen nodded. "I hope this hasn't tarnished your opinion of me."

"No, Glen, of course not."

"Good. Very good."

I looked around the dark room we were standing in. I thought at first we were in a storage room, but upon closer inspection, it looked like an unfinished display room. The pirate crap. Joy. "Was this what Cassidy was working on?"

"Yes. I'm not sure what to do with it all now. My expertise is in sunken ships and Spanish treasure, you see. Pirates? I can't say I'm well versed. That was all Lou." Glen sounded sincerely upset. I wondered if it was because he'd believed the nonsense Cassidy had been spouting as fact and now realized he'd been played, or if he was simply lamenting the lost money he'd poured into the pirate angle of the business.

Probably the latter.

Still, to say I wasn't curious about the display Cassidy had been concocting for Smith would be a lie. I was here, right? Where was the harm in checking it out? For all I knew, maybe it was the big, neon flashing sign pointing to the reason for all of yesterday's insanity.

"Glen?"

"Hmm?"

"Would you mind if I took a look at Cassidy's work? He was pretty adamant with me that he'd connected Captain Smith to piracy and, of course, you can understand why I'd want to know whether that was truth or conjecture."

"Oh, no, I don't mind at all. Let me get the lights." Glen shuffled around in the dim room before the overhead lights switched on.

The display cases were messy, still in the process of a cohesive story being prepared for each. There was a life-sized cardboard cutout of a stereotypical Hollywood pirate in one corner, and a wall-mounted television beside it with a dark screen.

"Interactive video?" I asked, pointing.

"It was supposed to play *Pirates of the Caribbean.*"

I rolled my eyes so hard, it hurt.

The rest of the setup looked to be a general history of piracy before it began to focus specifically on the Keys. Then I found a few handwritten notes atop a glass case that was practically empty.

"One-Eyed Jack," I read.

"Yes," Glen said, hurrying toward me. "Lou was obsessed. He was the Pirate King of the Florida Keys, more infamous than Blackbeard or William Kidd. But his career was shrouded in mystery, as was his death."

"Maybe he never existed at all." I looked at Glen's startled expression. "Pirates were eliminated down here by 1825. Maybe One-Eyed Jack was nothing more than a rumor—something one of the less savory wreckers came up with to scare visiting captains and crews, you know?"

"Oh, no, no, no," Glenn said quickly, shaking his head. He wore big glasses, like circa 1979, and shoved them back up the bridge of his nose as they started sliding down. "Lou was insistent. Jack was a real man." He picked up some of the notes. "See here. He estimated Jack was born around 1818. He was always described as a healthy, powerful man, even in his old age. Lou's research shows all mentions of Jack vanish from public record after 1871, so he suspected Jack suffered a tragic fate at sea, or even something more sinister. Murder, you know, possibly by rival pirates or even at the hands of the Navy! Can you imagine if Jack had lived and there was a resurgence of pirates?"

I grunted.

It just so happened these dates were horribly close to my own records on Smith. Born in November of 1818, died of unknown causes in (estimated) July of 1871. And yeah, Smith had cut quite an imposing figure. But his entire adult life was dedicated to the sea. That's rough, unforgiving work, so of course he was built like an ox.

Glen turned the page. "Look at this. Lou said the first mention of Jack being 'One-Eyed' is in 1861."

"Yeah. What a coincidence," I muttered. "The same year as Smith's accident."

"Was it?" Glen asked, startled and yet curious.

"It was," I ground out. "But that doesn't prove anything. I'm sorry to say this, but Cassidy was taking evidence A and evidence B and making them fit because it was convenient."

Glen sighed and set the papers aside. "Well… maybe… but I guess we'll never know for certain now."

I crossed my arms and was about to walk to a different display, when a little plaque sitting inside Jack's case caught my attention. "*Santa Teresa*? Another Spanish galleon?"

Glen leaned down to read the plaque through the front of the case. "Yeah. This one's a doozy."

"What do you mean?"

"There's conflicting reports as to whether the *Santa Teresa* was… real."

I laughed, but in the "are you shitting me?" tone, not the "I find that humorous" tone. "Why's that?"

Glen straightened, his back popping loudly as he did. "Ouch, geez…. Well, the *Santa Teresa* was supposedly built in Havana, Cuba, alongside the *Atocha*. It was meant to head back to Spain with the rest of the convoy, but it wasn't finished being built and they were so far behind schedule, they left without her. What little records historians have found seem to indicate a large quantity of silver coins was to be loaded on an awaiting galleon—presumably the *Teresa*—and it would head out on the next round making for Spain.

"But King Philip was so desperate for funds at the time, the *Teresa* was supposedly ordered to leave Cuba as soon as possible. So she headed out in October alone. We believe she's buried at the bottom of the ocean, destroyed by the hurricane that scattered the *Atocha*'s already sunken treasure."

Okay. Interesting, I had to admit.

"There's historical evidence to back this up?"

"A very small amount," Glen admitted. "Even I'm skeptical, but there's been two written accounts I've found, and the timelines are accurate."

"The Spanish kept such meticulous records of the *Atocha* and *Margarita*," I stated. "Why skip on keeping paperwork for the *Teresa*?"

"The rush to get it to Spain might have caused a lapse in protocol," Glen said. "And considering it was a last-minute build that never completed its maiden voyage? I could be swayed into believing its existence despite the lack of written documentation."

I pointed at the case. "Why's this here in Jack's empty display instead of on the walls in the main exhibit?"

"This was Lou's big thing—how he was tying the two subjects together."

I held my breath for a beat. "What do you mean?"

"Lou said One-Eyed Jack's last triumphant moment was when he found the treasure of the *Santa Teresa*. In 1871, worth around fifty grand. Today that's nearly a million dollars in Spanish coin lost at sea, recovered by a pirate, only to be mysteriously lost again. The value would likely skyrocket just based on who it belonged to and its history."

I gripped the case with one hand, feeling kind of shocked and excited and like the foundation of my world had been rocked ever so slightly. Also I was tired. "Can I lie down for just a minute?" I asked, already plopping myself onto the floor.

"Oh, oh, oh my gosh. You've got that sleeping thing. Can I get you anything?" Glen asked, suddenly all aflutter again.

I shook my head. "Just be a minute," I murmured before zonking out.

WHEN I woke up, it was to a weird sound.

Shink, shink, shink.

I blinked and yawned before slowly sitting up. Glen had settled on the floor beside me and was holding a necklace, tilting it back and forth so the pendant slid on the chain.

Shink, shink.

"Sorry," I said, rubbing my eyes. "Can't fight the sleep sometimes."

"That's okay. I figured if you didn't wake up in another minute, though, I might have to go get your friend so you didn't sleep on the floor all day."

"How long was I sleeping?"

"Almost ten minutes."

"Jesus."

"Must have needed it," Glen said thoughtfully, although it was obvious he knew little about narcolepsy beyond: I get tired.

"I guess," I politely agreed. I pointed at the necklace. "Is that a coin?"

Glen paused his motions and held the chain up from his neck. "Sure is. One of the pieces of eight from the *Atocha*."

"It's pretty."

"Yup. I had one made for my wife too." Glen smiled at the pendent. "I always liked the coins of this time period. No two are quite the same, and the stampings on the back, I always thought it looked more like an '*X* marks the spot' than a religious cross—"

I meant to put my hand on Glen's shoulder to stop him midthought, but in my… er… enthusiasm, I more like smacked him in the chest.

"Ow! Hey, Aubrey, what gives?"

"Say that again?"

"Ow?"

"No, the *X* thing."

Glen pushed his retro glasses back up the bridge of his nose. "The back stamp looks like an *X*." He held his pendent out, the chain still on him. "See?"

I took it and leaned closer. Of course I'd pointed the cross out to Jun already in the exhibit room, but I'd been caught up in the subtle style differences that hinted toward Mexican or South American in origin. But now that I was really looking… yeah.

X marks the spot.

Which made me think of the closet.

An X *on my heart.*

What if Cassidy's research wasn't a total pipe dream?

Captain Thomas J. Smith, aka One-Eyed Jack? Scourge of the Keys, Pirate King, and briefly, one of the richest men in the tropics?

It was crazy.

And not even normal crazy, but, like, total *batshit* crazy.

"I've gotta go," I said quickly, scrambling to my feet. I paused briefly as Glen huffed and puffed while standing up. "Can I take a few pictures of Lou's displays? Not to steal his work or anything, but I want—"

Glen waved his hand. "Go right ahead. What am I going to do with it all?"

"Jun. *Jun!*" I whispered loudly, hurrying back into the exhibit room a short time later.

He turned from watching a documentary on loop near a number of miniature replicas of Spanish ships. "There you are. Everything okay?"

"Yeah, sorry. I fell asleep," I answered quickly. "I just learned a few things that—maybe you're right about Cassidy being onto something."

"Are you serious?"

"As much as I hate to admit it, there does seem to be *some* historical evidence involved."

"Like what?" Jun asked, lowering his voice and backing me toward a wall.

"Get this. There might have been another galleon ship that was originally part of the *Atocha* and *Margarita* convoy. It was carrying at least a million dollars' worth of silver coins back to Spain—also lost at sea."

"What's the connection to Smith?"

I leaned closer, speaking more at my feet and forcing Jun to lower his head to hear. "Cassidy straight-up believed Smith was One-Eyed Jack, and *whatever* if he was or wasn't, but Glen had mentioned the backs of coins always reminding him of an *X* instead of a cross. Like on a treasure map." I grabbed both of Jun's biceps elatedly. "Kind of like the closet! What if that message was some sort of clue? What if that skeleton *was* Smith and it was a hint about his double life?"

"Now you're the one jumping to conclusions," Jun said.

"I know I am. I'm ashamed. But I've done more research on Smith than anyone, and he *was* a wrecker. So, instead of letting that knowledge cloud my judgment... I should start fresh and research *Jack* from the beginning. Treat him like a separate individual and see if their paths cross."

"You think you would be able to conclude whether the two men were one and the same?"

I nodded, looking back up at him. "Exactly. Cassidy was an amateur. I'm a professional."

"You're very excited," he pointed out.

"I know! I'm trying to contain it, but treasure hunting, Jun! What little kid didn't have this dream? And as a historian, the potential for new discoveries that could change everything we know is... it's *very* exciting, I gotta admit." My grin was making my face hurt.

Jun smiled that cute little quirk of his. "You make a good point."

I was about to speak again but saw Glen walk by us and I went after him. "Glen! Hey, can I bother you about one last thing?"

Glen stopped and turned around. "Sure, Aubrey." He looked up at Jun, smiled, and nodded politely.

"If I wanted to talk to other pirate treasure hunter sort of enthusiasts in Key West, where would I go?"

"Barnacles."

I blinked. "Uh… bless you?"

Glen started laughing, gut shaking. "You're funny. No, Barnacles—the bar. Over on Southard."

"You mean the den of ill repute?" I leaned close to Jun. "Used to be a brothel, way back in the day."

"Got it," he murmured.

"That's the one," Glen said. "It's a group of them. Lou used to hang out there. They meet for lunch and drinks every Tuesday and Thursday."

CHAPTER EIGHT

"WE SHOULD talk to these treasure hunters," Jun said as he walked to the meter to buy another ticket for his car before an enthusiastic traffic cop came by to smack him with a fine. "What do you think?"

"I think you're a mind reader," I answered, following behind him.

Jun dug into his pockets and fished out a few coins. "If they were friends of Cassidy's, perhaps one has insight as to why he broke into the Smith Home."

"Exactly," I agreed. "It directly correlates with the closet fiasco. Somehow. I know it does. The timing is too much of a coincidence."

Jun took the ticket the machine spit out and went to replace the old one on the dash in the car. "If that's the case, then we both need to be careful when talking to them."

"What do you mean?"

Jun shut and locked the door, looking at me from across the roof. "Aubrey. A man was murdered. We don't know by who. For all anyone knows, it was one of his treasure-hunting buddies—in fact, that makes the most sense."

"I wish you could strong-arm the cops into sharing info," I said. "At least see if the marlinespike had fingerprints or anything."

"Life would always be easier *if*—right?" Jun smiled and came around the car to join me again. "If anyone asks, you're simply offering your condolences."

"This is exciting, right? Say it is so I don't feel weird about it."

Jun put his arm around my shoulders, and we started walking back to Whitehead. "It beats the hell out of a hotel kitchen shootout."

"I'm going to pretend you didn't just say some yakuza dude fired a gun at you."

"It was a Chinese gang," he corrected.

I put my fingers in my ears. "La, la, la, I can't hear you!"

"I was okay," Jun insisted. "Just a scratch."

"Where?"

He stopped walking and raised the sleeve of his T-shirt to show a whitened patch of skin, almost like a ripple.

I touched it, frowning. "When was this?"

"Before we met." He put the sleeve back down.

"Now that I'm in the picture, no more getting shot at, okay? It'll make my hair fall out."

"We can't have that." Jun smiled and gave my hair a gentle tug. "I promise I'm careful."

We crossed the street and passed by an ice cream parlor with no less than eight hundred people inside, Key Lime & Forever, which was also surpassing fire safety capacity, and then a few lame tourist shops selling Key West trinkets and T-shirts you could find anywhere else in the country.

Jun came to an abrupt stop and smiled at something inside that I didn't see. "Stay right here."

"Huh?"

He walked into the tourist trap.

"Jun! Wait, you can find these shirts at JCPenney! Oh, I've lost him…."

I sighed and stepped to the end of the block, staring at the faint outline of the Smith Home hidden among all the tropical foliage. There was something in there I needed to know about. Something that would cause everything to make sense. Cassidy broke in, likely to… what, steal something, right? But in the captain's study? I tapped my chin thoughtfully. There was an old ship's compass worth a pretty penny. The desk and chair were original to the home, which was pretty amazing. There was an antique inkwell and pen, a pencil—which, believe you me, those were hard to find—the marlinespike….

Why steal any of those? If this had to do with treasure, how are any of those artifacts significant?

What about a map? I had some on display. One was Smith's. The others were authentic to the period, but only something I'd purchased to help fill the exhibit space. But it sort of made sense—what more could you possibly need to find treasure than a map, right?

"Here you go," Jun said, and before I could turn around, a hat was plopped onto my head.

"Why'd you buy me a hat?" I took it off to inspect it. A brown fedora. "Oh Christ, a fedora? You know this is a fashion no-no, right?"

"It's Indiana Jones's hat."

"Is it?" I looked back down at it.

"Sure, Indy."

"Okay, I'm biting. What's with the nickname?"

Jun took the hat from me and put it back on my head. "Indiana Jones said *X* never marks the spot, and he turned out to be wrong."

I grinned. "So I'm Indiana? That's pretty cool. Do I get a whip too?"

"Don't push it."

"Rawr."

Jun shook his head and pushed the brim down over my eyes.

"You're such a cutie," I said, following him once more. We kept walking along Whitehead. "Except that I'm mortified you're quoting *The Last Crusade*, when the obviously better movie is *Temple of Doom*."

"*Temple of Doom* doesn't hold a candle to *Crusade*."

"Take that back!"

"No."

"What?" I asked, flabbergasted. "This is like with Rihanna! *Who are you?*"

Jun took my hand and kissed it lightly. "Someone with better taste." He smiled widely, eyes crinkling before he let go, and I missed an opportunity to whack him.

BARNACLES WAS a dive bar. It was old as sin, and considering it used to be a brothel in the nineteenth century, that sordid history was practically fused into the support beams. The upstairs area was closed off these days and used for storage and offices, but way back when, the entertaining happened down here before the party was brought to one of the private, closet-sized rooms above.

There was nothing quite like the stench of low tide, yellow fever outbreaks, and gonorrhea to remind you of your time in the Florida Keys.

The building had been abandoned by the turn of the century and eventually restored and converted into a grocery store prior to World War I. Then, around the time I was in diapers, it was bought again and became the little gem it was today, where you could get shitfaced at nine in the morning on piss-warm beer and the inside smelled like thirty years of cigarette smoke and sweat.

It was too early for lunch when we reached Barnacles, but I didn't want to miss the chance to see who this group of treasure fanatics consisted of, so Jun and I sat at the back side of the square bar. We had a view of both sides, as well as the front, so we could watch those coming and going.

"I suppose a smart thing to have done would have been to ask Glen if he knew any of these dudes by name," I said, taking my new hat off and setting it on the seat beside me. "But I guess just look for a group ordering food."

Jun nodded, eyes flicking to the overhead television a few times. He cursed under his breath.

"What?" I asked, glancing at him and then looking around the bar.

He shook his head and pointed briefly at the television. "Rangers are down."

"I didn't know you watched hockey."

Jun glanced at me. "Is that bad?"

"No. I kind of like hockey. I mean, I'm *so* not a sports guy, but if I had to watch something, hockey is definitely the most entertaining. Plus hockey players are hot, have you noticed that?"

"Yeah," Jun said bluntly. "I have."

I scoffed. "Hey, eyes on me."

He chuckled and leaned over to give me a light kiss. It was pretty awesome.

"Get you gentlemen a drink?" a bartender asked, effectively ruining the mood as he slid up in front of us.

I pulled back from Jun and turned to look at the guy. Muscles, cropped hair—nice, but he had nothing on my boyfriend. "I suppose this is the wrong venue for a mimosa?" I asked, smiling widely.

"Corona. He'll have a water," Jun said, pointing at me.

The bartender gave me a critical look before nodding and walking away.

"Don't antagonize," Jun said to me.

I shrugged. "He shouldn't have ruined our moment."

"We'll have plenty more moments."

I flashed Jun a cocky grin and slid my hand under the bar top to rest on his thigh. "Is that so?"

Jun swallowed, his eyes locked with mine. "Yes."

"And what sort of moments will they be?" I crept my hand in between his legs.

Jun let out air, and I caught a shake in his breath. "Whatever you wish," he said.

I moved my hand a bit farther still, fingertips rubbing against his balls through his jeans. Jun gasped, and his thigh shook as he fought to remain still. I moved my hand upward, amazed to find that he was getting hard so soon. I'd barely done anything yet. We really were hopeless for each other if we were always seconds away from coming in our pants.

"Already?" I murmured.

Jun let out the smallest pant as I thumbed the head of his dick. "I want to make you feel good," he whispered.

I grinned, looked down at his crotch, and let go, putting my hands back on the bar. "I don't think you'll have any problem there. But what is it *you* want, Mr. Tanaka?" I leaned close. "To fuck my fine ass?"

Jun licked his lips.

That was a yes.

"Or maybe you want me to bend you over and do as I please?"

Jun didn't reply, but I saw the flutter in his throat. Getting him twisted up like this was making me horny as hell. I could honestly say I'd never expected to like this as much as I did—but teasing him, getting Jun antsy and desperate, squirming in anticipation for a guy his total opposite? Oh yeah, it was hot. And to think that people in the bar had no idea *I'd* been the one ordering him to choke on my cock this morning, not the other way around.

Jun shifted on his barstool. "You're in trouble," he said, clearing his throat.

I laughed loudly. "I bet I am."

Jun gave me some serious side-eye, but managed to compose himself by the time the bartender returned with one bottled beer and a glass of water with no ice. Jun slid a few dollar bills over, and the bartender left.

"Scrimping on the niceties," I muttered, then took a drink.

Jun silently sipped his beer.

No one looking to form a lunch date seemed to stop in for at least an hour. It was just me, Jun, muscley bartender—annoyed that I wasn't buying a drink so he never offered to refill my glass—some locals practically asleep on their tables off to the sides, and a group of obnoxious college kids screaming at the tail end of the hockey game from the right side of the bar. One drunk girl in the gaggle ended up fixated on Jun, even going so far as to send the bartender over with another bottle of Corona.

"I didn't order this," Jun said.

"She did," the bartender replied, pointing across the bar before walking away.

"Oh boy," Jun said, sighing.

"She's, like, half your age," I protested quietly, leaning closer to talk to Jun as we both stared at the girl. "What do you want me to do? Maul you?"

"That's mean." He slid the bottle away politely.

I winced. "No, *that's* mean." I glanced at the girl, who offered Jun a drunk pout. "I can grope you again. Because she's not backing down."

"Behave."

"Say the word and I'll be on your lap."

"Aubrey."

"No?" I looked at Jun. "I thought you might like that. Lying back as I do all the work." I lowered my voice but never broke eye contact now that I had him laser-focused on me once more. "Watching me ride you—watching the way I fuck myself on your cock, totally desperate to come all over your chest. Wouldn't you enj—"

Jun grabbed my face with both hands and planted a big kiss on my mouth, effectively shutting me up. His tongue caressed my lips, and I opened, letting him inside. Heat and Jun and a tang of beer.... Christ, now I really was ready to throw him down and climb up on that dick. He pulled away first, gently letting go.

I whistled. "Holy crap."

"Sorry."

"Did I really do that, or were you just telling the nice lady, 'no, thank you'?"

Jun thumbed the corner of his mouth absently. "You're in *so* much trouble, Mr. Grant."

"Oh, at this point, I can't wait, Mr. Tanaka."

When I thought to look back toward the college kids, Hopeful Drunk Girl was trying her luck with someone her age and orientation.

"Here comes a group," Jun murmured, nudging my arm.

I leaned toward him, looking around the bartender and shelves of liquor to the front door. Two guys and a woman came in, talking and laughing with the vibe of Conchs, not tourists who came to Barnacles to look like Conchs.

"Do you recognize any of them?" Jun asked.

"Yeah, all of them. Tourists can pay to be brought out for deep-sea fishing. The woman is one of the local captains. Has her own boat. Peg Hart is her name. And that guy on the left, I don't know his name, but he works for one of the Ghosts of Key West tours. The bald guy—Josh something—he's one of my contract painters for the Smith Home."

Jun grunted. "I wonder if they are casual friends or if they hunt treasure together," he said thoughtfully.

We watched the three motion to the bartender before pulling out chairs at a tall table to the left of the room. They sank into a comfortable chatter, sipping beers like they'd done this routine a thousand times.

"They don't seem too broken up," I whispered.

"If they are Cassidy's friends, they might not know about what happened yet."

"Or if they do," I said, "a million-dollar treasure split three ways instead of four? Could be reason enough for some people, you know?"

"Don't get ahead of yourself without first knowing the facts." Jun stood and grabbed the freebie Corona. "Ready to do a bit of acting?"

I hopped down, took my Indiana Jones hat, and nodded. "Yup." I slipped around Jun and headed over to the table. "Hey, everyone," I stated.

Josh So-And-So, I swear he was built sideways as much as Jun was tall, looked up from his drink. "Look at the tiny sprout we've got today. When'd you start working here, buddy? We'll have the usual—ask Frank in the kitchen what that means."

Oh for—I felt my eyelid twitch. "I'm… uh, not your waiter," I said awkwardly. "Aubrey Grant. I manage the Smith Home."

"Is that so?" Josh asked. "Didn't recognize you."

Peg laughed and shoved him roughly. "Didn't recognize the person signing your paycheck?"

"Must be the angle," Josh said jokingly. "I'm usually on a ladder, and he's so… short."

Ha-ha. Guess who wasn't being hired back to finish my restoration project?

"I'm Curtis Leon," the second man said, reaching out to shake my hand. "These are friends of mine. Peg Hart, and this Grade-A asshole you know already, Josh Moore. Pull up a seat."

Jun grabbed two chairs, and I sat first before he slid in beside me.

"Who's your friend?" Peg asked me, giving Jun a wink and chugging her beer.

"Jun Tanaka," I said, motioning to him. "He's visiting the island."

"Yeah? Well, be careful," she said to Jun. "Once you step foot here, it's impossible to leave. That's why I still have a husband."

Jun smiled politely in response while everyone laughed.

Ohhh... I knew what he was doing. He was being the nice guy, the quiet and unassuming one, like when he worked with Matt. Matt was usually the loud, in your face, *don't fuck with me* sort of Fed. The good-cop, bad-cop tactic.

Jun didn't expect me to be the bad guy, though, did he? Because, at best, I just do bitchy.

He was letting me lead because I knew these folks, or at least knew of them. I lived in Old Town, I worked here, I could (in theory) speak easier with them about Cassidy. If he did the questioning, maybe they'd peg him as a cop and get spooked. That is, if they were guilty of something.

"I don't think we've seen you poke your head in Barnacles before," Curtis stated.

"No, I'm usually at Sea Shack."

"Tourist trap," Josh grunted, crossing his huge arms, which were brown from years in the sun.

"Ah, I suppose, but the smell of cigarette smoke makes me want to light up," I replied, waving my hand vaguely.

"We all gotta die sometime—might as well go out doing what you love," Josh answered.

I glanced at Jun and saw his eyes narrow slightly.

"So, what brought you over this way today?" Curtis asked, clearly the most pleasant of the three.

"Lou Cassidy, actually," I said. "Was he close with you all?"

"What do you mean, was?" Peg asked, setting her beer down.

Curtis hung his head briefly before letting out a long sigh. "Lou's dead, Peg."

"*What?*" she cried out.

"Dead?" Josh echoed.

Curtis looked up. "I was visiting Glen over at Key Pirates early this morning. The police showed up and were questioning him about Lou. He... he was murdered late last night. I didn't want to say anything yet...."

Peg's eyes were as big as saucers, and something told me she wasn't faking this shock. So, not suspicious, although that alone wasn't reason enough to write her off as guiltless. "Dear God. What happened? That poor bastard!"

"That's actually why I'm here," I stated. "He was found in the Smith Home. It looks like he had broken in, and there was some kind of scuffle that…. Well, and he died," I simply concluded.

"You accusing Lou of trying to rob that place?" Josh asked defensively. "Lou was a damn good guy, and you're saying he would have risked his neck to steal what, *exactly*? A fucking deck of old playing cards?"

"Hey!" I piped up. "I didn't say that at all. And those cards are worth a few hundred bucks, thank you."

Curtis held his hands out, trying to silence the table. "Guys, come on. The fact is, we don't know what happened yet. Josh, Aubrey here is right. The cops said Lou was found upstairs in the Smith Home, and how can we explain his presence there? He wasn't an employee—he didn't have keys."

"Bastard had to have been drunk," Peg said sadly, shaking her head.

"I only wanted to give you all my condolences," I told Josh firmly. "I was told you were good friends of his." Okay, so that was more of a guess on my part, but luckily for me, I'd been right.

Curtis nodded and spoke for Josh. "Thank you. It's nice of you to come down here."

Peg held up her glass and wiped under one eye. "To Lou, the best damn hunter if there ever was one."

Curtis and Josh obediently raised their glasses, clinked against hers, and took long chugs of beer.

"Cassidy was a hunter?" I asked. I figured that didn't mean he hunted Bambi, and I was hoping to get a bit more out of the group before being dismissed.

Peg burped and patted her chest. "Treasure hunter. He was a natural."

"Oh." I rubbed my sweaty palms against my thighs. "Did he ever find anything, like… famous?"

"He was hot on the trail of One-Eyed Jack's lost stash."

"Peg," Josh said. "We don't need folks inviting themselves into the hunt."

"Believe me, do I look like the sort of guy who gets his hands dirty?" I asked Josh.

"Lou claimed a lot of things," Curtis interrupted. "He was still researching."

"I guess he was pretty dedicated to Jack," I said absently. "He was designing an exhibit for Glen."

Peg nodded. "Sure was. Jack was Captain Smith, you know." She finished off her beer and waved to the bar for another.

"I'm sure Aubrey has done his own research," Curtis told Peg. He looked at me and smiled. "Right?" He was kind of cute. Tall, well-built, messy auburn hair.

"Ah, right," I said. "I didn't exactly come to the same conclusion."

"Then you're wrong," Peg stated frankly. She combed back some dyed red hair from her eyes. "Captain Rogers identified Jack as Smith. It's in his diary."

"Peg," Curtis said, putting a hand on hers. "Aubrey probably doesn't appreciate being told he's *wrong*."

Rogers. Rogers… I knew that name…. I yawned and shook my head quickly, trying to fight off the desire for a nap. "Rogers was a—a merchant ship captain. European furniture, I believe. His ship was stranded on the reefs his first time out here, and Smith was the wrecker who came to his aid."

Peg shrugged. "Well, I don't know about any of that, only that Lou has his diary and there's some entry about Rogers seeing Captain Jack disembarking from the *Red Lady* and slipping into a shanty. The next thing he knew, out stepped Smith, looking every bit like a respectable gentleman."

I looked at Jun's profile quickly. Now I was awake. "Lou *owns* Roger's diary?"

Danger, Will Robinson!

Captain Roger's diary was reported as stolen from a tiny museum in St. Augustine about a year ago. But maybe Peg didn't know that. Maybe she also didn't know that, as the manager of a museum myself, I stayed on top of reports of theft, and with a history in pawnshops and a friend in antiques, we all kept in contact with one another and were pretty well-informed.

And it just so happens that stealing an item of cultural significance from a museum was a *federal* offense. Hmm. I'd be damned. Here I was, sitting right beside a federal agent too.

"Peg," Curtis tried again. "You're offending Aubrey."

"No, I—" I was cut off by Josh.

"I think *Aubrey* best leave anyway. Our friend is dead, and he's pegged Lou a common criminal." He pointed at Jun. "Take this fuck with you too."

"Josh!" Curtis shouted.

"No, it's fine," Jun said, finally speaking. He slowly stood, taking a moment to grab one last sip of beer and rub it in Josh's face that he wasn't the least bit intimidated. "You all have a pleasant afternoon."

I hopped down from the chair, watching Jun make for the door. "By the way," I said, grabbing my hat before looking at Josh. "He's FBI. You may want to not be such an asshole in the future."

Josh's face paled and he glanced at his buddies.

Seeing him finally at a loss for words felt really damn good. "Uh-huh. See ya." I walked out and joined Jun on the sidewalk. "Sorry about that."

He looked down. "Why are you sorry?"

I shrugged. "Well, I know Josh won't apologize for being a cock… so…."

Jun smiled slightly and put his arm around my shoulders, squeezing.

I put my hat on and tilted the brim back to look at Jun. "Captain Roger's diary," I began. "Did you know it was reported as stolen from a museum last year?"

He raised a perfect eyebrow. "Is that so?"

"Doesn't the FBI look into museum theft?" I asked in a playful tone.

"That they do."

"And if he broke into my museum with the possible intent to take something," I continued, "isn't it conceivable he has more than a stolen diary in his possession?"

Jun looked thoughtful before he moved his arm, pulled out his wallet, and chose a card. He took his phone out of his other pocket and dialed the number. "Detective Tillman?"

I put my hands on my hips. Jun was such a sneaky bastard.

"Agent Tanaka. I'd like to set aside some time to speak with you today about Lou Cassidy."

CHAPTER NINE

"BUT WHY do you think he agreed to talk with you?" I asked Jun. I paid the cashier in the shop we'd ducked into so I could buy some candy before I imploded and tackled the nearest person on the street to steal their cigarettes. "Do you think he found stolen artifacts at Cassidy's home and knows the FBI has jurisdiction?"

"I doubt that's the case," Jun said, holding the door open for me as we walked out. "But local law enforcement tends to listen when we pull the *agent* card."

"But the FBI can look into Cassidy now, if they wanted?"

"The Art Crime Team would likely want to, yes," Jun answered. "And if it boils down to me having to make phone calls to get Tillman's cooperation, I know an agent in Miami on the team that might be able to help."

I stopped walking. "Not… Matt or—"

"No." Jun crossed his arms. "Matt's still with Organized Crime. He took a transfer to Boston."

My shoulders loosened. "Okay. Good. I had to check." I ripped open a bag of Skittles, a few falling to the ground and bouncing across the sidewalk. "Crap."

"Come on, Indy." Jun led the way back to the rental car, and we got in.

I put the hat, which I was now likely to never live down, in the back seat before offering Jun some candy. "I took pictures of Cassidy's displays in the museum."

"Did you?" he asked before popping the Skittles into his mouth.

"I figured it might be important."

"Smart. With the owner's permission?"

"Totally."

Jun nodded, starting the car. "You'll need to direct me to Tillman's office."

I gave him directions to get out of Old Town, as we needed to head over to Stock Island, where the Monroe County Sheriff's major crimes unit worked. It was less than a twenty-minute drive, not that I went there often. I got nervous just driving to New Town, because that pushed the extent of my safety with narcolepsy. But Jun driving was fine. It was just too bad nothing was ever easy when tourists ignore Do Not Cross signs and bike on the wrong side of the road. In a sense, Key West was very much a miniature New York City.

I took out my phone and opened the photos folder. I swiped through the pictures I'd taken, ruminating on the idea that an additional galleon existed and that maybe, *just maybe*, Smith had lived a double life as a famous pirate. "What did you think of that band of merrymen?" I murmured.

"I believe that Peg honestly had no idea Cassidy had been killed."

"I agree."

"I'm not a fan of that Mr. Moore," Jun continued.

"You better believe I'm not hiring him back to finish the rest of the house's interior."

"That's not what I mean," Jun replied. "I don't like coincidences. Him having access to the house, as well as being the friend of the murdered intruder, doesn't sit well with me."

I plucked absently at the pink rubber case of my phone. "I don't like it either. Gives me indigestion." I looked at Jun's profile. "What are you thinking?"

"Was he ever left alone in the home?"

"Sure. I didn't babysit the painters. They finished the first floor about two weeks ago. I didn't want to schedule the paint job during the busy season, but the board took so goddamn long to approve the project, that was the only slot of time they had to offer me."

"By all accounts Josh could have discovered the broken window latch during their work in the parlor. Or even broken it himself."

Fuck. "I found remnants of paint on the latch yesterday," I answered. "Plus, he's a big guy. And he has a beard, like Ghost Smith." I looked at Jun again. "Is that probable cause?"

He shook his head. "Speculation."

"But you think he's guilty?"

"Of something," Jun said. "I'd be interested in knowing about any alibis he might have for last night."

"I'm making you get involved."

Jun glanced sideways.

"We should stop."

"It's just an unofficial meeting with Tillman," Jun said calmly.

"But this is your vacation. We're spending it being snoops."

"Technically I'm a concerned boyfriend with connections. You're Indiana, who's all excited about changing history."

I laughed and punched his arm lightly.

Jun chuckled. "Don't worry, Aubrey. I want to talk with Tillman. Let me do that so it puts my mind at ease. Then we'll get back to beach-lounging and sightseeing."

I started to reluctantly agree, but then the phone in my hand went off and I nearly jumped out of my skin.

Jun put a hand on my shoulder. "It's just the phone."

I shook myself firmly and started to swipe to accept the call. "Oh my God, it's that blocked caller again!" I quickly answered. "Hello?"

Static.

"Hello?" I tried again.

Jun took the phone from my hand and put it to his ear, driving one-handed. "Who is this?" he demanded.

I yanked the seat belt and leaned close, listening beside Jun.

And then the same deep, gravelly, creepy-as-fuck voice answered Jun. "Smith."

Jun pulled the phone back and looked at the screen. "Hung up."

I swallowed and took the cell. "I'm too smart to believe that the disembodied spirit of Captain Smith is haunting my phone. *Right*?"

"Yes." Jun kept his eyes firmly on the road.

"Except, what if the skeleton is Smith and I disturbed his final resting place. Like, a curse or something?"

"Aubrey."

"I know it's nuts, but there's a real mystery behind Smith's death. Now the skeleton in his house, the person I saw last night, and this? I don't believe ghosts, but—" I whined and waved my hands. "At the same time... I don't have an answer for any of it!"

"That's why we went to Key Pirates. And why we spoke with Cassidy's friends and now Tillman. Because someone living is behind this and they've upset you, so now they answer to me."

I snorted loudly. "Weird stuff always happens to me, but this? What the hell, right? I used to think the strangest thing I'd been a part of was a naked crackhead who came into Gold Guys back in New York, asking for fifty bucks in exchange for his testicles. But murder and ghosts?"

"And pirates," Jun added dryly.

"How could I forget," I grumbled.

"I'll make sure Tillman's on the right path," Jun promised. "I'm not leaving in a week and a half if I'm at all concerned for your well-being."

I looked down at my phone. I was gripping it hard between my hands. "Matt never said anything like that."

"Like what?"

"Just… defending me."

"Aubrey."

I looked at him.

Jun glanced away from the road and said, "I'm not Matt."

And thank God for that.

I smiled and nodded. "I know. I'm glad." I leaned my head against the passenger window. Not that I was as loopy as my pal Sebastian to enjoy crime solving and dead people or whatever it was that he'd been doing up in New York, but a part of me was *sort of* enthralled by this. Not the breaking-in and murdering part, but the historical part. I don't like being wrong, but I'm a big enough man (ha-ha) to admit when I am. And if there was a whole other life Smith led that I hadn't authenticated?

Exciting.

Much more so than spending the day shopping on Duval.

"Do you think there really is a long-lost pirate treasure?" Jun asked after a few moments.

"I'd be lying if I said I hope not."

Jun parked the car near the back of the sheriff station lot, shaded by palm trees on the left and hidden by a row of empty cars along the right. He shut the engine off and checked his watch. "We still have a few minutes before the meeting." He unbuckled the seat belt and looked at me. "There's time for a quick catnap," he offered.

Tempting. But I had a better idea, and not much can top a nap.

"How many minutes is a few?"

"About ten."

I looked around the parking lot, but there was no one hanging out. A few guys taking a smoke break, but they were all the way near the front doors of the station. I turned back to Jun and smirked. "We'll even have time to cuddle after."

"What?"

I pushed the console between us back and scooted close enough to unbuckle Jun's pants.

"Whoa, Aubrey, are you crazy?" Jun asked, grabbing my hands.

"Are you talking back?" I asked, raising my brows. I leaned over Jun, kissing him. "If you don't want to," I whispered, "just say no." I reached down and cupped him through his jeans.

Jun grabbed my face and held it as he kissed me back hard. "Make it fast," he murmured against my lips.

My mouth curled into a devious grin. "Considering you're already hard, I don't think that'll be a problem."

I still hadn't seen Jun's cock, and like the classy guy I was, the first time was going to be in a freaking parking lot. I unzipped his jeans and reached in to pull him free.

"Ho, ho, okay," I said, kind of laughing. "Jesus."

Jun sort of woke from his trance and looked at me critically. "What?"

"What's the saying—hung like a horse? What the fuck do you feed this thing?"

No joke. Jun's dick was huge and gorgeous. Not long, but wide— *stuff you like a Christmas goose* kind of wide. Forget blowing him, I couldn't wait to get him in bed and have that beast driving home because it was mocking me as if it were a personal challenge. Like climbing Mount Everest. Only the bravest would ever dare.

I quickly kissed him because I didn't want Jun thinking the wrong thing. "You're absolutely beautiful. I mean that. And you know what I'm gonna do now?"

Jun shook his head obediently, despite it not taking too many brain cells to piece together my plans.

"I'm going to cram this entire thing into my mouth." I kissed him again as he groaned. "Think I can do it?"

"Yes," Jun breathed. He moved his hand down to stroke himself.

I grabbed him to keep his hand still. "No touching. Keep an eye out. We can't have anyone seeing me going down on you, now can we?"

He shook his head once more.

I grinned and put my head in his lap, swirling my tongue around the head of his cock. Jun sighed shakily and planted his hand in my hair.

This was a jaw ache waiting to happen, but that really turned me on, like *whoa*, so without further teasing, I wrapped my lips around the head and went down.

Jun let out the most devastatingly perfect moan that I'd ever heard a man make. It sounded like not only was this the best head he'd ever gotten, but the moment compared to no other in his life. It didn't matter that we were fresh into this relationship and I'd jumped him in the parking lot of a station full of cops—oh my God, what the hell was wrong with me!—or that it wasn't terribly romantic. Everything was perfect because it was him and it was me and, after three years of friendship and loss and flirting, here we were.

Finally.

I pulled off with a wet pop and looked at him. "I want you to come in my mouth, got it?"

"Yes, yes," Jun panted, putting pressure on the back of my head, silently pleading for me to get back to business.

I couldn't resist twisting him up just a bit more, though. I put my index finger on his lips, nudging the tip into his mouth, where it met his hot tongue. "Show me what you want me to do to you."

Jun sucked hard in response, all the way down my finger. He slid his tongue up the pad like it really was a cockhead, and left little nibbles as I slowly pulled it free from his mouth. He was breathless and leaned forward to nab it between his lips again, but I didn't let him.

"Such a good boy," I whispered.

I went back down on him, working my way to the root. I closed my eyes when I finally managed to take all of his cock down my throat and his trimmed hair pressed against my nose. Jun cried out, his thighs shaking as he resisted slamming up and fucking my face until I lost consciousness. I grabbed on to his hips tight and started moving my head up and down. I sucked hard and fast because we were playing with fire, so the sweet nothings would have to wait until tonight.

Jun brushed hair back from my eyes, holding it so he could see my face. "I've dreamed about this," he whispered. "Aubrey…. So good…."

I moved back up to the head, moaning around the mouthful I had. Jun bucked up hard in response, battering the back of my throat, and I fucking loved it. I moved one hand from his hip to his crotch and pressed gently, groping his balls through his pants. Jun's breathing quickened, everything now trembling.

He really was *everything*.

I wondered how different my life would have been at this point if I'd met Jun at the bar instead of Matt three years ago. Would we have hit it off? Dated? Would it be as intense as it was now? What I was certain of at least was that, after the Mattocalypse, I appreciated men like Jun more.

Men like Jun, who treated me nice, who wasn't afraid to say he loved me, and practically worshiped the ground I tripped on. I dug that— being treated like a real boyfriend and not a fucktoy. I could definitely see us committed for the long haul. No matter where I lived or where in the world he was working, coming home to Jun was something I think I'd wanted for a long time.

Maybe… I'd even been in love with him for years but never realized it.

"Aubrey," Jun said. "I'm almost there. Please…."

Christ, he sounded so sweet when he begged. I'd have loved to say a few naughty things in reply and watch the way his body responded to dirty talk, *buuut*… I was sort of busy. I started jacking him off as I sucked the head. Jun squirmed in his seat, and I felt all of his muscles stiffen. And then came the fireworks.

Jun groaned, one hand still gripping my hair, the other wrapped so tight around the steering wheel, I could hear the material protest. He spurted into my mouth, powerful jets of cum that if I hadn't been a part of this morning's events, I'd have figured he hadn't gotten off in a week or two.

I eased off his cock, wiped the string of salvia from my lips, and settled on the edge of my seat. "Good?"

Jun chuckled. "Perfect."

"Hey now, don't let it go to my head. Leave room for improvement so I keep practicing."

Jun smiled and turned to look at me. He reached out and touched my face—always so gentle. "Wish we were home," he murmured.

"Why's that?"

"So I could hold you for a while."

Aww, geez… there goes the *pound, pound, pound* of my make-believe heart condition again. I tilted my face to rest against his hand before kissing the inside of his wrist.

Jun made a content sound and started righting himself and his clothes. "Do you have any more Skittles?"

"Hmm? Oh, yeah. Want some?"

"It's that or we need to find some cigarettes immediately."

I laughed loudly, dug through my bag of candies, and held the open package out. Jun took a handful and thanked me before he got out of the car. I followed, trying to discreetly adjust myself while telling my body to behave for now because tonight would be worth the wait.

Jun walked around to the passenger side, then patted bits of my hair down as he got close. "I'd told myself the entire plane ride here that we needed to go slow."

I snorted. "Yeah. Same. That worked for about, oh, a few hours."

"Can't fault us too much. There was a lot of Skype flirting before I got here." Jun smiled and with a nod, led the way into the station, munching on candy.

BURT TILLMAN was not too tickled to see Jun. Or me. In fact, he probably could have gone the whole day without even thinking of either of us.

"Agent Tanaka," he said, offering a stiff handshake. "I *am* in the middle of a homicide. I hope you understand my time is precious."

"I've no intention of taking you away from your case," Jun replied. "It so happens that Mr. Grant and I ran into a few of Cassidy's friends this morning and gathered a bit of information that might be of value to you."

Tillman eyed Jun, glared at me, then nodded and turned to lead us down a hallway. We entered a large room that had several desks with plain-clothed officers sitting at them. Each had towering piles of papers spread across their workspace, and a phone seemed to always be ringing from somewhere. Tillman walked toward the back, grabbed two plastic chairs, and hauled them up in front of what I presumed was his desk before he sat behind it.

Jun and I both took a seat.

"So?" Tillman asked.

Jun took over this part, and I was only more than happy to let him. Keep this between lawmen, you know?

"We spoke with a few people down at Barnacles today. Curtis Leon, Peg Hart, and Josh Moore."

Tillman nodded, rolling a pen between his thumb and index finger.

"Seems that Curtis was already aware of Cassidy's death."

"Yes, he was having breakfast with Glen Porter, Cassidy's employer, when I went down to speak with Glen."

"Were you aware they are amateur treasure hunters?"

"I vaguely knew," Tillman replied. "I know Peg—she owns her own boat. I've heard a few stories about the four of them going out to search for sunken treasure."

Jun leaned back in his chair, crossing his long legs and seeming completely at ease. "Peg mentioned a diary that Cassidy had, about Captain Rogers."

Tillman narrowed his eyes. "I'm not familiar with this man."

"He was captain of a merchant vessel from 1854 to 1871," I piped up.

Tillman looked at me. "Let me guess. The skeleton is Rogers and he killed Cassidy?"

"I think the skeleton might actually be Smith," I corrected. "Thanks, though."

Jun cleared his throat.

I didn't roll my eyes, but man, I came close to it. "Cassidy got the diary because it mentions Smith and One-Eyed Jack supposedly being one and the same, and I told you yesterday how hell-bent he was about proving me wrong. The point is, that diary was stolen a year ago from a museum in St. Augustine."

"I suspect a man that's stolen from at least one museum, with the intent of perhaps stealing from Aubrey's," Jun began, "likely has more than one hot item in his possession."

Tillman looked down at his mass of paperwork, thoughtful. "We've been to his apartment. Nothing like an old diary was found."

"I know an Agent Dixon in Miami who works with the Art Crime Team," Jun stated. "I'm sure she would be more than happy to assist."

Tillman sat back in his chair. "This St. Augustine museum would first need their local law enforcement to submit an entry to NSAF."

Tillman knew more about FBI policies than I did. *Check.*

Jun smiled. "Of course. But I'm sure with a few phone calls, I can get the ball rolling, considering the situation down here. What do you say, Detective?"

Ha, ha, ha, *checkmate.*

Tillman frowned.

"I'm not looking to take over or interfere with your case," Jun stated. "I'm only here for a week and half, and when I leave Aubrey, I want to sleep at night knowing that he's not being harassed or in danger at his place of business. That's all."

Tillman looked between the two of us.

I nodded and offered a smile.

After a beat, Tillman let out a heavy sigh and shifted some of his papers around. He picked up a small evidence baggie that held a key fob. It was bright orange and seemed to have some sort of room number on it. "We found this in Cassidy's apartment. It belongs to a unit at Store Yourself in New Town." He offered it and Jun accepted.

"What's the chance of getting a search warrant?" Jun asked, turning the fob around absently.

Tillman smiled this time and held up a form. "Just got it, twenty minutes ago. Cassidy has a record of theft. Appears he's been obsessed with this pirate Jack guy most of his life." He stood. "As a courtesy to you, Agent Tanaka, and because I'm not well versed in the diaries of merchant sailors from the 1800s... I'll extend the offer of you being present while I serve this. Unofficially, of course."

"Of course." Jun stood, and they shook hands again. "I suppose we'll bump into each other there. It just so happens that Aubrey is qualified to offer assistance regarding anything you might find in the unit."

Tillman looked at me. "That he is," he said tersely.

WE'D FOLLOWED Tillman from Stock Island to New Town and parked outside of Store Yourself about thirty minutes later. Jun turned the car off, leaned over me to unlock the glove compartment, and revealed a gun and holster.

"Whoa, you came to Florida packing?"

Jun looked at me briefly before grabbing it. "I don't go anywhere without a service weapon."

"Even on vacation?" Because I found that sort of... sad.

Jun didn't respond, just put the shoulder holster on. He opened the door and said, "Would you grab the suit coat in the back seat?"

I partially climbed over the console to reach the folded G-man coat before getting out of the car. "You came prepared."

Jun adjusted his weapon as he came toward me, took the coat, and hid the gun as he slid it over his shoulders.

"You think there's something dangerous inside the unit?" I asked, looking up.

"I'd rather not take any chances. Stay behind and out of the way, okay?"

Tillman climbed out of his car beside us and removed the folded warrant from an inner pocket before leading the way.

"Regarding Josh Moore," Jun said, the scuff of his shoes on the pavement echoing over his words. "Aubrey hired him to paint the first floor of the Smith Home. He finished that two weeks ago."

"Is that so."

"It might account for the broken window in the parlor," Jun continued.

Tillman stopped and turned to face Jun.

"He's similar in appearance to the description Aubrey gave of the second intruder."

Watching Jun work Tillman was pretty awesome. I think his good-cop thing was making it difficult for Tillman to even be properly annoyed, since Jun was technically helping. Just, you know, sort of passive-aggressively.

"I don't suppose he shared yesterday's whereabouts with you?" Tillman asked.

"He did not."

Tillman looked at me briefly before nodding and walking toward the business once more. "I'll look into it." He opened the front door, held it for us, then approached the counter. He flashed his badge at a disinterested woman.

"I've a search warrant, ma'am," he said, sliding the form over. "Unit 513, belonging to a Lou Cassidy."

She chewed her gum loudly, popping a bubble while glancing over the legal form—like anyone actually read that mumbo jumbo. "Fine with me," she stated after a moment. "He's a week late on payment. Will the police be paying that?"

Tillman just smiled. "Do you have bolt cutters?"

She sighed and got to her feet. "Yup. Head on through that door," she said, indicating a door to our right. "Unit 513 is down the middle aisle on the left side. I'll be there in a moment."

"Appreciate it," Tillman said, and I swore if he had a hat on, he would have tipped it.

Jerk never used his hat-tipping voice on me.

Then again, I had been sort of a sassy smartass with him the last few—er, all the meetings we'd had so far.

Jun opened the door leading to the units, holding it for Tillman and me before bringing up the rear. "I must admit," he said quietly. "Curiosity is getting the best of me."

"You and me both," Tillman called. "Man's apartment is a shrine to all things nautical. I can only guess as to what'll be in here." He stopped outside an orange door about four by four feet. He looked at me and Jun. "I'll be disappointed if it's Christmas decorations."

The office door opened behind us and echoed loudly as it slammed shut. The woman from the counter was walking toward us with a hefty pair of bolt cutters. "Here you are, gentlemen," she said, handing the tool over to Tillman. "Please don't make a mess. I'll be in the office if you need anything."

Tillman thanked her and waited until she'd slammed the door again. He took the clippers to the combo lock on the door, quickly snapping it. He slipped it free and pocketed the lock pieces before setting the cutters down on the floor.

Jun took my arm and gently maneuvered me to stand behind him. He removed his gun and took a readied stance as Tillman yanked the door open.

The missing skeleton from yesterday came tumbling out, breaking as it smashed into the linoleum floor.

CHAPTER TEN

I YELPED.

Or… more like… *okay*, I screamed.

I screamed way louder than I meant to, but *hello*! I was prepared for pretty much anything to come falling out of the packed unit but Skelly. I jumped back instinctively, despite the skeleton hardly posing any sort of threat.

Jun turned around and put a hand firmly on my shoulder. "You okay?"

My eyes widened, but I nodded. "Uh, yeah." I cleared my throat. "Startled."

Jun holstered his weapon.

Tillman crouched down, looking the skeleton over. "Don't suppose you could verify that this is the same one you saw yesterday, Aubrey?"

I gave Tillman a look. "Yeah, sure," I mocked. "Spitting image. How many other missing skeletons have there been in the last twenty-four hours?"

"Aubrey," Jun said in that "you're in trouble, and not the good way" tone.

Tillman stood, staring at me. "I may owe you an apology."

I crossed my arms. "I told you it was real."

"Makes me wonder if Cassidy was doing any sort of surveillance on the Smith Home," Jun stated, looking at Tillman. "To have gotten in and out as quickly as he did."

"We've not found evidence of that, but I'll be sure to check," Tillman said, nodding as if he sort of agreed with Jun's assessment. He quickly snapped on a pair of latex gloves from his coat pocket, then pointed a small flashlight into the unit. He ducked his head and climbed into the mess.

"What'll happen to the skeleton?" I asked, loudly so Tillman could hear. I moved away from Jun to the opposite wall of units, keeping the distance between me and Skelly as big as possible so I didn't touch any of the broken bones. "If it's really Smith, he needs to be put to rest in the family plot."

"First, it'll go to the county medical examiner," Tillman said.

"Smith was missing his left eye," I continued. "And his personal diaries talk of breaking his hand and ribs in his younger years. If those can be confirmed by a doctor—"

"Yes, yes," Tillman said, cutting me off as he came back out of the unit. "If it's Smith, I'll make sure you folks are able to do what you need for him." He held out a small, black leather book perhaps no longer than five inches. "Is this the diary of a merchant sailor?"

"Do you have any gloves so I can touch it?"

Tillman reached into his pocket before offering me a pair of latex gloves.

I took them. "It really should be handled with cotton gloves."

He frowned.

"This'll do for now," I added quickly before taking the booklet. Jun moved around the skeleton to my side, both men peering over my shoulders as I gently pulled the leather clasp free. "It's in amazing condition. Usually this clasp is the first part of the leather to deteriorate and break off."

I opened the book, the front page stamped in big letters: DIARY, 1867, NEW YORK. It had lovely artwork of fairies around the wording. At the time, it was a generic diary designed for the masses. The left page featured a list of memorable events occurring throughout the year, as well as information on stamps and postage. I caught a faded signature on the title page and brought it closer to try to decipher it.

"I hate entries in pencil. They're impossible to read—but I'm fairly certain this name is Edward R. Rogers."

"That's him?" Jun asked.

"That's him," I confirmed. I turned the pages carefully. Nearly every predated entry had a short line or two written by the owner. "I'm sure the man kept many years of diaries, but *this* is the one that was stolen, so the entry Peg mentioned, about Smith and Jack, it has to be in here somewhere." I looked at Tillman. "I don't suppose you'll let me read through it?"

He took the diary back—carefully, I noted. "Do you believe a long-dead pirate is the reason Cassidy was murdered?"

"Yes," I said automatically. "I believe that Cassidy was searching for a lost treasure, supposedly once salvaged by One-Eyed Jack. There may be a clue in the diary that can point us to Cassidy's motives and who may have been with him last night."

Tillman looked at the booklet. "Meet me back at the station." He pulled back the sleeve of his coat to check his watch. "I need a few hours to deal with this," he continued while waving a hand at the skeleton. "Say, four o'clock."

I WAS hungry and tired when we left Store Yourself, and really not in the mood to go back and forth from Stock Island eighteen hundred more times. But considering Tillman didn't have to let me look at that diary for any reason whatsoever? It was pretty cool of him to agree. And without tooting my own horn, it was true that I knew the most about Smith. If there was any chance I could find the reason for Cassidy being in the Smith Home that would in turn lead to his murderer, I don't think Tillman would pass the opportunity up, regardless of whether he liked me or not.

Plus, he was still playing nice with Jun to keep the Feds out of his hair in any sort of official capacity.

"Let's get lunch," Jun said as he started the car.

I lowered the passenger seat to lie down more comfortably. "Pick any place," I said around a yawn. "I'm going to take a quick nap."

"Would you rather go home?" Jun asked. "I can make us lunch—"

I waved a hand lazily. "It's okay," I murmured. "You know I can sleep anywhere. At work I sleep under my desk."

"All right," Jun said, and I could hear the smile in his voice.

Traffic through Key West could be hairy at times, since the town had been doing construction for what felt like forever. Sometimes it got backed up between New and Old Town, and for those who commuted to Key West from the Upper Keys for work? Forget it. It was as much of a headache as riding the L train to Williamsburg during rush hour. So I wasn't terribly surprised that, when I woke up, we were just getting back into Old Town.

"We could have eaten in New Town," I said around a yawn.

"Chain food," Jun said, deftly moving around a group of girls on bikes weaving in and out of traffic. "I can eat junk anywhere."

"I guess so. There's a nice little café on the next street, if you want something like that."

"Perfect." Jun took the turn I indicated and stole a parking spot on the side of the road before the car behind had a chance to cut him off and grab it. We got out, and Jun paid the meter again, then joined me on the sidewalk. He was still wearing his shoulder holster and coat.

"You don't have to keep wearing that."

He glanced down, almost like he'd forgotten.

"The donuts aren't going to open fire."

"Does it make you uncomfortable?"

"No."

Jun took my hand and changed the subject as we walked to the café at the end of the block. "When we both have vacation time again, I'd love to take you to Japan."

"Yeah?" I asked, perking up. "Even though I don't speak a lick of Japanese?"

"Doesn't matter. You'll be with me. Plus, there's enough English and romaji to get around."

"What the hell is romaji?" I asked.

Jun's mouth quirked. "Japanese words written in the Latin alphabet."

"Oh. Derp."

He chuckled. "Would you like that?"

"Totally," I said. "Do you have any family there?"

"No. My sister, Misako, and parents all still live in DC."

Jun was a born-and-bred American, but his parents were from Japan and understood the importance of having their children learn about their Japanese roots. He'd told me years ago about his family speaking English in public, and at home he and his sister were schooled in Japanese. By high school Jun was also fluent in Mandarin, something he and Matt had in common, which I guess was probably what brought them together on the job.

Jun opened the door to the café and followed me inside.

"Welcome to Southernmost Coffee and Tea," a chipper guy at the counter said. "What can I get you?"

I approached, eyeing the menu briefly before saying, "Decaf coffee and—oh my God, is that a maple candied bacon *cronut*?"

The guy glanced in the glass case. "Yup. It's pretty good too."

"That. I'll take that."

"For lunch?" Jun murmured behind me.

"Yes, for lunch!" I looked at the employee and shook my head. "I can't take him anywhere."

He laughed and motioned to Jun. "For you, sir?"

"Since we're having dessert for lunch, a regular coffee and the key lime cronut."

I paid for the... uh, lunch, and Jun carried the tray out to the porch. We sat at a free table among a number of other patrons, enjoying the picture-perfect day, cool breeze, and a very unhealthy meal. For a moment I was able to disregard the fact that we were knee-deep in a murder and long-lost pirate treasure mystery.

Jun was smiling and watching as I wrecked my cronut. "Good?" he finally asked.

"Yes," I said around bites. "Candied bacon, Jun. This is a gift to humanity."

He cut his cronut into more accessible pieces. "I figured key lime because, when in Rome...."

"Yeah, if you went ten days without trying at least one of the thousand things we key lime-ify down here, you'd be insulting the entire island." I watched Jun eat for a passing moment. "Hey."

He looked up.

"When did you tell your parents?"

"That I was an FBI agent?" Jun asked dryly.

"*No.*"

He chuckled and set his utensils aside. "I didn't tell them until I was in college." He took a sip of coffee.

"Why's that?"

Jun shrugged and set the drink down. "I suppose the same reason so many wait to mention it. I was afraid of how they'd react."

My heart beat a little harder. "Was it bad?" I asked, hearing my own voice drop to a near whisper.

But Jun gave me a little smile. "No. Not really. In retrospect, had I known what their reaction would be, I'd have said something earlier to spare myself the turmoil. But it wasn't the sort of thing discussed in our family." He leaned back, staring at his cronut for a moment. "I guess I sort of *assumed* they'd react poorly, which I then regretted for a long time. But my father is rather traditional, and with me being the oldest and the son...."

I leaned over and patted Jun's thigh. "But everything is okay with you guys?"

Jun put his hand over mine. "Yes." He let out a breath and picked up his fork once more. "It actually opened a dialogue between us that wasn't there before. I think my parents would like you."

My heart went *thumpy thumpy*. The idea of meeting his parents was both terrifying and extremely exciting. I stuffed another bite of cronut into my mouth and said around the food, "Earlier today, I was thinking about why Cassidy was in the home."

"Have any ideas?"

I took a sip of my decaf. "A treasure map."

Jun raised an eyebrow. "How'd you decide that?"

"Well, let's say, for the sake of argument, I've been wrong and that Smith *is* Jack."

Jun nodded.

"And that the *Santa Teresa* was a real ship, and it *did* sink, and there was a fortune lost somewhere in the waters off Key West."

"That's quite a lot of 'for the sake of argument,'" Jun pointed out.

"I know, but let's say in every instance I was wrong and Cassidy was right."

"Very well."

"Glen mentioned Cassidy believing Jack found the lost Spanish treasure in 1871, the same year he disappeared from public accounts. It's the same year Smith died under mysterious and conflicting circumstances. And yet, if he did discover the mother lode, where'd it go? How do that many coins just *vanish*? Maybe Jack hid them before he died. Maybe he even died because of the coins."

"I've never heard you say 'maybe' so many times when it comes to history," Jun said warily.

I made a face and shook my head. "Believe me, to say any of this without facts and evidence is making the cronut come back up, but it makes sense, doesn't it? Cassidy was convinced of all of this, and why else would he break into Smith's home but to look for a clue as to where the fortune was stashed? And since we're dealing with pirates, it has to be a map."

Jun sipped his coffee again. "I suppose I can see where you're going with this."

"The map is in the captain's study," I continued. "That's where you saw evidence of people."

"Yes, but I wouldn't be able to tell you if something was amiss more than the knocked over ropes."

"And until the police let us in, we can't say for certain if anything was taken by the Smith Ghost intruder," I concluded. "But I can guess."

"How?"

"One of Smith's actual maps was on display." I held my hands out, palms up. "This far into the game, I'd be shocked if it *hasn't* been stolen."

Jun was quiet in response, ruminating on the shaky facts and assumptions.

I took another sip of my decaf before asking, "Do you believe in ghosts?"

"Why?"

"Someone killed Cassidy. And… I know it was a man. A living, breathing man. But I can't deny that who I saw upstairs might as well have been Smith's twin. And the phone calls—*Don't go back inside*, and saying he was Smith."

"Someone is trying to intimidate you, that's all."

"So is that a no?"

Jun sighed. "In Japan there is an event called *Obon*. For many in this day and age, it's seen more as the time of year to have a family gathering, but it stems from the belief that in summer, the spirits of loved ones return to visit the homes of their relatives. Families travel to clean the graves of their ancestors, and shrines are given candles and fruit."

"What's your point?"

"My point is, these beliefs are hundreds of years old, and all around the world, you hear stories of ghosts. Perhaps this worldwide phenomenon originated for good reason." Jun smiled.

"Nice and cryptic, thanks."

"Do I believe Smith is haunting the home? No. But I do believe someone wants you to think that."

THE RADIO didn't really play Jun's preferred music—considering most of it was pretty explicit or indie, like *whoa*, but all the back-and-forth driving we'd done that day proved that occasionally something would come on that he liked. I just found it a little amusing that my straightlaced G-man knew all the lyrics to songs like Styx's "Renegade." He murmured the words under his breath, his deep baritone adding that little extra oomph a song about running from the law probably should have had to begin with.

"Did you know this song was released on their album, *Pieces of Eight*?" Jun asked.

"So?"

"Isn't that the type of Spanish coin that sank on the supposed *Teresa*?"

"Yeah, but—oh. That's freaky."

He chuckled.

"It's like a sign."

"But what sort?"

I shrugged. "Maybe we're on the right track."

I'd asked Jun if we could burn the last of our free time at the library before going back to Stock Island. Not that I hadn't spent hours and hours and *hours* researching and combing through the archives there already, but I'd always been looking for photographs and documents on Smith. And while I was sure Cassidy had done his fair share of work on Jack at the library, I couldn't be certain of how far he'd gotten.

The woman who managed the archives was… how do I say… *particular*. And by particular, I mean, if she wasn't impressed by the person inquiring their first time, she'd never let them dig through her endless supply of history. Yes, I know, it was a public library and they couldn't exactly restrict the public, but she was about two hundred years old and there was just no reasoning with a gal like that.

Miss Louise Marble had a real passive-aggressive way of turning down the folks who wanted to look through her records in the climate-controlled room. If she didn't like the person, or didn't believe them to be a serious historian, she simply said, "Oh no, we don't have anything on that subject in the archives."

I very well knew she did, but she'd clam up and just stare at the person until they left. If the research being done wasn't to the benefit of Key West, a reputation she was extremely protective of, you'd better believe nothing would be gained from the library. Now, because my work had been in favor of Smith's legacy, I'd proven my validity to Miss Louise fairly early on in my transition down to the Keys. She was still a bit persnickety regarding my "freshwater Conch" status, but was thrilled with the restoration I'd conducted on the home, so I guessed that was worth more to her than me not being a true local.

Lou Cassidy, though? Conch or not, he'd been trying to defame Smith in my mind, and most likely in hers as well. I doubt he'd gained much access. So now that I was essentially hunting down the same information, I'd need to be careful how I went about wording my research needs. I couldn't afford to be on Louise's shit list.

The Monroe County Public Library, with its pinkish building front, was on Fleming Street. Jun parked nearby and followed me up the steps to the front doors. I waved to a few employees who saw me come in before making my way to the archive area. The building had a hushed sense of calm about it, that particular sort of quiet that could be found nowhere but libraries. It was relaxing, albeit nap-inducing at times.

"Miss Louise," I said, louder than I would have spoken in a library, except that she wouldn't have heard me otherwise. "How are you, dear?"

Louise looked up from her work, her stern expression softening ever so slightly around the edges. "Well, well. I haven't seen you in some time, Aubrey. You just took what you needed and that was it, was it?"

See? Like a grandma you never want to be on the wrong side of because she'll remember how you upset her when your birthday came around and you'd get nothing but a check for four dollars and eighteen cents.

"I'd never, Louise," I answered. I offered a little takeout container—a cronut I'd bought before we left the café—because a little wooing never hurt anyone. "Apple crème. It's a limited flavor."

Louise took the container and gave the cronut a suspicious look through her bifocals before eventually smiling. "You're a good boy, Aubrey."

"Thank you."

She looked at Jun standing behind me. "Introduce me," Louise chastised.

"Oh, sorry. Louise, this is Jun Tanaka. He's visiting from New York. Jun, this is Louise Marble, the smartest woman on the island."

"Ma'am," Jun said, reaching out to gently shake her extended hand.

"Aubrey likes to suck up to me," she said to Jun before giving me a look that could peel paint. "But I don't mind because he's good at it. Except I still don't like that nose ring, mister," she concluded, giving me another hard glare. She didn't like my nose ring, my earrings, my hair, my shoes—but she wasn't hardly as critical of anyone else, and considering the access she gave me to the old records, I think her intense dislike was some sort of weird approval.

I just smiled. It didn't bother me. If I were her age—hell, I think she was ninety—I'd probably be telling kids to get off my lawn too.

She carefully set aside some old photographs she'd been pawing through and looked up at Jun again. "Are you Aubrey's boyfriend?"

Jun didn't answer immediately and instead glanced at me.

"Or do you prefer a different title, like partner or significant other? My brother, Herman, God rest his dumbass soul, was with his beloved Samuel Shell Jr. for fifty-three years and always referred to him as his best friend. I said, Herman, you shit, you ain't fooling nobody. They even got gay married in California, but Herman never called Samuel anything but his friend. To each his own, I guess. So which do you prefer?" She eyed Jun.

"Uh… boyfriend is fine, ma'am," Jun replied.

"Now. What do you want, Aubrey?" Louise asked after finishing with Jun.

I leaned over her desk, eyeing the photos with mild interest. "I was looking for a bit of information on Captain Edward Rogers."

"What *kind* of information?" she asked.

"You know, it's always pertaining to Smith," I said with a wicked grin. "I'm interested in their relationship."

Louise threaded her gnarly fingers together and stared hard.

"Not that kind of relationship," I corrected. "I know neither of them were—their *professional* relationship, Louise. That's what I want."

"Paperwork on Rogers is mostly limited to court records," she finally replied. "He retired to St. Augustine and never lived in Key West."

"Court records?" I asked. "What years?"

Louise scratched the tip of her nose as she thought. "Throughout the 1850s and '60s. You need exact dates?"

"It's preferable."

Louise didn't make to move from her seat. "Rogers worked with Smith three times."

"That's pretty bad luck, don't you think? Getting stranded and needing wreckers so many times for an experienced captain."

"Not every captain was as competent as Smith."

"True." I tapped her desktop absently. "Did Rogers ever appear in the court records as having dealt with wreckers other than Smith?"

"No."

Crap. Not sure what I was fishing for, but—

"Except when he reported piracy."

"When was this?"

Louise's face pinched up. "In 1867."

The same year as the diary Cassidy had stolen.

"What did the records say?" I asked, leaning down to be eye level with Louise.

She gave me a critical expression. "Neither Rogers nor piracy have anything to do with Smith, Aubrey."

"I know, I'm sorry. I've been learning more about Rogers and his time in Key West. I'm interested," I answered, which, hey, not total bullshit.

Louise looked away and studied her antique wristwatch for a good minute. "He originally claimed to have had a run-in with the *Red Lady*."

"The supposed ship of One-Eyed Jack," I stated.

Louise sniffed. "That would be correct," she said woodenly. "But he retracted the claim and let it drop."

"Did he report any stolen goods when meeting the *Red Lady*?"

"He said he was boarded, pirates began to loot, but then quickly abandoned his vessel. Rogers never said what, if anything, was actually stolen."

"Why do you think he'd have recanted on the story?"

"Oh, heaven knows," Louise exclaimed. "A resurgence in piracy wouldn't have been good, especially so soon after the Civil War. *If* Rogers had some sort of run-in, and I stress the 'if,' I suspect Key West would have dealt with it on their own. They were the only southern port under Union occupation during the war, and if the Navy came back down to deal with another wave of pirates—you know folks hold grudges for a long time. I doubt many would have wanted an influx of the US government again so soon."

"So they'd have scrubbed it from the record," I concluded.

Louise nodded.

I wracked my brain, trying to come up with enough plausible leads and players in history that one of them would have to cross Jack at some point throughout the years of his activity. But I had to simultaneously not let Louise know exactly what I was fishing for. What a pain in the ass.

"Louise? Who was the judge superior in wrecking court at the times Rogers would have been going?"

She didn't answer right away.

Ah-ha! I'd stumped her!

"Judge William Marvin, I believe."

Damn, she was good.

"Let me go get the ledgers."

"Do you need help?" I asked.

Louise slowly rose from her chair, her back hunched from age, but she was still pretty spry on her feet. "Your Mr. Jun can help," she said, waving a hand for him to follow.

I waited until Jun had gone inside the climate-controlled room with Louise before grabbing scrap paper and a pen from her desk. I needed a timeline to work with, so I wrote down the gist of everything I knew.

1850—1871 Smith was a wrecking captain. Worked with Rogers three times during his career.

1853 Smith built his house in town.

1861—1865 Civil War.

1861 Smith has accident at sea and loses his eye. Same year One-Eyed Jack is mentioned in records.

1867 Captain Rogers claims to have been attacked by the Red Lady *and then recants. His diary claims to have seen Jack enter a sea shanty and come out as Smith.*

1871 Jack supposedly finds the long-lost Spanish treasure of the Santa Teresa *before mysteriously vanishing from all records. Smith's death is reported in the same year.*

I sat on my knees, rested an elbow on the desk, and ran a hand through my hair as I stared at the dates and events. Rogers popped up in Smith and Jack's life more than I realized. Had it surpassed what could be considered coincidental? If Jack had really attacked Rogers's ship, why would a pirate basically say *lol jk*, and vamoose?

Unless… after the many times Smith had come to Rogers's aid, they were friends? And when Smith/Jack realized who he was attempting to pilfer, he decided against it?

I hit my forehead against the desk. I was basing this on zero historical evidence. However, it did raise an interesting thought: Did Rogers have anything to say on Smith/Jack's mysterious death? Would he have made a notation in his 1871 diary? St. Augustine was over a seven-hour drive, so no way I could go see for myself—but the staff was only a phone call away….

"Oh look, he's gone and fallen asleep on my desk," Louise chastised from nearby.

I raised my head. "I'm awake." I stood, folded my note, and tucked it into my back pocket. "Any luck?"

As she seated herself, Louise motioned to Jun, who was carrying an old ledger. He'd been given special gloves to wear while handling the book. "Set it down right here," she told Jun as she made space on her desk. Jun did as requested before handing Louise the cotton gloves, which she in turn put on.

I moved around the desk to lean over the book. "Was there ever anything odd about the court records between Rogers and Smith?"

"What do you mean, odd?" Louise asked as she carefully turned each page one at a time.

"I don't know. Did Smith ever charge Rogers less than his other wrecks?"

Louise stopped on one page and pointed at the tight, cursive script of the time. "The first court date between the two was in 1855. Smith was awarded 30 percent value of the ship and cargo."

"Quite lucrative," I murmured. "Was there any dispute?"

"No. Rogers went with it. But he was new to being a captain," Louise said before turning the pages. "The next date wasn't until 1857. It looks like Smith was awarded…." She paused and leaned closer to read. "Only 9 percent."

"That's odd," I said.

"Why?" Jun finally piped up.

I glanced at him, and he appeared extremely interested. "The average reward for saving wrecked vessels and cargo was 25 percent. It could dip as low as 3 or as high as 50, but Smith was pretty consistent with a good payout. Judge Marvin had a great deal of respect for Smith, and he was the one who ultimately decided the percentage, based on several factors, of course. I find it strange that Smith received so little."

"Was there ever an incentive for judges to award higher payouts?" Jun questioned.

"Everyone had incentive back then," Louise muttered.

I made a face and motioned Jun to stay quiet. There were judges not on the straight and narrow, just like wreckers, but Marvin and Smith were not to be spoken of that way, lest Louise take away my archive privileges.

"No dispute from either party on the percentage," Louise stated.

"Were Rogers and Smith friends?" I asked as she skimmed the pages for the final court date. "I mean, after they met on the first wreck. Perhaps Smith was doing Rogers a favor."

"It's possible," Louise said. "It wouldn't be the first time that Smith proved himself a gentleman. Ah. Final date was 1861. Same as the second, 9 percent and no dispute."

There was something fishy between Smith and Rogers. And if I discovered what, the truth of One-Eyed Jack would undoubtedly be uncovered.

CHAPTER ELEVEN

"OUT WITH it," Jun finally said once we were in the car again.

His voice broke through my little bubble of thought, and I looked up. "What?"

"You look like you've got some great mystery solved and you're ready to declare results."

"I've nothing to declare except my genius," I replied coyly. "You know that's not actually verified to have been uttered by Oscar Wilde."

Jun looked away from the road and at me a few times. "Smartass."

I laughed. "My ass is many things."

"What was that at the library? Your brain was firing on all cylinders."

I lifted up in the seat to remove the note from my back pocket. "Something is suspicious about Smith and Rogers."

"How do you mean?"

"Smith was never awarded so little for his wrecking work," I replied. "But twice in a row he nearly aided Rogers for free."

"Maybe they were friends like you suggested," Jun said.

"Maybe."

"You don't sound certain."

"Smith's personal diary wasn't terribly well-kept, but the few mentions of Rogers over the years—it was never anything that stood out to me. Like two ships passing in the night, pardon the nautical phrase."

Jun's thumb was tapping the wheel absently. "Do you believe they were involved in something illegal together?"

"No."

"Do you believe Rogers was a pirate?"

"I don't think so, no."

Jun cleared his throat. "Then I've another idea."

"What's that?"

"Lovers." He looked at me briefly. "It would certainly explain the lack of notations in Smith's diary, while, when in wrecking court, his discounted aid speaks to some sort of personal relationship."

"Smith was married," I stated. "But—ah! I feel like the two years of research I've done is as stable as a house of cards!"

Jun put a hand on my knee. "That's not true. As a historian, you've come at these revelations with an acceptable amount of reservation but haven't dismissed the evidence until you've thoroughly researched it. And if your conclusions change, Aubrey—they change."

"Such is life," I added.

He moved his hand back to the steering wheel. "That's right."

"I'm very hesitant to suggest Smith had a male lover, though I don't doubt that it's entirely possible. It requires… a phone call."

"Next time Smith rings, are you going to ask him?"

"Now who's being the smartass?" I asked, watching Jun smile. "The St. Augustine museum. I know they have a number of diaries belonging to Rogers. I'm curious about their contents, but especially 1871, when Smith died. Grief knows no bounds, after all."

"You think Rogers would have made a notation if they were involved?"

"Yes. Have you ever seen Theodore Roosevelt's diary from 1884?"

"I can't say I have."

"His mother and wife passed on the same day," I explained. "Within a few hours of each other. All he wrote was 'The light has gone out of my life.'"

"That's terrible," Jun said quietly.

I fiddled with my phone. "Well… the point is, he didn't even need to mention names. If Rogers and Smith had—*something*—perhaps there is an entry of similar despair."

And even though both men had been gone from this world for a long, long time, part of me hoped that wouldn't be the case. Despite a relationship being a clue to help unravel the story of One-Eyed Jack and who might have killed Cassidy, I didn't want the truth to be a secret love affair. Not because it meddled with the history, but because the endings of men like me—back then—were so often fraught with tragedy.

I SLEPT the rest of the drive back to Stock Island, which turned out to be too long, and I was groggy as fuck. I dialed a number on my cell before yawning and stretching my arms overhead as Jun and I walked across the station parking lot for the second time that day. I put the phone back to my ear just as someone answered.

"Museum of St. Augustine Nautical History, this is Amy."

"Hello, I'd like to speak with your manager, if they're around."

"May I ask who's calling?"

"Aubrey Grant, property manager of Smith Family Historical Home down in Key West."

"One moment."

Crappy hold music began to play.

I stopped outside the front door beside Jun. "If St. Augustine wasn't a seven-hour drive, I'd want to go see these diaries myself," I said before someone picked up. "Hello?"

"Mr. Grant? My name is Lucrecia Kennedy. How may I help you?"

"Pleasure, ma'am," I said. "I first wanted to share some good news with you."

"Is that so?"

"Local police down here have recovered a diary belonging to Edward R. Rogers, reported stolen from your museum about a year ago. Dated 1867."

"Oh good lord, are you serious?" she exclaimed. "This is incredible! When will we get it back?"

"I'm sure a Detective Tillman will be in touch with you soon regarding getting it to you."

"This is such good news! Thank you for the call," Lucrecia said. "We were beginning to fear it'd never be returned." She sighed, sounding relieved. "Was there something else I can help you with?"

"Actually, yes. As you're probably aware, I research and maintain reports on Captain Thomas J. Smith. I have records on my end that indicate he'd worked with Captain Rogers a few times throughout his career of delivering goods to Key West."

Lucrecia hummed in response. "Indeed."

"It was recently brought to my attention that the two men might have been better friends than I originally thought, and I'm hoping you are able to provide insight from Rogers's side."

"Oh. I see. Well, I'll help you in any way I can, but I'll be the first to admit that I don't do property management *and* historical research. So you may need to be specific in what you'd like me to look for among our artifacts."

"I'm interested specifically in Rogers's personal diaries. He first met Smith in 1855 and knew him until Smith's death in 1871."

"You want me to go through over fifteen years of—"

"No, no," I said, cutting her off. "Just 1871 specifically. Smith died sometime around July, give or take a few months in either direction. If you could look for any mention of Smith, a man named Jack, or anything that sounds like grieving."

Lucrecia let out a breath. "Okay. It may take me a little bit. When do you need this information?"

"ASAP?" I tried, wincing.

"ASAP," she repeated. "All right. We're pretty busy here right now, but I appreciate what's been done to recover our stolen artifact, so I'll give you a call tomorrow. Will that work?"

"That's perfect," I answered. I thanked Lucrecia before hanging up.

We walked into the station after that. A uniformed officer led us back to Tillman's desk. I took a seat across from the detective, who was simultaneously on the phone and typing at his computer. He glanced at me and motioned to the small diary settled inside a plastic evidence bag. I'd borrowed a pair of cloth gloves from Louise on our way out of the library, and I pulled them on before gently removing the booklet.

Careful with the leather clasp, I slowly opened the diary and began to skim each entry in search of the one where Rogers realized Jack and Smith were the same man. Most of the entries were of no great importance. Rogers talked about the weather a lot, but I guess a man who spent so much time at sea would likely find a great interest in it. He mentioned his mother now and then, as well as a sister, but he seemed to be a bachelor, which admittedly added fuel to the lovers' fire.

Somewhere in mid-April I'd realized Tillman had gotten off the phone, and he and Jun were speaking, but that's when I read two words that made my heart race.

Red Lady.

On April 23rd, Rogers recounted his run-in with the vessel, *Red Lady*, a pirate ship he described as *the likes of which I've never seen before. She was beautiful and marvelous, and cut through the choppy waters with every intent of making widows out of my crew's wives. I'd hardly been a babe out of my mother's arms when Porter sent pirates to the gallows. And then, like a ghost in the night, here appears the captain I've heard whispers of for the last six years. I was deathly afraid.*

And yet, just as quickly did the Red Lady appear at our side and her men board us, did her captain call them back. I admit that I saw him! Jack. One-Eyed, the locals say. Huge. Frightening. But I cannot speak as to why he let us live.

Jesus Christ. No wonder Cassidy stole this diary. And the St. Augustine museum had no clue the marvels they had tucked away. *No freaking clue!*

I turned the page. A few of the dates were left blank before Rogers noted on April 27th that he went to the court to warn them of his meeting with Captain Jack. *The locals are fearful of this man and ask I not speak his name, but when I demanded to know what is to be done of such a nuisance, they shy from calling the Navy in. Damn Southerners.*

April 28th: *I couldn't sleep and walked down to the wharves. In the dead of night, I swore the Red Lady was docking! Could her captain be here? What man at the docks has been paid off to allow this criminal to set anchor? I was too afraid to stay and watch!*

April 29th: *Ashamed I abandoned my vigilance at the wharves, I returned in the early hours. It was then I saw what I still cannot explain. This Captain Jack! He disembarked and disappeared into a shanty. But when he emerged, it was my dear Thomas.*

Unbelievable. This was an eyewitness account by a very creditable, honest man.

Cassidy was right from the start. *Damn it!*

I flipped through several more pages, but the last piece of evidence I could find before Rogers went back to his run-of-the-mill entries was on May 5th.

I have recanted. I cannot do the right thing. My heart has been compromised.

Do the right thing? Rogers must have meant he couldn't report Jack if it meant putting Smith in danger. He couldn't go through with it and told the courts he must have been mistaken. Because of his heart.

My phone started ringing as I considered how Jun's theory of lovers was looking more real by the second. "Hello?" I said distractedly.

Static.

I straightened in my chair and looked up, but Tillman—in an act of camaraderie—was talking to Jun about the contents of an open folder in his hands. The two of them were paying me no attention.

"Who is this?" I asked quietly.

More static.

"Smith?" I whispered.

"Aubrey," his crackly voice said.

I held my breath.

"You'll be dead too."

"TILLMAN'S GOING to request incoming call records from your cell provider," Jun said. He swung his hand lightly in mine as we walked along Mallory Square at sunset. "That's why you signed those consent forms—so he can figure out who keeps harassing you."

"It wasn't *harassing*," I mumbled. "He said I'd be *dead*! That's a bit more serious than harassing, don't you think?"

It had been the longest day of my life. I'd been up since the asscrack of dawn and felt like a week's worth of time had passed in what was in reality about twelve hours. But in the course of one day, we'd somehow stumbled upon historical proof that Smith was a famous pirate captain, that he might have salvaged a long-lost sunken treasure now worth a cool mil, and had a possibly intimate and more likely heartbreaking relationship with one Captain Edward Rogers.

Bob Ricci wanted me fired for doing my job, Adam had an awkward crush on me, we'd discovered the remains of who was almost most certainly Captain Smith after their mysterious disappearance from the closet, and Josh Moore was a pretty decent candidate for murderer of the week, in my opinion. We still didn't know exactly what Cassidy had been killed over, but I was convinced it was a treasure map of some sort. Of course, I wasn't allowed in the Smith Home to confirm if any artifacts *had* been stolen and find where the map could potentially lead us!

I'd have loved a stiff drink or three about then, but Jun wouldn't have approved of mixing pills and liquor.

"That's why Tillman is on top of it," Jun said. He let go of my hand and touched my lower back, making me go all weak in the knees. "And it's why you're not leaving my sight and we're officially dropping this little Easter egg hunt we've been on."

"We've nearly figured it all out," I said as I came to a stop and looked up at him.

"Figured *what* out exactly?"

"Well, I—you can't deny the story unfolding about Smith is quite fascinating."

"Sure. It's interesting," Jun agreed. "But the man's been dead for nearly a hundred and fifty years. You're still alive, and I'd like to keep it that way."

"You know, if I could get into the house, we'd be able to narrow this down."

"The treasure map?" Jun questioned. He glanced off to his left and led me to a merchant's jewelry stand.

"We both know something had to have been stolen from the captain's study," I replied, following him. "The facts we've uncovered tell me that Jack… *was* a real pirate, and he probably met a terrible fate—considering Smith was inside the walls of his own home."

"We don't know those remains are Smith's yet," Jun said. "And that doesn't prove who killed Cassidy."

The woman running the stand glanced between the two of us but decided it was best to not say anything. Jun leaned over to examine the goodies.

I kept talking, despite his obvious attempt to sidetrack me. "No, but it proves the likelihood of the treasure being real. And if we confirm that something is missing, I bet it'll lead us to the killer trying to dig up wherever Smith—er—Jack hid the fortune."

Jun picked up a colorful ring. "I think the number-one priority is to let Tillman track this person via your phone. It'll likely get faster results than running all over the island, looking for buried Spanish silver."

Of course, Jun was right.

"That's handmade," the merchant finally said.

Jun turned the ring over a few times. "Very impressive." He offered it to me. "Like it?"

I perked up as he dropped it into my palm. It was an octopus tentacle that wrapped around several times and was painted with a shimmery rainbow motif. "It's so cute!"

"How much?" Jun asked the woman.

"Sixty dollars."

Craaaap. Pretty and pricy.

I sighed and handed it back over to Jun, but he shook his head and took out his wallet. "Wait, Jun, you don't—"

"Do you want it?" he asked, staring down.

"Well… yeah, but—"

He just nodded and opened his wallet to pay the woman. "Thank you."

She smiled. "It's one of a kind."

"So is he," Jun said, petting the back of my head briefly. "Come on, Indy."

"You didn't have to buy this," I said as we started walking again.

"If I wanted to?"

"You're too charming for your own good." I slid the ring onto my pointer, turning it this way and that to catch the sinking sun's rays on the colors. "I really love it. Thank you."

Jun's mouth quirked to the side in a smile. He petted my hair again, leaned down, and kissed my forehead. "You're welcome."

"What should I make for dinner tonight?" I asked, looking up from the ring.

He shrugged.

"Oh! I can make a really good seafood marinara pasta. I put shrimp and baby clams in it."

"Sounds wonderful. Do we need to pick anything up at the store?"

"Nope. It's all at home."

Jun looked to the side, eyeing another merchant stand. "I'm going to grab a drink for the walk back to the car. Thirsty?"

"Water, please."

Jun maneuvered around a few groups of people and got in line behind two women ordering some mixed drink served in a coconut. I stared down at the ring again, leaning back against the railing that overlooked the ocean. It wasn't the gesture of buying the ring that I loved, although major boyfriend points because I'm too cheap to have gotten this for myself. It was the stupid simple fact that Jun didn't make fun of me for liking octopuses.

It sounds so lame, I know. But they're special to me, and Matt said I was creepy for liking them. When we had been dating, he asked me what I wanted for my birthday. I begged for a trip to Boston to visit the aquarium. Instead, he bought me a DVD of tentacle porn.

Hilarious.

So yeah, it was a cool ring, but it was *a lot* more than that.

"Grant!"

I looked up. Standing maybe fifteen feet away was Josh Moore with a plastic cup in his hand.

When our eyes locked, he dropped the drink and roared, running forward. "You son of a bitch!"

I pushed myself off the railing in a rush and jumped sideways as Josh tried to grab at me. "What the fuck?"

"Keep your fucking nose out of our business, you little twerp!" Josh grabbed the front of my T-shirt and yanked me close. He reeked of cheap beer, and his sunburned face was twisted up in sheer rage.

"Let me go!" I shouted, clawing at his meaty hand. "Dude! Are you insane?"

"Sending the cops after me?" Josh growled, ignoring the sounds of startled tourists moving away from our commotion and not helping. "Think you're untouchable because you're getting some dick that has a badge? I'll make you pay."

And a fist came at my face faster than I could react. Drunk or not, Josh landed a good hit to my jaw. My teeth chattered together, and I bit my tongue, tasting the tang of blood. Fear and adrenaline surged through my veins, and my raised-on-the-streets-of-Brooklyn-before-gentrification reflexes kicked in. On impulse alone I spat in Josh's face, and a wad of blood and saliva drooled down his cheek.

He let go to wipe at it, and I jumped up, decking him hard.

Well—hard for me, but I'm tiny and he's no less than the size of a small mountain, so while he staggered to the side but remained standing, I felt like I'd broken every bone in my hand.

"Son of a fuck!" I screamed, cradling my fist. I looked at Josh and saw his cheekbone was bleeding. My ring cut his face. Served him right!

"I'll rip your goddamn heart out!" he snarled.

Holy crap!

Jun grabbed Josh's arm from behind and yanked it hard, forcing Baldy McShit-Faced to spin awkwardly on his feet so they were looking at each other. Josh slugged Jun, and I swear to God, Jun let him, because in the same intake of air, Jun had Josh pinned on the ground facedown, arm twisted up behind his back, with a knee holding him still.

He looked up at me. "Call the police."

It sort of took a second for Jun's voice to register, because my head was still playing that incredible takedown even though my eyes were seeing something totally different.

"Aubrey!"

I shook my head and blinked. "What? Police—yes!" I fumbled for my phone and used the hand not throbbing to call 911. All the while, Josh swore obscenities at me and Jun, The Man, God, his mother—and the onlookers clapped like we were a group of street performers.

"LET ME see." Jun cradled my chin and tilted my head up as I removed the ice pack a cop had offered for my face.

The police had come to Mallory Square and picked up Josh, who was belligerent and still trying to fight even after they got him handcuffed. We ended up at the local station too, which ruined any semblance of a romantic—or at least normal—evening, especially after Jun had been adamant that we were stepping away from this hot mess. But we needed to give statements, and Jun felt it necessary that Tillman knew about Josh.

Jun's eyes narrowed slightly, that one tiny change in his expression speaking volumes more than any angry words he could have spewed.

"Did it bruise?" I asked.

"Yes." He had me put the ice pack back and then crouched. He picked up my right hand and removed the second ice pack. "Can you move your fingers?"

"Yeah, it's okay," I said as I wiggled them all. "I didn't keep my wrist straight. I've usually got a mean right hook, you know."

"I don't doubt it." Jun pressed my puffy hand in between his own briefly before letting go.

"How's *your* face?"

"Fine."

"That was a pretty awesome takedown you made," I said. "Will he be booked for assaulting a federal agent?"

"I wasn't technically on the job," Jun replied as he stood back up.

"Mr. Grant and Agent Tanaka. Again."

We both turned to see Tillman coming in through the front door, shaking his head.

"Detective," Jun greeted.

"I'm considering having you put on payroll at this point, Agent," Tillman said wryly.

Jun's mouth did that little quirk thing. "Sorry to bother you. I'm sure you'd like to go home at some point."

Tillman just pushed his suit coat back and put his hands on his hips, doing that cop pose again. "The arresting officers brought me up to speed. Will you be pressing charges, Aubrey?"

"Hell yes, I'm pressing charges!" I retorted. I lowered the ice pack on my face. "He fucking punched me! I'll have to pancake foundation on to hide this."

"I spoke with Mr. Moore after the two of you left my office earlier. He didn't have an alibi for his whereabouts last night," Tillman said after a beat.

"Home alone watching television," Jun muttered.

"Basically," Tillman agreed.

"Did you tell him about me? He claimed I sent the cops after him." I pressed the pack against my jaw again. "He said he was going to rip my heart out. The guy's a few fries short of a Happy Meal."

"Of course I didn't," Tillman said sternly. "But you can rest easy knowing he won't be going anywhere outside of jail soon."

"Do you think he killed Cassidy?" I tried. "He's hammered. Maybe it's killer's remorse?"

Jun and Tillman looked at each other and spoke telepathically. When did they suddenly become so buddy-buddy? Cops, man. Seriously….

"What?" I asked, looking back and forth.

"I'll keep you apprised," Tillman stated, shaking Jun's hand.

"Thank you. Have a good night, Detective." Jun nudged my shoulder, and I stood awkwardly to follow.

"Wait, what happened? You guys just talked with your eyes!"

Jun hushed me until we were outside of the station. "If it's all right with you, I'd like to go home."

"Yeah, that's fine, but what was the telepathy you guys did?" I asked again, following Jun to the rental car.

He opened the passenger door for me, then gently shut it after I got in. Jun walked around the front of the car and slid in behind the wheel. "It's hard to say about Josh."

"He had the means," I said, raising one wimpy finger. "He could have easily broken the window himself. And with free rein of the house, who's to say he didn't find what they needed in the study and then carry out stealing it when I was supposed to be away on vacation?"

Jun didn't look at me as he pulled onto the road.

"And motive—Christ, if the treasure is real, a sweet million is excellent motive. But I guess forensic evidence is really what Tillman needs, huh?" I continued. "Fingerprints on the balcony door maybe, or even on the marlinespike? Maybe some stray paint in a suspicious place? You know, Josh has my cell number.... He could have been making those creepy calls."

"You've brought up a point that I've been hesitant to speak about," Jun said.

I turned back to him, watching the passing orange streetlamps briefly light his profile. "What point?"

"Josh is certainly a person of interest," he said after a pause. "And if he's behind the breaking and entering as well as murder, you said it's been two weeks since he had access to the home."

"Right."

"And yet they waited until the night you were supposed to be away from work."

"Uh, yes," I hesitantly answered. "What're you angling at? Cassidy really does have surveillance in there somewhere?"

"No. Someone who's associated with the property told them to wait because they knew about your vacation."

"I REALLY don't feel comfortable eyeing my employees as suspects," I said around the toothbrush in my mouth. "I don't want to sniff out the rat."

"I didn't ask you to." Jun leaned down and rinsed his mouth with water.

"But you think someone I work with is in cahoots with Josh, or at least Cassidy."

Jun straightened and wiped dripping water from his chin. "I think there is a high probability that is the case."

"Based on your gut?" I stared at Jun in the mirror's reflection.

"My gut's been doing this for eighteen years," Jun answered. He moved his hand over my shoulders in a comforting manner before sliding it down to my lower back. "You say folks know the alarm system at the home is testy? Maybe they suspected nothing but a cruiser would drive by with you on vacation."

I pursed my lips around the brush. "I'm liking this less and less."

"So am I."

"Can't we just ignore all the bad shit and have fun hunting down a lost Spanish treasure?"

Jun patted my butt before walking out of the bathroom. "Come to bed, Indy."

I finished up and rinsed my mouth. I turned off the light to the bathroom and then the loft as Jun pulled the comforter back on my bed and lay down. I ran across the room and jumped on the mattress, landing partially on top of him. He grunted and laughed, grabbing on to me.

"That's Dr. Jones to you, mister." I leaned down and kissed him.

"Begging your pardon," Jun murmured between kisses.

I took Jun's hands and yanked them up over his head as I settled on his hips. "This okay?"

"Yes," he breathed. "It's after ten, though. Don't you need to sleep?"

"There are few things more important than sleep," I replied. "But sex with you is one of them."

"I'm honored."

I leaned down to kiss him again and wiggled my ass against Jun's crotch. I grinned when he sucked in a sharp breath of air. I sat up and yanked my T-shirt off, tossing it somewhere in the room. "Touch me."

Jun's hands were immediately on me, deft fingers sliding up my sides and playing with the barbells in my nipples. He moved his grip to my back, holding me still as he put his mouth on my chest.

I groaned and slid my arms around his neck to keep him there, rocking my hips lazily. "I'm gonna fuck myself so good on your cock."

Jun shuddered and his mouth faltered a bit.

I smiled to myself. "Yeah, you want that, don't you? Want to just lie back and watch me ride you."

He let up on my nipple, and the cool air of the cottage hit the spit-slick skin, giving me goose bumps. Jun's mouth latched on to mine, tongue thrusting in and coaxing mine to come play until we were both left gasping for air. "I've dreamed of being in your bed since the day we met," he whispered.

"Yeah?" I smiled and kissed him again, tugging his lower lip with my teeth.

Jun groaned. "Y-yeah."

"Did you ever think I'd be bossing you around?" I adjusted how I was sitting so that I could better thrust against Jun's own erection.

He gasped. "I—I think a part of me recognized that tendency in you."

"Hmm… you realized it before I did."

He laughed. "I'm thankful."

I kissed him again. "I'm happy to provide anything you need." I climbed off Jun and crawled to the edge of the bed to open the nightstand. "Lose the pants," I said over my shoulder, which I heard him quickly do. Regardless of the fact that, as of yesterday morning when Jun arrived in Key West, we hadn't technically been dating, I'd still done the adult thing and purchased bedroom products. Because the joke was so on me if I thought I could withstand his charms and devilishly perfect looks the entire vacation.

I kicked my pajama pants off and knee-walked back to Jun's side with a condom and lube in my hands. "Know what you're going to do?" I asked, straddling him again.

Jun shook his head. "No," he whispered.

I took one of his hands and pressed the bottle of lube into it. "Now do you?"

Jun uncapped the bottle, and a moment later, one hand grabbed me, kneading a cheek firmly. His slicked-up hand touched me next, gentle and cautious as his fingers explored my hole.

I wrapped both arms around his neck and grabbed a handful of Jun's hair so I could tilt his head back and kiss him. "Next time," I murmured, "we'll keep the lights on, and you can fuck me from behind."

Jun's hot breath ghosted against my mouth, and his fingers pushed into me. "So I can appreciate your body art?" He gasped, and I'd swear he was the one being stretched, from the sounds of pleasure coming from him.

I groaned and rocked back. "That's right." The massive octopus tattoo on my back had thick, inked outlines made to look like brushstrokes. It was pretty hot if you asked me.

"So tight," Jun whispered.

"It's been a while since I've even used my dildo." His fingers thrust in harder, and I cried out. "Holy fu—yes!"

"You have a dildo?" Jun asked between kisses.

"D-does that upset you?"

"No." He grabbed my ass with both hands briefly, squeezing and pulling the cheeks apart. "I think it's sexy."

"It's pink."

Jun laughed breathlessly and started stretching me again. "I'm not surprised."

I let Jun continue for another minute before I pulled away, pressed my hands onto his chest, and shoved him back down among the pillows. "Stay right there," I ordered.

"Yes," he agreed, voice quiet, but just that one word dripped with passion and need.

I smiled and slowly slid down to his thighs so that Jun's erection was in front of me. I wrapped my hand around it and gave it a few lazy pumps. I'd put his girth out of mind since the car blowjob, but damn... Jun really was huge. This was going to be the biggest dick I'd taken. I thought of crossing myself and saying a prayer before getting on that pogo stick, but I just started laughing at the mental image.

"What?" Jun asked.

"No, nothing," I replied, opening the condom. "Ever been turned down because of this weapon?" I asked as I slid it over him.

"Ah... yes."

"Wow, really?"

"Yes."

"What a shame." I moved back up to his hips. "Before we get down to business... I don't want this to be a mood killer, but *sometimes*— rarely—my cataplexy is triggered during sex."

Jun sat up a bit, but I pushed him back down. "Is there anything I should do?"

"Cross your fingers that it doesn't ruin our fun."

"I'm serious."

I shrugged, despite the dark room. "Just keep me from falling off the bed and take it as a compliment that I literally lost muscle control because of you."

Jun didn't respond.

"Laugh, it's a joke."

"Ha-ha."

I grumbled and leaned down to kiss him hard. It only took a few of those before Jun was grasping at my body once more. I sat back up and reached behind to hold his dick as I slowly eased down. Jun's hands gripped my thighs, and I could feel him shaking as he kept his body still.

"Holy fucking Christ," I said, gasping loudly.

I'd get used to a boyfriend this big, right? *Right*? Then again, there was something so fierce and raw and animalistic at having my insides scraped away with every inch I slid down on. Maybe getting used to it wasn't what I wanted. The thrill sent sharp spikes, erratic and random, from the top of my head to my toes, from my nipples to my balls. Everything was on fire and I felt as if I was being consumed. Pain and a bit of discomfort bloomed into something incredible.

I finally sat on Jun's lap, his entire cock in my ass, stretching me as wide as I could go. I took a breath and shuddered as another wave of intense euphoria washed over me. Putting my hands firmly on his chest, I hesitantly rose up, and the burning sensation returned. I hoped like hell that the two orgasms I'd given Jun today wouldn't prolong him now, because no way was I lasting long. I couldn't even be embarrassed by that truth. He felt like how I imagined heaven was.

Jun moved his hands, running his palms along my back. He brought his legs up, digging his heels into the mattress like he was ready to pound into me, but was waiting as to whether or not I'd allow it.

"You like this?" I asked, feeling light-headed.

Jun groaned loudly in response. "Yes!"

I hesitantly rocked my body against his own, and the push and pull on my ass made my toes curl. I focused for a moment, testing my control as I tightened muscles around him. It made us both gasp.

"Ready to please me?" I asked Jun, tweaking one of his nipples.

"Tell me," he begged.

"Tell you what?" I asked coyly. "To fuck me hard? You want to hold me down and ram your cock in as fast as you can, don't you?"

Jun was shaking, his grip on my hips so hard, there was no doubt he'd leave marks.

"No," I said. "You'll have to wait."

Jun shuddered, but I knew he liked the answer.

I sat up straight and used his chest as leverage again to push up and down, fucking myself on his massive cock. My own dick slapped his lower stomach as I moved, but I ignored it. It felt good. Jun must have liked it too, because each time I came down and it hit him, the sounds he made sent me over the moon. In no time the head was drooling precum all over Jun's sweaty skin.

I touched myself just enough to swipe the liquid with my thumb before leaning over and pushing it into Jun's mouth. He wrapped his lips firmly around it and sucked hard. I'd have never imagined my fingers being an erogenous zone—but that tongue. *That tongue.*

"Sit up," I ordered. "Kiss me."

Jun immediately moved, resting on his elbows to meet me as I came down to kiss his mouth. The angle change was just right, and the next movement I made had me crying into the kiss.

"Oh fuck," I moaned. "*Fuck*!" I pulled back, shoving Jun down again and gripping his pecs. I rode him hard, letting go of any intention I had of giving Jun the reins. I might have the dick up the ass, but I was calling the shots. I slammed down on him, our skin hot and slick, the slapping of our bodies filling the quiet of the cottage.

I grabbed myself, jerking nearly painfully, as I desperately hurtled toward the brink of oblivion. "I'm gonna come all over your chest," I said, vaguely impressed that I'd managed a complete sentence when I was so full of cock that breathing, let alone thinking, had taken a back seat to my immediate need of orgasm. "You want that?"

"Yes," Jun moaned. "Please!"

I grabbed the back of Jun's head with one hand and got him to sit up again. "Where do you want to come?" I asked, panting as I kept moving against him. "Tell me, now."

Jun's hold on my hips tightened to the point that I'd be feeling those bruises as much as my throbbing ass the next day. "Your back and ass."

I leaned close and kissed him, and the taste of Jun's mouth, his erratic breathing mingling with mine, and the slab of cock rammed up my ass like a steel rod finally did it for me. I choked on my own moan, cum spurting against Jun's body and dribbling down my fist. I felt like I was about to black out—the bliss was sensational beyond belief.

"Aubrey," Jun gasped.

The desperation in his tone sort of brought me back to earth, and I stopped moving to awkwardly sit up from his lap. I winced as he pulled free, but didn't even have time to lament the loss or consider the relief before Jun had me on my stomach. I wasn't sure where the condom ended up, but he beat himself hard, dick and hand brushing my ass as he sought the same release I'd found.

I heard his breath catch and then felt a warm rope of cum hit my asscheek and another land on my lower back. Jun collapsed on me after, managing to hold himself up enough so that he didn't have his entire weight bearing down on me. I'll be honest—I did immediately pass out, probably triggered in part from the sex, but it wasn't for very long. When I opened my eyes again, I was still on my stomach, and I felt Jun's tongue moving along the contours of my body.

I grunted.

He raised his head up to mine and kissed the side. "Awake?"

"Uh-huh."

"Enjoy it?" I could hear the smile again as he spoke.

I slowly stretched and rolled onto my side to look up at him. "Oh yeah. Just—give me a minute…. Brain cells."

Jun laughed and kissed my lips. "Come over here and lie with me." He sat up, tugging me with him.

We both moved to the head of the bed and flopped back against the pillows. Jun gathered me up and wrapped his arms around me as I draped myself over him. We were a tangle of sticky limbs, our blood cooling and breathing evening out.

"I love you," Jun whispered, kissing my head once more.

I loved him too.

Definitely.

CHAPTER TWELVE

THE IRONY of a narcoleptic with insomnia was not lost on me. But the sad truth was, when it came to sleeping through the night, I often tossed and turned because of all the exhaustion and naps throughout my day. I mean, sex was a damn fun way to knock me out for several hours, but I did end up waking nonetheless.

We'd shifted around, Jun's naked form pressed up against my back with an arm slung over my waist. I touched his forearm, tracing the cords of muscle that flexed slightly in his sleep. I twisted my head toward the nightstand and reached out for my phone. I winced at the light as I turned the home screen on to check the time.

Three o'clock…. Geez.

I put the phone back and shut my eyes, trying to focus on nothing.

I picked up the ticking of a wall clock from downstairs, loud enough to be mistaken for a freight train in the middle of the night. I listened to a car roll down Simonton Street, Jun's breathing, and the sound of my freezer dropping ice cubes into the bin before filling back up with water.

Great. Wide-awake with nowhere to go.

I laced my fingers with Jun's and thought, in no malicious way whatsoever, that it must be *so nice* to sleep uninterrupted. This would be a good time for the Smith Home alarms to go off, since I was already awake. But that wouldn't happen, since the house was shut down for a stupid police investigation—honestly, how long did it take to dust a doorknob for fingerprints?

I mean, don't get me wrong, I knew that a murder investigation took precedence. And time. Nothing worked as fast as television would lead us to believe. But the more convinced I became that Smith's map had been taken by the second intruder and murderer at large, the more anxious I was to get inside and check for myself. All it'd take was a quick peek. I mean, hell, it wasn't like if they found evidence of me being there, it would suddenly put me under the magnifying glass of Burt Tillman. I worked there. I *religiously* worked there. I bet you'd find my epithelial tissues or whatever in every single nook and cranny of that place. I bet they'd even be on the ceiling.

And Bob Ricci, telling me I was forbidden to be in the house and threatening my job? Yeah, fuck him. I didn't respond well to bullying tactics.

So... I guess what I was trying to ask myself was, would it really be so bad if I hopped on over to take a look? Sure, I could just lie here naked with Jun, and really, who in their right mind would say no to that? But I was already awake and it'd take, like, twenty minutes, tops. What if the map really *was* gone? It could be important for Tillman to know, even though he'd likely just be angry. Deep down in his heart I knew he'd appreciate the tip when it became relevant. And besides all this, there was also the fact that I had to call Ms. Price in the morning and defend my job. What if she asked about the state of the home or Bob had been feeding her lies? What was I supposed to say? Make something up without having seen the third floor for myself?

I looked over my shoulder at Jun, gauged that he was deep into REM, and slowly eased out from his hold. I got to my feet, dressed in the dark, then grabbed my phone. I turned the flashlight on so I wouldn't trip and fall down the spiral stairs in my attempt to sneak out, but I caught sight of Jun's gun and holster on his suitcase, and it gave me pause. He hadn't put it away before we fell asleep, although admittedly I did sort of sidetrack him.

I'd never held a gun before.

Not that I wanted to, but... *Ghost Smith*. Except he, er, Josh, was currently in jail. So the odds of going to the house and being attacked were pretty fucking slim to none, but those phone calls, telling me not to go back and that I'd be dead—Josh incarcerated or not, I didn't want to take any chances and be caught with my pants down.

Jun was still sleeping. I hoped like hell he'd stay that way, because he would kill me for doing this. I slowly eased the weapon free from his holster, surprised at its weight. Jun wielded it like an extension of himself, but it felt too heavy to be of any use. That was okay, though. I wouldn't have to fire it. Just having a gun would scare off any potential intruder.

Not wasting another minute, I hurried down the stairs and picked up my crappy Chucks from beside Jun's shoes at the front door before tiptoeing to the back. I paused to dig out my Vespa keys from under a pile of junk on the unused dining room table, then fetched my helmet from where it sat on the washer. I slipped out the back door, juggling the handful of crap while stomping into my shoes and then putting my helmet on.

Safety first!

I pulled the seat up on my pink Vespa to stash Jun's pistol among some week-old mail, a map, an extra hoodie, and a bag of Twizzlers I'd bought and forgotten about. What a travesty! I slammed the seat down, hoisted the Vespa off its kickstand, and walked it to the front of the house. I brought it to the street before I sat, turned the ignition, and made a quick getaway in hopes of not waking Jun.

In the middle of the night, I could get to the Smith Home in under five minutes easy. Speeding down the streets, the cool tropical breeze whipped through my clothes and sent shivers up my arms. The neighborhood was empty of the typical daytime madness, and despite being a town to party in, 3:00 a.m. was pushing it for most folks. The only traffic I encountered on the way to the house were a few chickens crossing the road—a joke that got old real fast, believe me.

I turned onto Whitehead Street, and the Smith Home seemed to almost emerge from the canopy of surrounding trees. It was kinda creepy at this hour. But hey, at least there were no lights on in the windows, or apparent shadows moving about the house. I rolled into the employee-only driveway, parked beside the gift shop, and cut the engine. I heaved the Vespa back onto its kickstand, grabbed Jun's scary gun, snuck to the back gate, and let myself onto the property.

That strange bubble that seemed to encase the house was there once again as I walked along the dark paths in the garden. It's not that it was quiet at three in the morning; it was like sound was simply unable to pass through the gate. It became muted. Faraway. Sometimes it almost felt like if I screamed, no one would hear me.

Weird, right?

I hurried up the front steps and crossed the porch, only to find the cops had put one of those stickers on the door that if you opened it, would cause a tear and they'd see someone had trespassed. I'm sure Tillman wouldn't need more than one guess as to who did the entering either. I huffed and put my hands on my hips, about to cuss the detective out, but then I remembered the broken window latch around back. I'd already proven I could finagle my way in, so I went down the steps and circled the house to the opposite end.

This door had been stickered over too, but the windows? Sticker-free and Aubrey-size. I went to the corner window that looked into the parlor, shielding my hands around my face as I peered in. Totally pitch-black. I couldn't make out a single thing inside. I took a deep breath, told myself not to be a scaredy-cat because I was Aubrey Grant and had once chased a pickpocket who was dressed like Batman off the subway, and shimmied the pane open.

I stuck my leg in first and then ducked my head inside. I held on to the frame and bounced back on one foot to carefully get my other leg inside while not bumping or breaking any nearby antiques. Standing in the parlor, I let my eyes adjust and breathing slow, and considered flicking on the lights. In fact, I should turn all of them on. Set this house ablaze in warm tungsten because I couldn't shake off these damn heebie-jeebies. But if I did that, I might as well have been on the porch with a megaphone, proclaiming I was breaking and entering.

Just my phone's flashlight it was, then. I followed the small beam out of the parlor and across the downstairs to peek into the dining room. Dark. Empty. Ghost- and intruder-free. I circled around to the stairs and started up. My palms were sweaty and Jun's gun weighed about a thousand pounds in my hand, but I was fine. I could do this.

I had to take my house back.

Well, not *my* house, but I digress.

Anyway, a gun would stop someone dressed like Ghost Smith. Unless… you know, there was still that little chance Ghost Smith was… *a ghost*. In which case a bullet wouldn't do much. Fuck. I should have brought salt or something. That's what they used on *Supernatural*.

By the time I'd reached the second floor, I realized my thoughts had detoured drastically from guns and intruders and ghosts and whatnot to being centered mostly on how hot Jensen Ackles was. I chuckled and then froze when I heard a creak that hadn't come from my own steps.

I stopped breathing.

I didn't move a muscle.

Be chill, I told myself. *Be the Aubrey Grant you were at the beginning of the week.*

I wasn't afraid to stand up for myself.

I wasn't a wimp.

I took all of life's curveballs and carried on.

But most important, I would *never* hear the end of it if I told Sebastian about this and admit I ran away before investigating. He was my junior, after all. I have to keep face with the kid.

Squaring my shoulders, I boldly walked into the master bedroom, flashing my phone in all of the corners and clearing it of any persons, physical or spectral. I did the same in the children's room and concluded what I'd heard must have simply been the house settling. So onward to the third floor.

I walked up the second set of stairs, no longer trying to be quiet. The Smith Family Historical Home was my life, damn it. Someone could try to take it from me, sure. But they'd have to deal with me kicking and screaming the entire time.

"Okay," I called as I reached the landing. "I know I'm alone, but on the off chance I'm not, I've got a huge gun and I don't know how to use it, so don't fuck with me."

The house was silent.

"That's what I thought," I answered back.

I walked into the study, shining the light around. The rope barriers had been left on the floor, untouched by the investigating police. And like I'd predicted, it was the ones to the far right of the room, where maps were framed and hanging on the wall—leaving Smith's desk and small artifacts untouched. I carefully stepped over the ropes.

Color me fucking surprised as I stared at a big empty spot where Smith's original map was supposed to be. I was angry that I'd been robbed, but this was good for two reasons: one, it leaned heavily in favor of Jack's Spanish treasure being very real, and two, I kept digital photographs of every antique in the house for cataloging and insurance purposes. So I still had access to the treasure map's details.

I just wish I knew what it was about *this* map in particular. I'd guessed correctly that it would be missing, but for the life of me, when I closed my eyes and recreated the image in my mind, there was nothing… *treasure mappy* about it. It was simply a topographical map of Key West that Smith had made harmless notations on. I shined my light on the other charts still hanging on the wall, but they weren't original to the house, and nothing jumped out at me as *thar be silver here!*

So what was I missing?

What did Cassidy and his killer know that I didn't?

There was something obvious I was overlooking. It had to be right in front of my face and I'd just written it off as nothing.

I walked out of the study and went back to the storage closet where this entire fiasco began. I unlocked the door and went inside, shining my light onto the false wall and staring hard at the wallpaper. It covered the entire interior of the closet, but was also inside the nook behind the false wall.

It was a cream color, wonderfully preserved, with shimmery stars and crescent moons in random patterns. This was the anomaly in the house. The anomaly in the entire tale unfolding before me, really. Everything followed a timeline, from the 1850s straight on until Captain Smith, aka One-Eyed Jack, bit the big one and his body mysteriously vanished in 1871. And yet, this style of wallpaper was from the mid-1880s, and it appeared nowhere else in the house. In fact, I believe it was a style seen more in New England and—

"I'll be damned," I murmured. Now I knew why it always struck me as such an odd style. It was actually a ceiling paper.

I put my elbows on the wall and leaned into the nook. The ceiling paper was better preserved here than the rest of the closet. The stars were vivid and sharp, varying in tones of gold, copper, and silver, while the centers had mismatching dots of color. I shifted my phone and Jun's gun to the same hand and reached out to brush my fingertips against the paper. I'd seen stars like this before—in *this* house.

"Son of a—"

"Aubrey!"

I flailed, fumbled, dropped my phone, and held the gun up in a panic. "Stay back!" I shouted.

"Jesus Christ, it's me!"

Oh crap.

"Jun?"

"Who did you think?" He replied, dark silhouette holding his hands up in defense. "Put that down right now."

I lowered the pistol, Jun immediately came forward, and snatched it from my hands. "I'm sorry," I started.

The light shining from the phone on the floor cast distorted, angry shadows on Jun's face.

He checked the safety and clip before tucking it into the back of his jeans. "What the hell are you doing?" he demanded, moving closer and towering over me. "I don't know where to direct my anger first."

"I was only—"

"Breaking and entering."

"I work here!"

"It's a crime scene, Aubrey!"

"Yeah, but—"

"You stole my handgun," he continued. "You took a federal agent's weapon, and you're waving it around out in the open like an idiot. Do you *want* to go to prison?"

"I didn't steal it!" I argued. "I borrowed it! I wasn't going to shoot it. I just wanted to feel safe."

"You'd feel plenty safe if you weren't sneaking around at half past three in the goddamn morning!" Jun said, voice booming and scary angry. "You could have blown my head off. You could have shot *yourself*!"

Geez. I wasn't just skating on thin ice; it had cracked underfoot and I was drowning. "I discovered what was missing," I tried desperately.

Jun narrowed his eyes. "Out," he said, his tone dropping low and frankly proving to be even scarier than when he shouted. "We're going home now."

"Jun, we can't. There—"

"Aubrey. Don't."

I swallowed. I didn't move, didn't say a word as I stared at him.

Taking his gun…. God, *fuck*, what was I thinking? I felt tears pricking the corners of my eyes as the very real fear of Jun breaking up with me and leaving immediately settled like a rock in my stomach. I tried to apologize, but nothing came out. My throat was dry, parched like I'd been stranded on an island with no well. I reached out for Jun, and he stopped me, beginning to push my hands back before he froze.

Jun turned his head at the same time I looked around him toward the open closet door and the third-floor landing. Halfway up the steps, staring at us from between the banisters, was Captain Smith. Only a second or two passed between the three of us, but I swear it might as well have been an hour. Jun and I staring at him, Smith staring right back. He was as real and solid as the first run-in I'd had with him, and now Jun saw exactly what I'd been hysterical about.

My knees buckled, and I grabbed at the nook. I used my hold on the wall to keep myself sort of standing, while my cataplexy fought to drag me into a useless heap on the floor. "S-Smith!" I sort of slur-shouted.

It was hard to make out details in the near dark, but I knew Smith froze. A ghost had no reason to be on alert. So an intruder. A living, breathing human. For some reason dressed as Captain Smith.

"FBI," Jun said in a commanding voice. "Freeze!"

Nope. Smith turned and bolted down the stairs, feet pounding and the house shaking as he made a mad dash for safety. Jun took off after him, flying down the steps and vanishing from sight.

"Fuck, wait! Jun!"

I let go of the wall and grabbed my phone before I staggered and stumbled to the stairs. I looked to the second floor and saw Jun race along the hall and make a sharp turn before continuing down the next flight. I gripped the railing and tried to hurry after the two without killing myself. At the second floor, I had to stop and give my muscles a moment to gather strength before I continued to the main floor. I was halfway down the next set of stairs when I heard the parlor window slam open and bodies scramble out of it.

Come on, come on!

The cataplexy wasn't as awful as it could have been, and by the time I reached the parlor, I was okay, but alone in the house. I ran for the window and all but dove out of it to try and catch up to Smith and Jun. I jumped off the back porch steps and turned to my left in time to see Jun vanish into the surrounding heliconias and leap over the picket fence.

I was in no shape to do that—I'd only just given up smoking! Damn it! I tore off into the gardens, reached the fence, and hoisted myself up before landing hard on the sidewalk outside the property. I wiped my palms on my pants, turned around, and looked for them. I saw Jun racing down Greene Street, so I took off after him.

Smith was at least a block ahead, with Jun closing in on him. I pushed myself harder, blood pumping and adrenaline racing. Our feet pounded the pavement, echoing along the empty street. We ran by a sushi restaurant, a hot sauce shop, and half a dozen bars, all shuttered and silent. A chicken startled somewhere nearby, squawking and flapping its wings.

A trash can was overturned ahead of me by Smith, the metal rattling loud enough to wake the dead. I watched Jun leap the obstacle with ease, but no way were my short legs taking me over it. I'd end up face-planted in a half-eaten cheeseburger for sure. I dodged sideways, barely missed tripping over the lid, and kept going. My lungs were burning, and I had a stitch in my side now, but Smith hadn't stopped and neither had Jun.

We reached the boardwalk, and Smith didn't hesitate to run up a set of stairs and along the winding path. If Jun hadn't been so close on Smith's heels, he might have gotten lost in the dark twists and turns. The few drunk people still hanging around, maybe waiting for the sunrise, let out shouts of surprise as we ran by. The only immediate thought I had at this point was *Jesus Christ, I'm going to die*. Not even back in high school gym class had I ever run like this. But somewhere in between wishing for sweet death, I thought, *Jun should have some sort of FBI logo on his body*. Not that a T-shirt or jacket would protect him any better, but anyone could claim to be something, you know? I could claim to be Santa Claus, but without the beard and suit, I thought I wouldn't be taken very seriously.

I didn't want to see Jun hurt because of the fuckup I'd made.

Sea Shack was looming in the distance, a shadow against the darker sky. The boats docked to the left bobbed and rocked in the gentle coming and going of the waves. I stumbled when I dared to glance at the water and crashed to the ground, bruising and scraping my knees. I swore loudly and gripped my scratched, bloodied hands.

When I finally looked up, hissing through clenched teeth, I saw Smith jump into one of the boats. An engine turned over and failed.

"Out of the boat!" Jun shouted. He stopped running and took a firing stance.

Then a shot pierced the quiet of the island.

Jun ducked and ran for cover.

Oh God, oh God. Jun hadn't fired—Smith had!

I scrambled to my feet as the boat's engine turned over again and another shot seemed to shatter the night like a hammer to a mirror. I dove behind a trash can and peeked around the side. I watched Jun lean out from behind a small white building that housed the electrical controls for the pier's lights, but he didn't have a chance to fire before Smith took a third shot.

The engine sputtered once more, and then it seemed like Smith gave up, climbed back onto the dock, and shot in Jun's direction as he began to run again. Jun fired back this time, and Smith clutched his bicep and stumbled forward but kept running. Now it was official. Jun would have to account for that bullet. I'd gotten the FBI involved when all the poor man wanted to do was enjoy a little R&R in a tropical paradise.

Instead?

More of the shit Jun dealt with on a daily basis.

Dead bodies. Criminals. Shootouts. Just… you know, instead of chasing suspects down smelly back alleys in New York, Los Angeles, or Boston, Jun was doing it with the ocean on his left and palm trees to his right. It really wasn't much of a consolation prize, though.

"Jun!" I shouted, slowly standing.

Jun came out into the open and took sure strides toward the middle of the walkway, looking at where Smith had vanished down another road toward a residential area. "Stay where you are," he told me before going to the boat.

"Like hell," I called, hurrying after him, ignoring the burning pain of my scraped knees.

I could hear sirens nearby. The shots had roused at least one Good Samaritan.

Jun got to the dock's edge and peered into the boat, gun aimed and ready if there was anyone inside.

"Jun," I said again, reaching his side and then freezing when he held his hand out to stop me.

I peered into the boat and saw the cause for concern.

Peg Hart—dead.

CHAPTER THIRTEEN

THE SIRENS were right behind us.

I turned away from the boat to see police cars pulling into Sea Shack's parking area. Jun turned as well, gun now aimed at the ground in a nonthreatening manner. I could practically feel him vibrating at my side. I looked and caught a stain on his shirt and arm.

"You've been shot!" I exclaimed.

Jun shook his head tersely. "Just a scratch," he replied.

"Drop the weapon!" an officer called out, standing behind his car door and aiming a gun at us.

I put my hands up.

Jun slowly set the gun on the ground. "I'm a federal agent," he said as a few officers approached. "I have identification in my back pocket." He put his hands behind his head as one of the officers roughly grabbed him and started searching Jun for more weapons.

"For Christ's sake," I called when the second officer ordered my hands behind my head. "He's FBI," I told the first guy. "You going to buy him breakfast after that frisk?"

"Stop, Aubrey," Jun said firmly.

The first officer finally pulled Jun's badge from his pocket and opened it. "Special Agent Jun Tanaka." He looked back and, after a beat, handed Jun the badge. "My apologies."

Jun tucked the badge away and collected his gun, giving the officer who was checking me a hard look. "He's with me."

I lowered my hands when the cop backed away.

The first officer extended his hand to Jun, who briefly shook it. "Officer Brown. We got a call about three suspicious men seen running along the boardwalk and multiple shots fired," he stated.

"Four shots were fired by the subject I pursued here on foot," Jun answered. "I returned one shot after I was hit." He turned a bit to show the blood soaking his T-shirt sleeve. "Mr. Grant was unarmed and ran for cover," Jun finished, pointing at me.

"I'll call for an ambulance," the second officer said as he tilted the remote speaker on his shoulder and began reporting the situation as he walked back to the vehicles.

"I chased the subject from the Smith Historical Home," Jun said.

"That's pretty far," Brown said, impressed.

Yeah, and I felt every cigarette I ever smoked the entire way.

"I believe the subject to be involved in an ongoing homicide investigation headed by Detective Tillman out of Stock Island. However, my current cause for concern is what's in the boat the subject tried to escape on."

Brown's expression faltered. "And what's that, Agent?"

Jun turned around and walked back to the water's edge, pointing. "This individual is a friend of the first murder victim."

Brown peered into the boat, and I leaned a bit to catch the color drain from his face, but he kept cool. "Tillman, you said?"

"Yes," Jun answered.

"I'll get him out here right away," Brown said, getting on his own radio.

JUN REFUSED medical treatment at the hospital. He sat with one of the EMTs, who was cleaning and wrapping the wound on his bicep. "Are you okay?" he asked me.

I realized I had my arms wrapped so tight around myself, it looked like I was gripping my stomach so I wouldn't hurl. "Me? Yeah." I dropped my hands to my sides.

He nodded his chin in my direction. "You scraped your hands."

I looked down at them. My palms were caked in dirt and dried blood. I shrugged. "Just a boo-boo." Jun was staring hard when our eyes met again. "I've got Hello Kitty Band-Aids at home I've been dying to use."

He frowned.

"I'm sorry," I said, glancing at the EMT and back at Jun. "I just wanted to help. The only time I've ever run away from a problem was with Matt, and I gave up a life in New York that I loved because of it. I gave up my friendship with you. I didn't want to make that mistake again. Does that make sense? I didn't want this mess to ruin everything, and I felt it would have if I didn't confront it and try to… help fix it."

Jun didn't respond but stood when the EMT gave him the all clear. He came toward me, got right up in that nonexistent personal space New

Yorkers were used to having invaded, and put his hands firmly on my shoulders. "Yes, it makes sense."

"But you're still pretty pissed, aren't you?" I stared up at Jun.

"Oh yes."

"Are—we going to break up?"

His eyes narrowed behind his glasses. "No. Unless you…."

"No, I don't want to!"

"Then no, we aren't."

My shoulders slumped under his hold. "Good."

"But that doesn't change the fact that you acted completely out of line."

"It seemed like a better idea in bed. I couldn't sleep."

"The next time we're neck-deep in a murder and you can't sleep, wake me up. There are plenty of noncriminal activities we can engage in."

I heard a car door slam and looked toward the parking lot. Detective Tillman was walking toward us. "Quick," I murmured, tugging Jun down a bit closer after grabbing a fistful of his T-shirt. "Smith's topographical map was missing from the study."

Jun glanced sideways at Tillman before back to me. "What does that prove?"

"Nothing. Not a fucking thing, because there's nothing special about the map."

"Josh is in jail," Jun said. "Yet this Smith impersonator came back—to the third floor."

"There's something up there. Another clue," I said fast.

"What?"

"I don't know!" I glanced at Tillman, who was getting close enough for me to make out the stern, tired expression on his face. "There's… more than one map, perhaps. But—maybe it's not a map. Not in the traditional sense. If it took this long to uncover Smith's secret life as a pirate, we can be certain he was smart about how he hid the treasure."

"Agent Tanaka," Tillman called.

Jun looked at Tillman briefly. "We're looking for someone big, tall. Fairly young and fit enough to outrun me," he continued. "And someone who knows how to accurately represent Smith. Think, Aubrey."

"Tanaka!" Tillman called again.

"Th-there's two people," I blurted out. "Bob Ricci, who's really pissed with me regarding the whole closet-skeleton thing yesterday. He's a big man and a historian. It *could* be him."

"And?" Jun prodded.

I swallowed hard. "And… there's one person who fits the physical description who was with me when I first called the police," I whispered.

"Adam," Jun said for me.

I nodded, biting my lip hard. I liked Adam. It hurt to suspect him of *anything*. He was a good boy, and good boys didn't fucking kill people. But the evidence that this was an inside job was stacking up fast. The treasure-hunting group must have originally all been involved in the search for One-Eyed Jack's sweet pot, if our chat at Barnacles was anything to go by. So Josh broke the window latch to provide a convenient way of getting inside without someone having to steal my house keys. Then Cassidy and Adam/Bob went inside, something happened between them, and Cassidy ended up dead. Adam/Bob returned again tonight because the map must not have provided enough information on the treasure. But then Peg was killed. Was—*crap*. Was Adam/Bob killing off the hunters so he didn't have to share the bounty?

Josh landing himself in jail, Adam/Bob wouldn't have planned for, but now that left just him and Curtis Leon. Was Curtis going to be the next body to wash ashore?

"He'll return to the house," I said. "There's no way he'll give up when he's this close. We can set a trap. Jun, we have to stop him before another person is—"

Jun grabbed me, kissing me silent.

I could hear Tillman let out sigh close by.

Jun gently broke the kiss, his mouth hovering a breath away from mine. "Don't say anything," he whispered.

IT TURNS out that when the police needed to be sweet-talked, I was not the best candidate for the job.

Who knew?

I sat cross-legged on the ground, out of the way of the commotion, police, and first responders. I watched Jun from afar as he talked with Tillman. He held himself like a man in charge, which… considering he'd fired his service weapon, meant he was at least involved a bit now. And for a man in a bloody, wrinkled, punk band T-shirt he wore yesterday, he still came off like a badass G-man.

A few men lifted Peg Hart's lifeless body from her boat, *Mistress*, and onto the wharf. Her dyed hair was wet and plastered across her face. She was missing a flip-flop. It was almost too much—I'd spoken to her just yesterday.

I drew my legs up and wrapped my arms around them as I buried my face into my knees. I started to shut everything out so I could sleep, despite my location.

"Indy."

I looked back up. Jun was standing over me. It was a good sign if he was calling me by my nickname. I think. "What?"

He crouched down to be eye level with me. "How long do you think it'll take to find the other maps?"

I blinked a few times and felt my heart speed up. Jun knew I wasn't a wimp. He *knew* I had strengths and skills different from his own, and upset with me or not, he was depending on me like I did him. "I'm— well, I'm not sure. The database on my work computer has a complete inventory of our antiques. I can go through them and look for similarities between the map and other items."

Jun nodded and helped me to my feet. "I bought you some time."

"Really?"

Tillman and a uniformed officer were approaching us.

"Open the house. Treat it like an ordinary day."

"Even with Adam there?" I asked.

Jun nodded. "If it's him and he believes we don't suspect him, he'll be more likely to try again tonight."

"I should act annoyed," I suggested. "Like I just want to be on vacation and I don't plan on coming in tomorrow."

Jun's mouth quirked. "There you go. But be careful, Aubrey. If it's…. Don't be alone with him, okay?"

"Aubrey," Tillman interrupted. "You remember Officer Barney?" he asked, motioning to the man at his side. "He'll give you a lift back to the Smith Home and will stay until your staff arrives."

"Sure, thanks," I answered.

Tillman was already moving in the direction of Peg. "If you'll join me, Agent Tanaka."

"Call me for anything," Jun murmured, slipping away from my side.

I caught his hand briefly and squeezed his fingers before he pulled back, made a fist, and knocked it against mine. I grinned widely, watching Jun follow Tillman.

We were a team—albeit a pretty unconventional one.

A special agent and historian.

Uncovering the truth in both the past and present, trying to stop history from repeating itself with more senseless deaths, all in the name of a pirate's buried treasure.

I mean—we *fist-bumped*!

Jun Tanaka was happy-ever-after material if there was such a thing.

IT WAS half past five by the time I was back at the Smith property. I yawned, jaw cracking, as I stood beside the perking coffee machine. If I had to readjust the strange life I lived to include murders and deadly races for treasure, then by God I was going to forgo the stimulants that were at home anyway and have some real coffee. I picked up my X-rated coffee mug—what had Jun called it, *Tako to ama*?—and poured some cream into it from the mini fridge directly behind me in the break room.

My hands were still disgusting. I grunted and went into the adjoining bathroom, wincing and cursing as I washed the scratches and cuts clean with soap and water. I pulled out a small first aid kit from under the sink and sat on the floor, carefully applying medicine and about a dozen boring, adult Band-Aids to my palms. I looked like a kid who was playing pretend doctor or something. I flexed my hands a few times, the Band-Aids crinkling uncomfortably, but it'd do for now.

The coffee was ready in the break room, and I filled my mug. I took a tiny sip and groaned. Nothing hit the spot like caffeine. I walked through the makeshift aisle and turned the corner to my desk.

"Smells good!" Barney called from the gift shop's main floor.

"You're welcome to a cup," I answered, turning on my computer. "There are extra mugs in the break room."

Barney's head appeared above the wall of crap that shielded my desk. "Appreciate that."

"No problem." I smiled as he went to help himself before I turned back to the computer screen.

Once upon a time, the database had been a nightmare on an Excel spreadsheet, created by the guy who had the job before me. It was clear when I took over that, one, he wasn't all that interested in doing about 80 percent of what this job entailed, and two, he didn't have a clue how to use Excel. One of the first projects I began at the home was getting real software to input data and photographs, so our inventory was accurate, complete, and at-hand for insurance purposes. This program was pretty cool too, because it was so customizable that I could search by location and narrow it down to everything in a particular area of the home. And since Ghost Smith kept returning to the third floor, that was where the search started.

I brought up a photo of Smith's topographical map and enlarged it to the size of my screen before sitting back and staring at it. I was trying to figure out what in particular about the map made this group believe the treasure's location could be ascertained by it, when I noticed the star.

The star—like the ceiling paper. Exactly like it. I knew I'd seen it before!

I leaned forward, zooming in even more on the picture. The star had been drawn on after the fact. The ink was a different shade than the hand-drawn map, and compared to the notes Smith had written on the map, it appeared to have been added by another individual. Smith had a shaky hand—even in his younger years, there was always a small tremor in his writing—but whoever drew the star was sure and strong in their motions.

So… there was a star on Smith's map, made by someone else, that matched the paper in the closet, added by someone nearly ten years after Smith had passed. The only person living in the home at that time was Mrs. Smith, who by all accounts had lost her touch with reality upon her husband's passing and remained in mourning the rest of her life. But Captain Edward Rogers was still alive, living in St. Augustine.

A single heartbreaking thought occurred to me just then.

What if *Rogers* had put Smith in the wall? Smith vanished in 1871, no one found his body, and he was proclaimed dead. But his lover… what if Rogers never stopped looking for Smith? And somehow found him and *maybe* the treasure he'd likely been killed trying to protect.

It was too much conjecture—but that message in the nook? *An X on my heart*. Smith certainly didn't write that about his own heart.

Regardless of the bittersweet romance that I both did and didn't want to be true, the fact remained that Smith's body was put into the wall (because I didn't need a medical examiner to confirm it, call it *my* gut instinct), and it had to have been well after he died. His wife would have noticed a decomposing body. And this star on the map matching the paper was too coincidental.

Except—*why* put Smith in a wall and cover it over, meaning to hide him away forever?

Was Rogers afraid of something happening to the remains?

I zoomed out on the map and hit the print button. I swiveled around and grabbed the paper from the printer, holding it out to look at. The star was located in the middle of the water. That must have been why Peg was murdered. Whoever was behind this, be it Josh, Adam, Bob, or a real *Ghost Smith*—they must have mistaken the star as the location of the treasure. Peg brought them out on the ocean, and then she was killed so she couldn't demand her fair share, only for the murderer to realize the star didn't mean what they'd thought. They returned with the intention of taking another look in the Smith Home, and here we ended up.

I picked up my mug and took another sip of coffee. I nearly set the printout aside when my eyes caught something. A second star. Diagonal from the star in the ocean, near the opposite bottom. It was located directly on top of the Smith Home. And then suddenly it all sort of clicked.

Smith hadn't brilliantly hidden his untold riches from the world.

Rogers had. And he'd even laid out their entire story—now someone simply had to assemble the clues.

The stars were the *X*s.

And *X* always, *always* marks the spot.

CHAPTER FOURTEEN

I REALLY hadn't planned on napping, but between the Mallory Square fistfight last night, followed by the best sex I've ever had, a gunfight before sunrise, and scrutinizing every single little artifact in my database before we even opened the doors for the morning rush—who the fuck could blame me? And I crashed hard. We're talking drool on the pillow and tongue hanging out of my mouth like a dog, hard.

I grunted when a finger prodded my chest.

"Aubs."

"Uhn."

"Aubs, wake up."

I rolled away, putting my back to the intrusion.

A sigh. "*Aubrey*! Wake up!"

I startled and jumped, nearly hitting my head on the desk I was sleeping under. "What?" I asked, rubbing the sleep from one eye and turning to stare at Adam. *Oh crap. Be cool.*

"You alive?" he asked, giving me a less than patient expression.

"Er—yes. Thank you for that. I think my eardrums are still intact too."

Adam scooted back a bit so I had room to get out from under the desk. "Your alarm went off twice and you didn't get up. I had to take drastic measures."

I crawled out on my knees before climbing to my feet, back popping as I straightened. I yawned and picked up my phone, which I'd apparently ignored, to check the time. "It's already nine?"

"What happened to your face?" Adam asked suddenly, voice low and harsh. "And your neck? Did *Jun* do that?" He sounded outraged.

"Huh? No. No! Well, the neck, yeah—but that was consensual," I said, touching the remnants of the bite mark Jun had left yesterday morning. "Some drunk dickwad punched me at Mallory Square last night," I continued, keeping my answer vague as I motioned to the bruise on my jaw.

Adam furrowed his brows, staring hard before he eventually changed the subject. "Bob Ricci is here."

I dropped my phone. "He's what?"

Adam jutted a thumb toward the gift shop's main floor.

Fuck me sideways. What now?

I was in the funny position of being alone with two dudes who might or might not have killed some people. Frankly, if it had to be one over the other, why *not* Bob? Fucking asshole. I actually disliked him. Please let him be Mr. Baddie.

"When did he get here?"

"Last night," Adam answered.

"Last—what?"

Adam narrowed his eyes a bit and pressed both of his big hands to my cheeks. "Are you sure you're okay? You feel warm."

"Whoa! Yes, fine! Thank you," I said quickly, slithering out of his hold.

Adam awkwardly lowered his hands. "Sorry. Uh, Bob said he stayed at Turtle Bay Inn. He came in just a minute ago asking for you. Want me to tell him you're busy or… something?"

"No, no. I can talk to him," I said. I cleared my throat and finger-combed my wild hair.

"Your shirt's inside out," Adam whispered just as I started walking toward the doorway.

I stopped and looked at him, then down. Yes, sure enough, that's what I got for dressing myself in the dark. "For Christ's sake." I yanked it over my head, not in a state of mind to care if someone besides Jun saw my body bling, before righting the shirt and putting it back on. What was I wearing? A cartoon octopus with a top hat and monocle, holding a cup of tea. Naturally.

"Aubrey…. Get into a fight with a feral cat?" Bob asked as I walked into the main room. He was an intimidating guy, even without the constant bad attitude. Nearly as tall as Jun but with none of the warmth or sense of safety. He hit the gym on a regular basis, judging from the slightly too-bulky muscles that were pulling at the seams of his polo shirt. And he always had a five-o'clock shadow, regardless of how recently he'd shaved. Bob Ricci was the kind of manly man who probably beat up guys like me back in high school to prove his testosterone levels.

"Good morning, Bob," I said, ignoring the question. "I wasn't expecting you here."

"The same can be said about you," he replied, crossing his arms over his barrel chest in some kind of macho-man intimidation tactic. "But I saw that scooter of yours in the driveway."

"It's a Vespa," I corrected. *Be respectful of the Italian wasp.*

Bob didn't respond immediately. "Let's go talk somewhere."

"Here's fine," I answered, because I wasn't supposed to be alone— not that Adam as my backup was what Jun wanted.

Bob shook his head and walked to the door that brought tourists into the garden. "Let's go," he said again.

What else could I do? I begrudgingly followed. This Friday morning was turning out to be another picture-perfect March day in the Keys. The sun was shining bright through the canopy of trees. Birds tweeted and whistled above us, and butterflies fluttered here and there in the warm air. Bob walked along one of the back paths, away from the home and in the direction of a small koi pond. He stopped once he entered the opening, sliding his hands into his pockets as he stared at the sun's reflection on the water.

I skirted around him to a tiny case beside the water pump and removed a bag of fish food. "So?" I ventured as I tossed a handful into the water and the otherwise lazy koi began jumping for their breakfast.

"I thought I said you weren't to be on the grounds until I spoke with Price?"

I calmly closed the bag and put it away. "Yeah, about that…. We had the house closed because of a pesky murder investigation and no one from the board came down to help me. So when I was told I could open today by police…." I paused and looked at him from my crouched position. "Someone had to do their job."

"Weren't you supposed to be on vacation anyway?" Bob asked tersely.

I squinted a bit as the sun peeked out from behind a small puff of clouds. It was hard to read any sort of expression on Bob's face. "Yup. My boyfriend's visiting."

His jaw tightened in the corners. Oh, well okay, *that* I could decipher. Bob didn't like the idea of me slobbering on a dick.

"Where is he?"

"Home. Why are you here, Bob?" I stood.

Bob took a step closer, crowding me in ways I didn't like. I had a flash of imagery—one hard shove to my chest, falling into the pond, held down, water in my lungs….

I stubbornly held my ground. "Here to breathe down my neck? Why'd you come in last night?"

"What?" he asked, taken aback.

"Staying the night at Turtle Bay? Why?" I prodded. "Adam's naïve enough to believe whatever excuse you gave him—wanting to avoid morning traffic, maybe? Spending the weekend in the Keys after dealing with me? Why'd you *really* come down last night?"

"I'm not here to play twenty questions with you," Bob growled.

"What's your relation to Peg Hart?" I asked, hoping saying the name would give me something—a hesitation, a crack in his angry expression—*anything*.

Instead, all I got was "Who?"

"Where were you last night? Say, around three?" I kept going.

"That's none of your—"

Somewhere in the recesses of my caffeinated, exhausted mind, I remembered Smith stumbling as he ran away from Jun. That's right, Jun had shot him! It clearly hadn't done more than graze Smith, but a nick was a nick. I grabbed Bob's huge beefy arm, yanked it toward me, and shoved the sleeve of his polo shirt up.

"Nothing," I whispered. Maybe it had been the other arm? I grabbed his right arm and did the same. No evidence of a bullet wound, and I didn't think Bob would have healed overnight, no matter how many green juices he drank a day.

"Get the hell off me, you creep!" Bob shouted, shoving.

And I lost my footing.

I think I screamed something—probably "Fuck you, Bob!"—but I was too busy flailing my arms and trying to regain my balance to pay much attention. I toppled back and became submerged in cool, fishy water. I immediately panicked and thrashed violently as I fought to right myself. I don't do oceans, pools—fuck, not even tubs. Because all it would take was one sudden sleep attack or cataplexy episode for me to drown.

I'd inhaled a mouthful of water going down, and the treads of my worn-out Cons lost traction on the slippery pond ground while I attempted to shove up and break through the surface. A fist grabbed my shirt, and oh God—this was it. Bob was going to kill me. He was stopping his last obstacle before absconding with the treasure and retiring to some no-name island in the Bahamas, never to be seen again. Meanwhile, I'd be dead in a pond full of fat fish, leaving it up to Jun to identify me.

In the last bit of frenzied life I had, I grabbed the hand holding my shirt and fought violently to tear free. But I had no air, and I could feel the strength in my arms leaving me. This just wasn't fair....

My head came up suddenly and I choked, spitting water and gasping for air. The hand let go on my shirt, and I immediately toppled back underneath the surface before it hoisted me up again. Sputtering once more, I looked up through the wet hair in my eyes at Bob, leaning over the edge, keeping me upright.

"You stupid fuck!" he roared.

"Y-you pushed me!" I said, gagging on the taste in my mouth and spitting again.

Bob hoisted me up more, grabbed my hands, and pulled me to the ledge. "Get up."

"I can't," I protested, still breathing hard. "Just—hang on."

"Oh, come on with that narcoleptic crock," he said.

I looked up, slamming my fist weakly on the bricks that circled the pond. "You think I wear this medical alert bracelet because it's pretty?" I protested. My legs were completely Jell-O, and I was barely hanging on to the side with what upper body strength I had at the moment. I was so scared that I wasn't actually afraid, if that made sense. Just skipped it and went right on to rage. I was going to kill Bob, as soon as I could climb out of the pond.

Bob swore enough in that moment to make a sailor blush before grabbing underneath my armpits and yanking me out of the water with admittedly impressive strength. He set me on my feet, then held me when I wobbled forward. With a look of disdain, he kept one hand on my chest and the other under my arm, before shuffling back so he didn't get wetter than he already was.

I didn't say anything, just stared at my sad state and focused on regaining my breathing.

"Bobby!" a high-pitched female voice called suddenly. "Bobby, you said it'd only be a minute!"

I knew that voice.

Looking up, I saw Liz Blake, the receptionist for the board's Marathon office, coming around the corner. She was wearing sunglasses, a big hat, bikini top, and shorts that could probably be referred to as *bootyshorts*. Wow—I'd never seen her in anything but office attire.

"Bobby?" I echoed. "*Bobby?*"

Bob swallowed and glanced over his shoulder. "Hang on, Lizzie."

"Lizzie," I said expectantly.

Liz's mouth made an *O* in surprise. "Mr. Grant! Yikes… you okay?"

"Sure, Liz," I responded in a near comical tone as Bob hesitantly released me, and I remained standing. "Just took a dip, is all."

She glanced at the koi pond and raised her glasses up. "In there? I don't think it's for swimming, Mr. Grant."

I managed to not say anything bitchy and instead wiped water from my face and pushed my hair back.

"I won't tell Price about the destructive acts you've made to the house," Bob murmured. "If you… keep quiet about this."

"*Destructive acts?*" I asked. "You're kidding, right? You won't tell Price to fire me for doing my job if I don't tell her that you nearly drowned me and that you two are having an affair behind Horner's back?"

Liz's eyes widened, and she put the sunglasses back down to hide her expression.

"Now see here—" Bob started.

"Yeah, I don't think you're in a position to 'see here' with me, Bob. How about you two just go."

"It was an accident," Bob insisted.

"Don't piss me off more than I already am," I warned. "Just leave. Enjoy your weekend tryst."

Bob's glare was so intense, he could have raised the dead by sheer force of will alone, but it wasn't going to work on me this time. He wasn't involved in the murders and lost treasure; he really was nothing more than a raging cock who I now had copious amounts of dirt on. So as I stood there dripping wet, soaked underwear riding up my ass and shoes making squishy fart sounds as I shifted back and forth, I put my hands on my hips and gave Bob my best "I dare you" face. And you know, the jerk finally backed down. In fact, he didn't say a word, just turned, took Liz's hand, and the two made a quick escape through the garden.

Once I heard the door to the gift shop slam shut behind them, I started to follow. Unfortunately, Adam was now our number-one suspect, because while Bob had been in Key West last night, had the means of getting into the Smith Home, and could have easily given Jun a run for his money—there was no wound on his arm, and I know I saw Ghost Smith get hit. If there was a way I could check Adam's arm… but without… manhandling…. *Uuugggh.*

I opened the door and walked into the shop, ignoring the few tourists who eyed me curiously while I *shlop*ed, *shlop*ed across the linoleum and into the back. At least I kept a change of clothes in the filing cabinet alongside my pillow. Mostly they were ratty things I wore when there was dirty work to be done around the property, but anything was better than my current state.

"Why are you soaking wet and smell like fish?" Adam asked, hovering in the doorway, watching me drip at my desk as I took out the clothes.

"I went swimming."

"What's going on, Aubs? Why was Bob here?"

"It's nothing—don't worry about it."

"I wouldn't, except that you're my friend. I care about you."

I turned, staring at Adam.

He cleared his throat. "As a friend," he said again. "Plus, you look like a hot mess. No offense."

"That assessment is true enough. I'm supposed to be on freaking vacation."

"So go home," Adam replied. "Herb's in the house doing tours, and I can man the shop, no problem."

I narrowed my eyes, studying him warily. Was he trying to get me out of here so—

"I know how excited you've been for Jun's visit," he said, voice barely a whisper. He looked behind him into the shop briefly before turning back to me. "And I'm sorry about what I said on the phone. I want you to be happy, so you should go."

God, I felt awful for doubting his sincerity. Because what if it *was* a ploy to get me off the property? What if Adam's crush was the only thing keeping my head on my shoulders and this was his way of trying to keep me alive while also getting what he wanted?

"Soon," I said, hoping I didn't sound like I was wary of him. Excusing myself, I went to the bathroom and stripped. I dried myself as best as I could with a handful of disposable paper towels, then washed my hair in the sink for good measure. Leaving my dripping-wet clothes hanging across the curtain bar, I put on the paint-covered, albeit dry, garments. My Band-Aids were gross now, so I had to peel all those off and toss them. There weren't many left in the kit under the sink, and on the off chance I got tossed into another body of water, I decided to not bother wasting them.

Adam was at the counter again after I grabbed my phone from my desk and came out of the back. He handed a group their tickets, directed them to the side door, and gave a brief explanation of reaching the house through the garden before wishing them a pleasant visit. I had nearly slipped out behind the tourists when he stopped me.

"Aubs, hold up."

I paused, holding the door open. "What?"

He put his hand out, offering something. "I forgot. I found this when I was helping Herb open the house." He dropped a button onto my palm. "I didn't think we had buttons on display, but maybe a cop moved it by accident."

I looked down at the button. It was fairly large, black, with the initials TJS scrolled into it with green. "Where was this?"

"Parlor."

"Why were you in the parlor?"

Adam looked taken aback. "I—Herb and I were sweeping. He takes forever, you know that. He'd still be sweeping if I didn't help." He pointed at the button. "It was on the floor."

I looked at it again.

TJS.

Thomas John Smith.

"Thanks," I said quickly, walking out the door.

"Wait!" He grabbed the door before it banged shut. "Did I piss you off or something? I'm sorry if—"

"No, it's okay," I called over my shoulder, already walking into the garden. I waited until I heard the door quietly close before I took my cell out and loaded my Skype app. I rang Sebastian and hoped like hell he was around to answer.

My bespectacled friend appeared on the screen a moment later. "Aren't you on vacation?" was the first thing he asked.

"What do you know about buttons?" I blurted out.

"Buttons? Can you move somewhere where the light isn't making you glow like an alien?"

I looked around and ducked under a sapodilla. "Better?"

"Yes." Sebastian pushed his glasses up the bridge of his nose. "Buttons keep your pants from falling down."

"You dick."

"I thought I was your cutie?" he countered.

"Monogram buttons," I replied, holding up the one in my hand. "See it?"

Sebastian leaned close to his screen, squinting. I felt kind of bad for asking him to decipher what he probably couldn't see very well, since his eyesight was pretty poor, but random button knowledge was him, not me. At least I hoped.

"What're the initials?" he asked.

"TJS."

Sebastian sat back, shrugging. "Does that mean something to you?" He picked up a cup from the desk and took a sip.

"It does," I replied.

"What's the condition?"

I stared at the button. "I'd guess it was a replica."

"Then what's it matter?"

"My skeleton fiasco hangs in the balance of this button," I said, sounding way too snippy. "I'm having a hell of a day. I just need your help."

"Where's Jun?"

"Long story."

"Are you two—"

"We're okay, I swear," I interrupted.

Sebastian hesitated for a beat. "Monogram buttons were popular on men's suits and outer coats. Usually black with the initials in color."

"Period?"

Sebastian rubbed at his bristly chin. "1870s?"

My heart skipped a beat. "Positive?"

"Mostly. It's not like I've read every book there is on nineteenth century fashion. I can look into it further if you wanted me to."

"No, it's not necessary. You've made me very happy," I said, finally smiling that morning.

"You won't be after receiving my consultation bill."

CHAPTER FIFTEEN

I STOOD at the back of the property, stared up at the house, and shielded my eyes from the late-afternoon sun. There were no windows on the third-floor study. Not on this end. The front, sure. Every room had at least one window that overlooked Whitehead Street. But back here, there was no window in the study with a view of the garden.

I raised an old photograph high, holding the snapshot dated 1854 up against the current home. There used to be a window in the study. One year before Smith met Roberts. I swiped through the pile of pictures in my hand to 1855, the same year the two met through wrecking. There was severe damage to the third floor, and the scrawled handwriting on the photo said *hurricane season*.

After the house was repaired, the window disappeared.

And I'd never thought anything of it until now.

Turning, I set the pile down on the nearby bench and picked up a large sheet of paper that had been rolled tight for too many years. I got down on the ground and flattened a copy of the original construction prints on the walkway. I ran my finger along the perimeter that became the study. Twenty-four feet in length. And the closet on the third floor, according to the 1853 draft, never existed.

Son of a bitch, amirite?

It was added to the house after the hurricane damage, and it wasn't because the Smith family could use some extra storage for linens. I stood with the plan, letting it roll itself back up. I grabbed the photos and ran across the grounds, then up the porch steps to the back door. Inside, Herb was talking to a woman maybe a few years older than myself.

"There he is," Herb stated.

I paused midstep in the foyer. "There's—me?"

"Aubrey Grant?" the guest asked, giving me a once-over, like "oh this train wreck of a kid can't be the manager."

"Depends on who's asking," I answered, sounding extremely paranoid.

And she caught that, laughed a bit uncomfortably, and raised both eyebrows. "Lucrecia Kennedy. We spoke on the phone yesterday about Captain Rogers?"

"Oh. *Oh*! Ms. Kennedy! I'm so sorry." I moved forward, fumbled the photos and papers to one hand, and shook hers. "It's been a long day. What on earth are you doing down here?"

"I researched what you asked for last night," she began. "And I found something that I simply couldn't explain over the phone."

"Really?"

She looked around the house. "This is quite beautiful. You've done a wonderful job with the property. Our little museum is nothing like this, you understand. Our staff... none of us are on-site historians." Lucrecia looked down at the large bag in her hand. "But even I know this is important."

Crap.

"Sure, come with me," I said but didn't move. "Anyone in the house, Herb?"

He perked up and shook his head. "Nope. Last tour left about ten minutes ago."

"Good. Follow me," I said to Lucrecia. I hurried to the stairs and took them two at a time to the second floor.

"I hope I'm not interrupting something important," she called from behind, trying to keep up.

I reached the second floor and did a little *gross, gross, oh my God don't think about it* jump across an area rug that had been situated over the blood staining the wooden floor where Cassidy had died. "Nothing that can't wait a few moments," I called. "Sorry, we're going up to the third floor. My office is rather nonexistent, and there's nowhere else we won't be immediately bothered." I hustled up the next set of steps.

At the third-floor landing, I walked to the corner where the closet was situated. I set my piles down alongside some sheets of paper I'd been doing math on, a measuring tape, cloth gloves, and the printout of the missing topographical map.

"Reorganizing displays?" Lucrecia asked upon reaching the landing and looking over my shoulder.

"Something like that."

She hiked up her skirt a bit and got down on her knees, opening the bag she'd brought. "Edward Rogers died in August of 1880. We have newspaper clippings verifying his passing. I never thought anything of it until you mentioned you wanted 1871 diaries."

"Did he keep one?"

"Yes. We had it in storage. Tourists see one diary, they've seen them all, you know? But it's empty."

"Empty?"

"He signed the front page but never made a single entry," Lucrecia clarified. She carefully removed a packaged leather booklet, exactly the same as its 1867 counterpart, which Cassidy had stolen. "And it doesn't appear that he kept any others after that year—until this one: 1880."

I grabbed my gloves to put them on. "Any mentions of Smith or Jack?"

"Smith," Lucrecia answered. She handed it over.

I opened it up and gently flipped through the pages. "They're all blank."

"Yes," she said again, and I caught her chewing her bottom lip. "Until July seventh."

I thumbed deeper into the journal to reach the entry in question. All it said was *I've found him.*

Smith had been dead nearly ten years by then. Rogers, that poor bastard. He never gave up looking for Smith's body after its mysterious vanishing and he was officially declared dead.

I glanced at Lucrecia.

She looked solemn. "It's blank again until August second. It's Rogers's last entry."

I swallowed and turned the pages. My ears were ringing, and it was like all of the air had been sucked out of the house. I reached the date and had to practically force myself to read.

I am mad with hysteria and grief that I cannot shake. I cannot cope. As Thomas's friend, I should have delivered him home to his wife, who has never retired her mourning. I should have seen him laid to a proper rest. But the devil's inside me. My heart is broken beyond repair that any man could make to it.

Edith would have never respected Thomas's burial wishes. What wife would agree to put her husband in the ground with his dearest friend instead of her? And who do I have who would carry out the wish for me? So I've left Thomas to protect our sanctuary and every piece of eight I never asked for. We would have managed without it. If only he had asked me first! He'd still be alive.

This will be my final entry. I cannot bear a life without him, now that the sliver of hope I've held on to all these years is gone. I will use my grandfather's dagger. Seems only fitting. I do beg, that if there comes a day when Thomas is found through the clues I've left—whether that soul sees in a man what I saw in him, or is simply someone whose kindness I do not deserve—please fetch me and rest us in a small plot together.

This is all we've ever wanted.

Edward R. Rogers.

I felt… *shattered.*

Like I was dying inside with Rogers as I read his final words.

I hadn't expected this to be his fate. Not really. I knew Smith had been killed for the treasure—Cassidy and Peg suffered the same tragedy over a hundred years later. But the self-inflicted death of one heartbroken man who wanted nothing to do with riches? Just wanted to be with the person he adored? And to think, Rogers hid Smith away because it was as close as he'd get to resting at his side. I couldn't—I literally *couldn't* imagine what life must have been like for them. Meeting in 1855 and falling in love when not only was it dangerous, but illegal. And to have kept their romance hidden for nearly fifteen years….

I didn't realize I'd started crying until a tissue appeared in my line of vision. I snatched it quickly and wiped my nose. "Sorry," I murmured. "Hits close to home. The gay part, I mean—not the other stuff."

Lucrecia just nodded. "I cried too, when I read it last night. The newspaper clippings hadn't said he'd died by suicide. We've been sharing inaccurate information for years."

I dried my eyes and set the diary down on the floor between us. "This all started over a pirate's treasure."

"Really?" she asked, her voice rising.

I nodded. "I thought none of it was true and it was just local rumors and bullshit. But it really happened. It's exciting, the notion of changing history with such an incredible find, but…." I took a deep breath. "Then I read these dairies of the men involved and have to remind myself they were real people with tragic endings."

Lucrecia dipped her hand into the bag again but paused. "So…. Your Thomas Smith was a pirate?"

I nodded.

"Rogers wasn't, though?"

"No, but… I think Smith stole for Rogers."

"What do you mean?"

I wiped my face once more and met her gaze. "The wrecking industry took a nosedive during the Civil War. I think Smith turned to piracy to make money. What Rogers wrote, about the pieces of eight he never wanted?" I touched the diary. "I think the investments Smith started making in a property upstate around that time might have been—"

"For the two to run away together," Lucrecia stated. She'd done none of the research I had on Smith's money and properties, but I think, as a human, she understood. That basic instinct to care for what you hold most dear. Smith and Rogers were in love and desperate to build a haven they could escape to.

I cleared my throat and started packing the diary away. "I appreciate you driving all day to come show this to me. I'm a snotty, puffy-eyed mess now, but I hope you won't judge too harshly."

Lucrecia smiled. "No, honey. Like I said, I cried too." She let out a breath. "I have one last thing to show you. It was part of Rogers's estate that was donated to our museum. It never fit with the nautical theme, though, so it was kept in storage. But after reading that entry, I sort of put two and two together regarding its importance."

"Do I need to get more tissues?" I asked warily.

She winced but ultimately shook her head and carefully removed a cardboard box. She opened the top, discarded the wrappings, and tilted it toward me. It was a long dagger, but I wasn't familiar with its origin or period.

"It's a rondel dagger," Lucrecia stated. "I had it authenticated back when it was first given to us. Sixteenth century, Italian in origin. Maybe a family heirloom, since he mentions it belonged to his grandfather."

"It's terrifying." I reached in and carefully held the blade to examine. "Holy crap. It's four-sided."

An X on my heart.

I SHOVED everything I needed for that night into the third-floor closet, then swung the hook into the lock as my cell rang. I straightened and pulled it free from my back pocket. Jun—again. He'd called nearly half a dozen times to check in throughout the day. "Hey, Jun."

"Hi, Indy. Is everything going okay?"

"Yeah. Nothing suspicious yet, but I should probably make to look like I'm leaving."

"And you're certain—" Jun started.

"One hundred percent," I replied, cutting him off. "I know it's him. The button came off a near-perfect costume. It doesn't belong to the house—how could Smith have monogram buttons made popular during the decade he was dead? Tourists wouldn't notice such a minor inaccuracy on a costume, though."

"Then we'll be there," Jun answered, no tone of doubt in his voice.

I started walking down the stairs to the second floor when I stated, without much thought to the digression, "Rogers killed himself."

Lucrecia Kennedy had left for St. Augustine about an hour prior and had loaned me the dagger and diary. She said her museum would be honored if they were displayed in the Smith Home—but I wasn't sure it was something my heart could handle. Did the truth need to be known? Yes, absolutely. Every bit of it, even if Smith's piracy tarnished his legacy and I upset a bunch of locals. But to put a spotlight on a weapon that ended the life of a lonely man? I didn't want their story to be remembered that way.

"What are you talking about?" Jun asked.

I stopped on the bottom step and slowly sat down. "He spent almost ten years trying to find Smith's body," I said, voice shaking. "And then he hid him in the wall. Rogers didn't want Smith to share a plot with his wife."

Jun didn't say anything.

"And then he killed himself," I said, choking up.

"Aubrey," he said gently.

"I shouldn't let this bother me," I replied, clearing my throat. "I'm a historian, and it's not very impartial. Just… you know."

"I know," Jun said simply. He understood.

I loved him.

I needed to tell him.

I'd loved him for a long time, and it'd taken three years to realize it, but I fully planned on making up for that blip on our radar. Jun was going to have one hell of a good future with me.

Cross my heart.

"You still there?"

"Sorry. Yeah." Over the phone wasn't how I wanted to say the L-word, though.

"We don't have to do it this way tonight," Jun began. "We can catch him another—"

"No, this is surefire," I insisted. "He's got a lot to go away for, and I don't want to ruin our chances."

Jun let out a small breath. "Then everything is ready?"

"Ready, Freddy."

"Be careful," Jun said. "Promise me that."

"I promise. Will you be careful for me?"

"I will."

I said goodbye and stood. The light outside was a fiery orange and pink as the sun set. There wasn't much time before darkness fell. I took a deep breath, squared my shoulders, and hurried to the first floor. Herb was going at his usual tortoise speed of shutting off lights and closing the home up for the night.

"I'll see you later!" I called.

"Leaving already?" he asked, poking his head out of the dining room.

I opened the front door and glanced back at him. "I'm supposed to be on vacation," I said, which wasn't a lie. "Got a boyfriend to tend to. Oh! Herb, do me a favor?"

"Yup?"

"Don't set the house alarm."

He cocked his head to one side. "Why?"

"It gave another false read early this morning," I lied. "I'm just keeping it off. I'll talk to the security company after my vacation."

Herb nodded and smoothed his mustache. "If you say so. Have a good night."

I ran out after that, jumped off the porch steps, and slipped and slid on smashed sapodilla fruits as I made for the back gate of the property. I sneaked out to the little driveway, forgoing my helmet because I was running out of time. I brought my Vespa off the kickstand and waved to Adam as he put the Closed sign in the door before shooting onto the road.

Wind whipped through my hair as I made a right onto Greene. I slowed to work through the crowds at Duval before taking another right and driving until I hit Eaton Street. At this point I'd nearly made a big square around the property of the Smith Home. The sky was mimicking a pastel painting as I slid into the nearest available parking spot. I hid Pink Princess in plain sight among a half dozen rental mopeds before walking back the way I'd come from. I was certain I was acting like a maniac, but I needed it to appear like I'd left the Smith Home for good that night, and I couldn't afford to be caught as I made my way *back* to the property.

There was a method to my madness, which was why I was cutting through the backyards of private homes and inns. I went slow enough to give Adam and Herb time to leave, so the evening had taken on that deep blue tone before the dark arrived in full. I eventually reached a fence in someone else's yard I had to scale. And I did scale it, which impressed me to no end—but then I fell off the other side and into the Smith garden. At least there was no one around to see that.

I brushed the front of my clothes, thought briefly about why I gave a shit if these rags got dirty, and made for the back door of the historic home. I stopped at the porch steps and looked up, studying the darkness through the windows. I'd be lying if I said I wasn't totally terrified about the stunt I was about to pull off, but what I'd said to Jun was the truth, and that's why he and Tillman were on board.

If I wasn't there to do this, the killer could very well escape with a million dollars and never face a penalty for the deaths of two people who never deserved such brutal fates. And, well, if I fucked up… it *was* my idea. No one to blame but me.

Taking the house keys from my pockets, I went up the steps and unlocked the back door to let myself inside. I didn't advertise my presence, and completed a full sweep of the house to confirm it was currently empty. Just me and a million dollars hidden in a secret room. I raced up the two sets of stairs to the third floor and went to the closet. Inside, I turned on a lantern we kept for power outages. I didn't want to use the house lights and scare away my midnight prowler from trying a third time to get the clues he needed.

Too bad for him, I'd figured out Rogers's hidden message first.

First, I picked up a pencil and the topography printout, then studied the ceiling paper of stars and moons until I found the exact two stars on the wall that matched the map. I circled them both and used a tape measure to draw a diagonal line, connecting them. Next was the wooden lid to Smith's compass in the study. On the inside was a tiny drawing, faded with age, but I'd deciphered it to be the Dry Tortugas—a small cluster of islands about seventy miles west of here, first discovered by the Spanish and home to shipwrecks and forgotten forts. Along the island shapes, there was a star, which, when I studied the wall again, had a matching partner on the ceiling paper. I circled it before turning the lid sideways. The length of it measured exactly from the star until it intersected with the previous line. I followed it with my pencil.

The last item had been Rogers's own diary, so thank God Lucrecia had visited that day; otherwise, I'd be tearing this house apart, looking for the last star. I hadn't found it the first time I'd thumbed through the 1880 booklet with her, but after skimming the empty pages again as she readied to leave, I found, on the very last page in the back, a map drawn in the same sure, strong hand as the stars on the topographical map and compass lid. Finding the matching star on the wall, I traced the length of the diary, and it also intersected with the first line.

Stepping back, I stared at the marks I'd made.

An *X*.

The first star, in the waters off the Keys, was where Smith and Rogers met. The second on Smith's house must have signified Rogers's visits and their secret rendezvous. The compass lid—it had to be the location Smith had recovered the *Santa Teresa*'s wealth—and the last, where Rogers found Smith's lost remains and the hidden treasure he'd died protecting.

I pulled my cell out of my pocket and loaded up an app that broadcasted a live video feed. Jun and Tillman would be able to see everything happening in the house, and the video would also be recorded and saved for use as damning evidence in a courtroom. I slipped into the hall and propped it in a corner on the floor so the camera had a full view of the upstairs area. I gave my audience of two a thumbs-up before going back into the closet. This part wasn't really in our schedule of catching the bad guy, but it was something I had to do.

For Smith and Rogers.

Because *I* was the someone who understood what Rogers saw in another man, and if there was a way to bring them both peace, even a century late, I'd do it. So I grabbed a face mask and pair of safety glasses from the closet floor before picking up the sledge hammer I'd snuck inside.

X *marks the spot.*

I swung hard at the *X*, putting a hole right through the wall within the nook. It crumbled fairly easily due to age and the fact that it was a false wall behind the first false wall I'd discovered. A few more swings and I had a big enough gap that I could see a door. I set the hammer down and broke the wall with my hands, tossing debris to the floor.

It really was something incredible—one of those moments that was too storybook to be true, and yet there it was, staring directly at me. The hurricane damage to Smith's home had been serendipitous, and he'd taken the opportunity to have a hidden room built, using a narrow amount of his study, and then hid the door behind the original wall with the latch, then hid that inside an ordinary closet.

Most people would assume he'd keep valuables in there, or perhaps sensitive documents, but no. While holding the lantern, I squirmed through the hole and tried the doorknob. The door swung open on squeaky hinges to reveal a tiny space with a cramped bed, chair, and basic bathing supplies on a small table—everything arranged in such a manner that it was as if the occupant had only stepped out for a moment.

This was the sanctuary Smith's body had been protecting.

Their secret space when Rogers would visit.

Besides the simple pieces of furniture covered in a thick expanse of dust and cobwebs, the room was absolutely filled with cloth bags. Some were rotting away with age and neglect, silver coins spilling into piles across the wood floor.

All around me was a million dollars' worth of lost Spanish treasure.

I took a few steps forward, moving deeper into the room. Positioned on the pillow of the bed was a diary. Likely Smith's. I coughed behind the mask and waved at the dust in the air as I approached. I regretted not having cloth gloves, but fuck, I didn't have a lot of time. Leaning over, I thumbed the pages, looking for… anything, really.

Smith hadn't written entries in it. There was just one note scrawled inside. He must have known how dangerous it was to own the treasure—how hot it'd be and how many people would easily kill to have it. So he'd written out his last wishes.

My family is well cared for. I have dedicated the best years of my life to making fortunes for them, so that they would never know the humble beginnings from which I came. They will carry on. My sincerest apologies, Edith. I do love you—you are my dearest friend. But I am not in love. And at my age now, I realize that's all I really want.

Should I not make it home alive from my last adventure, please see I am put to rest in our local cemetery. And, as I'm certain he will outlive me, save a plot for Edward.

Captain Thomas J. Smith.

I set the diary back on the pillow.

"Will do, Captain," I murmured.

A creak of floorboards and the shuffle of objects caught my attention. I jerked my head up, straining to hear. It was coming from the left wall—*the study*. I ran to the open door and climbed through the hole in the wall. I snatched up Rogers's dagger in my free hand and stumbled out of the closet. The lantern swung about, light dancing wildly around the hallway and briefly illuminating the big outline of a man in the study doorway.

"Aubrey," Smith said.

I pulled off the safety glasses and tossed them to the floor before lowering the mask to rest around my neck. "Hi, Curtis."

Curtis Leon, guide for the Ghosts of Key West tours and treasure hunter extraordinaire.

He reached up to peel the fake beard off his face. "How'd you figure it out?"

"Your buttons," I answered, taking a step to the side so I didn't block my phone's camera.

Curtis looked down briefly at his costume, thumbing the buttons on his outer coat. The lowest one was missing. "Buttons, huh?"

"Smith never wore monogrammed buttons," I continued, speaking loud so my voice didn't shake. "They didn't become popular until after his death. But they look great on your costume. I'm sure the initials make your character easier for tourists to recognize, right?"

He smiled slightly, almost sincerely. "Figures. Of all fucking things to give me away." Curtis stared at me from across the hall. "You found the treasure, then?"

"Oh yes."

"All of it?"

"Yup." I cleared my throat. "What now?"

"I can't let you live," Curtis answered.

"Like Cassidy and Peg?" I countered.

"I didn't mean to kill Cassidy. It was an accident."

"Peg wasn't." I squared my shoulders. "The cops told me she'd been strangled to death."

"The cops," he repeated, a hint of mocking in his tone.

"That's right."

"You should have brought them with you tonight, Aubrey."

My belly felt like it was on the loop-the-loops of a rollercoaster. I was nauseous and my knees were shaking. "I'm not going to lie down and die for you."

"No?"

"You'll have to catch me first." And with that, I threw the lantern at Curtis and ran for the stairs.

I heard the crash of the lantern above as I practically flew for safety, feet barely touching the stairs as I moved to the next step. Curtis's thundering feet rattled the stairs as I reached the second floor. I didn't turn, didn't look back. I ran down the hall and threw open the back balcony door. On Wednesday night, after stumbling over Cassidy, when I'd heard Curtis make his escape but was unable to follow, he'd climbed the porch and shimmied down the nearest palm tree to the ground. Now I was about to find out if I could master the same technique. I figured, since my life quite literally depended on it, I'd manage.

I ran onto the porch, throwing the rocker to the floor behind me to slow Curtis if he decided to follow this way, but as I climbed onto the railing and chanced a look over my shoulder, I saw Curtis pause in the doorway before heading to the first floor to cut me off.

Good.

I took a quivering breath and jumped from the second story porch. I slammed into the palm tree and nearly lost my grip before I wrapped my legs tight around the trunk.

Holy Mother of Fuck, what was I thinking?

I swallowed hard and started to shimmy down as quickly as possible, awkward to do as I still clutched the dagger in one hand. When I was close enough to the ground, I jumped safely to the porch. I tripped and fell to my already bruised and scraped knees, swearing loudly as pain shot all along my nerves. I struggled back to my feet.

"Don't move, Aubrey," Curtis said, walking out the back door with his pistol aimed at me.

I froze in place. Not a twitch, not a breath.

Curtis cocked the weapon. "I'm sorry about this. I really am."

"I think you're full of horseshit," I managed.

"It's a *million* dollars," Curtis replied, like I'd agree to him offing me if he just explained it a bit more.

A second gun came into view, pressed against the side of Curtis's head. "You're under arrest," Jun said. "Lower your weapon, now." He was wearing a jacket that identified him as Key West police, since he didn't have his FBI gear, but it worked in a pinch.

The standoff lasted maybe another second. Or a minute. Hour? Who fucking knew? All I was concerned about was that there was one gun too many in this triangle of potential death.

But Curtis slowly lowered his gun.

"Drop it," Jun ordered.

Curtis did.

Tillman came out of the bushes on the right side of the porch with a pair of handcuffs. He snapped them on Curtis's wrists and started giving the dumb fuck his rights.

Jun glanced at me, the briefest once-over to make sure I was alive and not bleeding profusely, before he moved to join Tillman.

But a gunshot rang out, loud like a crack of thunder during hurricane season. I jumped and put my hands over my ears instinctively, then scanned the area frantically, *desperately*. Where'd that come from?

Curtis dropped to his knees and fell sideways, blood pooling around him.

Tillman turned to the back door, gun raised, but then I watched him fly off his feet, hitting the porch hard as another crack echoed across the property.

"Drop your weapon!" Jun shouted, raising his gun as Herb appeared from the shadows.

Herb?

Semiretired, waiting to die, crappy tour guide, porno-stash *Herb*?

"Never let a kid do what you can do yourself!" Herb shouted. He cocked his antique gun and fired point-blank at Jun.

It was like slow motion horror as his body jerked violently and fell.

"*No!*" I screamed.

I saw red.

Nothing but raw, sheer fury coursed through my veins.

I wasn't going to lose Jun to this fucking pirate treasure.

I couldn't let myself become the modern-day Rogers.

I raised the dagger still clutched in my hand and threw it with every ounce of strength and ferocity I had within me.

CHAPTER SIXTEEN

I STOOD in front of a new tombstone. The earth was still freshly packed. The morning air held that sweet, cool scent of disturbed soil that I imagined existed deep in the wildest of forests. And like a forest, besides some birds chirping nearby, it was quiet.

Some vacation this turned out to be.

I blinked back a few rogue tears and wiped my nose on the back of my hand.

"Indy."

I glanced up, shielding my eyes from the morning sun as I looked at Jun. "What?"

"You okay?"

I nodded. "Yeah."

He stroked my hair for a few moments before handing over a bouquet of fresh flowers. I took it with a murmur of thanks and set it in front of the slab of granite.

"You did right by them," he said.

"I hope so."

Jun put his arm over my shoulders and pulled me closer until I wrapped myself around his back and chest, giving him a tight, sideways hug. "You did," he said again. "You fulfilled both of their wishes."

Thomas J. Smith had been identified by the local medical examiner, based on the physical facts we had on the former sea captain and part-time pirate king. After discussing it with Ms. Price and the rest of the nonprofit board, they all agreed to paying the expenses for him to be laid to rest in the local cemetery, based on his last wishes. More importantly, we had a lengthy chat with the city of St. Augustine and the museum that had been entrusted with Rogers's estate, as he had no living relatives, and Edward's body had been moved down to Key West. So Jun and I ended our vacation by paying respects to the couple, finally together after over a hundred years, one treasure hunt, and a few murders later.

"How's Tillman?" I asked after we'd both been silent for a while.

"He's doing fine. Recovering nicely."

I hugged Jun a bit tighter.

Herb had shot him without a second of hesitation last week, and in those horrifying seconds that followed, as I watched Jun fall, I thought I'd lost him. Thank God his vest did its job underneath the jacket he'd worn. And as for Herb….

"Herb?" I asked.

"He had a tetanus shot prior to being stabbed with that dagger."

I grunted. "Good thing." Did I sound bitter and sarcastic, or was it just me?

Jun tightened his hold. "He'll be going to prison."

"I wish Curtis was," I muttered. "I mean, he should have paid for all he did. Dying was the easy way out."

Jun just petted my head in response.

At what point other people began showing up in the cemetery, I wasn't sure, but suddenly we weren't alone anymore.

"Let's go home," I said. "Enjoy our last day together."

Jun agreed, taking my hand as we left Smith and Rogers alone. "What will happen with all those pieces of eight you found in the room?" he asked eventually.

"The board is going through the lengthy process of laying claim to it," I answered. "Florida has some whacky lost treasure laws they need to get around to keep it."

"I suppose they won't toss some your way for all the trouble?" he asked, and I could hear the smile in his tone without having to look at him and confirm it.

"Ms. Price *did* mention a bonus was in my future."

"Maybe we can take that trip to Japan sooner."

I stopped and finally looked up at Jun. "I love you. Did you know that?"

Jun's mouth quirked and his eyes did that little twinkly thing they do. "I did. But it's wonderful hearing you say it."

"I've been thinking, about… maybe moving back to New York."

His hand tightened in mine. Just a little, but I noticed. "Really?"

I nodded. "Don't get me wrong. Living in a tropical paradise is pretty sweet, and I love my job but… seeing you on a weekly basis seems way nicer than a few times a year."

"Don't give up everything for me, Aubrey," Jun said gently.

"I gave it all up because of Matt," I clarified. "This is me taking my life back." I smiled. "Don't you think?"

Jun put a hand on my jaw, holding it as he kissed me. "You're sweeter than candy, Mr. Grant."

"So are you, Mr. Tanaka."

Jun took my hand again, and we continued toward the front gates. "You know," he said. "Tillman got the ID of the caller leaving those harassing messages."

"Curtis," I muttered.

"No."

I made a face. "Josh?"

Jun shook his head.

"For fuck—*Herb*?"

Jun stopped just inside the cemetery walls and looked at me. "They came from the landline in the Smith Home."

"That's not possible. Only the tour guides use that phone to call the gift shop. You know, if they need something and can't leave the house unattended."

Jun raised an eyebrow.

"And I got calls while the house was locked down by the police," I continued.

"They came from inside the home," Jun said again.

A shiver crept deep down, right into my bones, and I looked across the sea of headstones, picking out the flowers we'd left for the gentlemen.

It wasn't possible.

Right?

C.S. POE is an author of gay mystery, romance, and paranormal books.

She is a reluctant mover and has called many places home in her lifetime. C.S. has lived in New York City, Key West, and Ibaraki, Japan, to name a few. She misses the cleanliness, convenience, and limited-edition gachapon of Japan, but she was never very good at riding bikes to get around.

She has an affinity for all things cute and colorful and a major weakness for toys. C.S. is an avid fan of coffee, reading, and cats. She's rescued three cats, including one found in a drain pipe in Japan who flew back to the States with her. Zak, Milo, and Kasper do their best on a daily basis to sidetrack her from work.

C.S. Poe can be followed on her website, which also has links to her Goodreads and social media pages. She can also be followed via her email newsletter on the website.

Website: www.cspoe.com

THE
MYSTERY
OF
NEVERMORE

SNOW & WINTER: BOOK ONE

C.S. POE

Snow & Winter: Book One

It's Christmas, and all antique dealer Sebastian Snow wants is for his business to make money and to save his floundering relationship with closeted CSU detective Neil Millett. When Snow's Antique Emporium is broken into and a heart is found under the floorboards, Sebastian can't let the mystery rest.

He soon finds himself caught up in murder investigations that echo the macabre stories of Edgar Allan Poe. To make matters worse, Sebastian's sleuthing is causing his relationship with Neil to crumble, while at the same time he's falling hard for the lead detective on the case, Calvin Winter. Sebastian and Calvin must work together to unravel the mystery behind the killings, despite the mounting danger and sexual tension, before Sebastian becomes the next victim.

In the end, Sebastian only wants to get out of this mess alive and live happily ever after with Calvin.

www.dsppublications.com

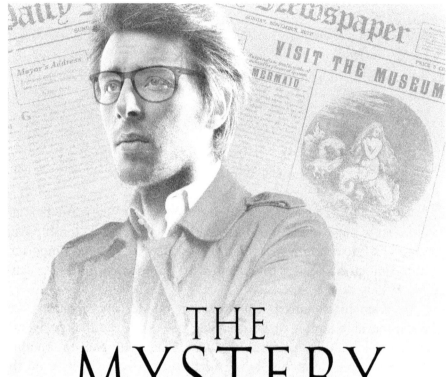

THE
MYSTERY
OF THE
CURIOSITIES

SNOW & WINTER: BOOK TWO

C.S. POE

Snow & Winter: Book Two

Life has been pretty great for Sebastian Snow. The Emporium is thriving and his relationship with NYPD homicide detective, Calvin Winter, is everything he's ever wanted. With Valentine's Day around the corner, Sebastian's only cause for concern is whether Calvin should be taken on a romantic date. It's only when an unknown assailant smashes the Emporium's window and leaves a peculiar note behind that all plans get pushed aside in favor of another mystery.

Sebastian is quickly swept up in a series of grisly yet seemingly unrelated murders. The only connection tying the deaths together are curiosities from the lost museum of P.T. Barnum. Despite Calvin's attempts to keep Sebastian out of the investigation, someone is forcing his hand, and it becomes apparent that the entire charade exists for Sebastian to solve. With each clue that brings him closer to the killer, he's led deeper into Calvin's official cases.

It's more than just Sebastian's livelihood and relationship on the line—it's his very life.

www.dsppublications.com

S.A. Stovall

VICE CITY

Vice City: Book One

After twenty years as an enforcer for the Vice family mob, Nicholas Pierce shouldn't bat an eye at seeing a guy get worked over and tossed in the river. But there's something about the suspected police mole, Miles, that has Pierce second-guessing himself. The kid is just trying to look out for his brother any way he knows how, and the altruistic motive sparks an uncharacteristic act of mercy that involves Pierce taking Miles under his wing.

Miles wants to repay Pierce for saving his life. Pierce shouldn't see him as anything but a convenient hookup… and he sure as hell shouldn't get involved in Miles's doomed quest to get his brother out of a rival street gang. He shouldn't do a lot of things, but life on the streets isn't about following the rules. Besides, he's sick of being abused by the Vice family, especially Mr. Vice and his power-hungry goon of a son, who treats his underlings like playthings.

So Pierce does the absolute last thing he should do if he wants to keep breathing—he leaves the Vice family in the middle of a turf war.

www.dsppublications.com

For more
great fiction
from

DSP PUBLICATIONS

visit us online.

WWW.DSPPUBLICATIONS.COM